ONLY STARS

KNOW

THE MEANING

OF SPACE

ONLY STARS KNOW

THE MEANING OF SPACE

OF SPACE

A LITERARY MIXTAPE

Rémy Ngamije

SCOUT PRESS

NEW YORK   LONDON   TORONTO   SYDNEY   NEW DELHI

Scout Press
An Imprint of Simon & Schuster, LLC
1230 Avenue of the Americas
New York, NY 10020

First Scout Press hardcover edition December 2024

SCOUT PRESS and colophon are registered trademarks of Simon & Schuster, LLC

Simon & Schuster: Celebrating 100 Years of Publishing in 2024

For information about special discounts for bulk purchases, please contact Simon & Schuster Special Sales at 1-866-506-1949 or business@simonandschuster.com.

The Simon & Schuster Speakers Bureau can bring authors to your live event. For more information or to book an event, contact the Simon & Schuster Speakers Bureau at 1-866-248-3049 or visit our website at www.simonspeakers.com.

Interior design by Hope Herr-Cardillo

Manufactured in the United States of America

10 9 8 7 6 5 4 3 2 1

Library of Congress Cataloging-in-Publication Data is available.

ISBN 978-1-6680-1246-8
ISBN 978-1-6680-1248-2 (ebook)

For readers:
Both met and unmet,
Taking the long way round,
Searching—over, under,
around, through—and finding.
The hope: Hold the light,
The prayer: Hold the light,
The anthem: Help is on the way.

JUKEBOX FOR JOKERS
(OR, CONTENTS)

A-Side continued...

LITTLE BROTHER $1.39

(OR, THREE IN THE MORNING)

Tornado $1.55

(or, The Only Poem You Ever Wrote)

THE SAGE OF THE SIX PATHS

(OR, THE LIFE AND TIMES OF THE FIVE Os) $1.77

From the Lost City of Hurtlantis
to the Streets of Helldorado (OR, FRANCO) $2.27

B-Side continued...

$1.15 **The Giver of Nicknames**

𝔗𝔥𝔢 𝔒𝔱𝔥𝔢𝔯 𝔊𝔲𝔶 $1.47

SEVEN SILENCES OF THE HEART $1.59

Granddaughter of the Octopus $2.09

NINE MONTHS SINCE FOREVER

$2.41 (CICERO'S INTERLUDE)

A-Side continued...

HOPE IS FOR THE UNPREPARED

(OR, ME) $2.49

B-Side continued...

ONLY STARS KNOW
THE MEANING OF SPACE

(LOVE'S INTERLUDE) $2.59

SOFA, SO GOOD, SORT OF

(OR, JOHN MUAFANGEJO) $2.77

END
CREDITS

$3.02

I may be statistically inconvenient
but I know I'm not unique.

—Michael Kelleher, "Sunbather's Diary"

This ain't got shit to do with shampoo
but watch your head and shoulders

—Naughty By Nature, "Hip Hop Hooray"

THE HOPE, THE PRAYER,
AND THE ANTHEM
(OR, THE FALL SO FAR)

Okay. Listen. This is how it's going to go, kid: in a week's time you'll be thirty, and there's nothing you can do about it.

Thirty.

The age when, according to Franco, Rinzlo, Lindo, and Cicero—your homies—you'll be cast in your final form.

"No more evolutions," Franco said gloomily.

"Pokémon to Pokéman and that's that." Rinzlo, more certain than certain.

"Only sucks if you're spending your thirties alone," Cicero said matter-of-factly.

Lindo saw you look away. "Too soon, Cic," he said.

Much too soon.

—An extract from your diary when reality hit: *Thirty.* Jesus. Fucking. Christ!

1

▶ ‖

At twenty, with life figured out in the special way literature undergrads have, you said at thirty you'd be headlining literary events around the world. There'd be rumors of an affair between you and Zadie Smith. The literary establishment would bay for her book, eager to see if she went full Alanis Morissette on you or partial Adele. You'd never confirm or deny the tryst, smiling secretively at Hay Festival panels.

After your first pieces showed up in *Granta*, your debut novel—a contemporary street tale bristling with boyhood bravado—would pay the rent. The second book, some historically inspired story of a liberation struggle hero, would mark you as one of the continent's literati, well on your way to ticking your way down the shopping list of success compiled for you when you were born. This one, your parents decided as they held you, was touched by destiny.

That's why they named you The Way, the Goal, the Destination on the Horizon.

They dreamed of you when dreams were all they could afford, back when they lived in the Small Country. Your mother typed away at breakneck speed in an office somewhere; your father hustled over-the-counter medication. They met at the sweaty discotheque with the flickering blue fluorescent lighting, their eyes drawn to each other like opposing magnetic poles. From the first funky hip-shake to the Cornelius Brothers and Sister Rose's "Too Late to Turn Back Now," they were promised to each other.

He said she danced like she was proposing to him. She said he danced like he accepted. He said, "Yes."

She said she didn't ask. She didn't have to: he was bought goods.

As he walked her home, the humidity gave them feverish sheens. His face glowed from the dancing; her cheekbones shone with delight at his presence. At her place, she kissed his cheek and watched him walk into the darkness, the equatorial night swallowing his ebony physique. She thought him a dream until he showed up at her work the next day. Everyone darted glances at him as he walked between the aisles to her desk. She drew him onto the balcony.

When would he see her again?

"Soon," she said.

"Forever would be better."

She laughed. "Forever would be nice."

They emerged from her village's church, married, showered with ululations. You hovered in their hearts when they bought their first house, when they buried her mother, and his father. Your mother wanted a baby. He said, "Me too."

"A boy," she said. "With your smile."

"Or a girl," he said. "With your eyes."

They'd be happy with the womb's lottery: a healthy baby made from the best parts of them.

They prayed for you after her first miscarriage. They weren't believers, but they prayed every day for nine months when she fell pregnant again. Their enemies were banned from the house lest any bad energy seep into her womb and turn you against life. Your father rushed home from work to press his head against her stomach. Your mother shooed him away. He joked that his job was a ploy to keep you to herself. "It's only fair," she said. "If it's a boy, it will be a matter of time before he outgrows me and I become an embarrassing nuisance. I might have more time with a girl before a boy takes her away too." Your familiar weight and how it made people treat her differently, your father's reverential protection and provision—she didn't want to relinquish the status you brought her.

You wanted out.

Out you came—the First Sundering—painfully, bloody.

Finally.

They prepared a room and a home: for your first day of school and your achievements, for your freedom and the Second Sundering—a wife and grandchildren. They readied themselves for these things from the moment you breathed and screamed.

When they could prepare no more they simply hoped in the way only people who know what it is to lose can hope. All you know is the one hope they ever voiced, to be what they yearned to be most when they were in search of refuge: safe and landed, the owner of things.

The owner of permanent and inheritable things.

Not to worry, you told them: title deeds would follow your great deeds.

First: a modern house in a manicured suburb fond of recycling. Second: a wife (quarter Venezuelan, two-thirds Eritrean, three-sixteenths Themysciran Amazon). Third: twin daughters with curls casting agents killed for (Harvard on the horizon for the elder, a future human rights lawyer; Cambridge for the younger progeny, another writer in the family).

Then the third acclaimed novel: something about complicated parenthood and the gear changes of interracial marriages.

PRAISE FOR THE THIRD NOVEL:

"A magisterial, perspicacious, and layered story which self-assuredly explores the pitfalls of modern marriage while affirming the enduring promise of love."

—Publishers Weekly

"The voice of a continent."

—Some Important Literary Figure

Ah. Look at you.

I SAY I SAID *LOOKATEW*!

A residency in New York (the epicenter of the Zadie Smith affair) would yield the fourth multiple award–winning Afro-American tale: slaves and gold from Ghana; colonialism in the Congo; diaspora, drugs, and detention in the United States, all topped with an earth-shattering romance between Some Black Guy and Some White Woman. It would astound audiences everywhere, lay siege to the *New York Times* best-seller list like a Mongol army come to reshape the geopolitics of the world—the book quoted for intellectual points.

Who could've known a boy from the Small Country, raised in the wide and dry New Country, could climb so high? Your neighborhood was known for its dedication to beer, biltong, battery, teenage pregnancies, and souped-up STI Golfs revving from gonorrhea to HIV in sex seconds flat. Readers like you were treated like lepers, shunned from the dust-patch soccer games with biblical fastidiousness.

You always knew.

For *kontrol* you'd purchase a farm in the New Country, some unimaginably large landmass stolen from a long-ago massacred indigenous tribe. Your old man would retire there to feign feudal interest in farming. His grief would finally unwind itself from his neck, fall to the ground, slither away into the undergrowth, sprouting feet and arms as it went along, a beautiful black face with close-cropped hair, and a radiant gap-toothed smile. It would hold you in its patient gaze.

"*Komeza*," it would say before fading away.

Carry on.

You'd say, "Yes, Mamma. I will."

Your father would breathe deeply, from the wrinkled skin on his forehead down to his toes, and let out the throaty laugh he stowed away as he crushed your hand in his at the funeral, leaning on you for support. Your younger brother was nearby, but it was upon you his full weight rested. The first thump of soil on the coffin nearly made you faint. The grave felt like a Charybdis capable of devouring the universe, flushing creation from this life into the next—a Final Sundering. But on the farm which stretched from east to west a sun would rise without its mourning glory. Your father would find peace. In the autumnal sunset on this farm of farms you'd whittle away at a possible memoir. There'd be tours to plan, lectures to prepare, awards to adjudicate, grants to graciously accept.

—Your cursive vow before The Fall: *nine years and 358 days to greatness.*

▶ǁ

At twenty-seven you were still plugged into the club scene. The fatigue showed. One time, at this moist joint, a light-skinned item with eyebrows from YouTube and hair from Peru chatted you up. You stepped outside so she could smoke. She said she liked the song thumping through the walls. You said music was eating itself: everything was a cover of a remix—you used the word *pastiche*.

"You sound like a sour oldhead." Her weave Nike-swished away.

You knew Pink when she had pink hair and made R&B jams. You and Enrique Iglesias threw back to "Bailamos" before he ditched the mole.

You were a yoof no longer.

You started evening art classes to pass the time and left them because some artsy fool you hated from the first brushstroke called one of your pieces pastiche. Everyone agreed. Even the Colored girl whose work would be at home in Oscar the Grouch's dustbin on *Sesame Street*. (She's exhibiting at MoMA soon.) The two of you might have had something before she agreed with Dude Who Actually Paints Well and Kind of Has a Point but Fuck Him and His Family Back to Adam and Eve.

—Your observation when you forfeited a future in the Louvre: *Art is the bread of life, artists are the gluten—that shit isn't for everyone.*

Next distraction: dancing at the salsa club at the end of the world, a lonely outpost of rhythm. Your boys laughed at you. You didn't care. You had to try new things before this snow-globe city drove you mad. You were going to *cumbia* the shit out of that dance floor. Buena Vista Social Club's "Chan Chan" became your ringtone. You practiced *ochos* while you seasoned your two-minute noodles and scrambled eggs, dreaming about slo-mo walking into a San Juan club with Héctor Lavoe's "La Murga" as your soundtrack, announcing the arrival of *El Salsero del Desierto*, the high-noon cowboy and melody mercenary come to clear out the riffraff and guns in the valley.

The salsa bug lasted until the Spanish girl in your classes swatted your balls away from her wickets for a soft six instead of hard sex. She was in the country doing volunteer work in the *lokasie* and didn't know anything or anyone in the Oh-Six-One. Sparked, you took her to *braais*, hikes, and spoken-word performances.

She said she'd never seen the *Godfather* trilogy.

"GERRARRAHEEYA!"

You had the trilogy at home. Her suggestion: meet up, practice salsa, cook, and watch the films, alternate between your places.

Three nights with the dark-eyed *mariposa* who struggled with timing and—*Dios mío*—couldn't execute an outside turn without taking out half the dance floor? "*Sí*," you said.

¡Sí! ¡Sí! ¡Sí!

The first night you made a stir-fry with meats unknown, an offer you said she couldn't refuse. (Earlier, when she'd texted she was en route, you busted out Celia Cruz—"O! Yeah, come over!"—but she didn't get it.) The second night, for *Part II*, she made pasta Alfredo. (You wisely decided not to use the quip.) On the third, your last home game, you teamed up for a joint hurrah and made gnocchi. After the end credits, you sat and decided to run DMC game on her by having a deep, meaningful conversation. The expanding universe with its Neil deGrasse Tyson film spoiler-physics told you to kiss the girl but *sha-la-la-la-la-la my oh my* she put a gentle hand on your chest and said no. *Muchos apologiendos* later—you insisted on making up Spanish around her—she hoped you'd remain friends.

You skipped classes, avoiding her. Then, one day, she showed up with a dreadlocked, earthy-smelling, tour guide boyfriend. You were on Duolingo for this Catalonian *blanquita*, and she went full native on your ass.

¡Mierda!

The salsa studio saved you the embarrassment of quitting by finishing its last dance with rent rates that spun it off the tenant's roster: it closed and didn't reopen. Franco and the guys said *cero y nada* about you being king of the Oh-Sex-None for gassing the Spanish girl's pursuit.

This wasn't the end for you, kid.

Couldn't be. Wouldn't be. *No fucking way.*

Twenty-eight would be the *año* of writing. All you needed was some cultured inspiration.

Cue birding. For a month you enthused about crimson-breasted shrikes and martial eagles. But bird-watching was a bar of boredom so high you couldn't Fosbury-flop over it. Instead, you hit the gym like draft day was approaching. Twice a day, six days of the week, waking up at fuck-me five o'clock for cardio and then hitting the weights in the evening until the cleaning staff came to wipe your sweat off the benches before taking their midnight taxis back to the hood. Gym was a different kind of church: form was faith, reps were religion, sets were sacraments. The ensuing female attention was crazy. You chewed through them like Pac-Man with three bonus lives, it's a miracle you didn't eat a ghost and die.

Playing the game put the worst parts of you on blast and repeat.

—Your retirement speech when you hung up your player jersey: *Pussy is a destabilizing force, like oil in a West African country.*

Franco said you were making a mistake: "Trust me, if you're gonna play the game then you've gotta play to the whistle, and then ten minutes after that."

Nah. You gave it all up. The only things you'd sleep with, you said, were books, working through the literary canon. But, fuck, James Joyce was a trial, and Tolstoy was a chore. (You finished *War and Peace*, though, and enjoyed letting people know you did.) You gave the classics a skip. You'd try them later when you were famous, when you had time to make time.

The writing?

Ha! There was always a distraction. Like the needlessly competitive pickup basketball games. Once, you drove for the hoop, hit Lindo with the wettest Shammgod, finger-rolled for a stylish two points, and landed funny. You were in pain for days. The doctor's diagnosis prescribed a road trip to Cape Town for special surgery. You knew it wasn't happening—you didn't have medical aid. You were no Ray Allen, and with your layup game shot to shit, you could keep the failing construction industry supplied with cheap bricks. Windhoek, you decided, was a city of old men with diseases and young men with injuries. You sighed your way to the bench, playing every other weekend to save your bad knee.

▶❚❚

Soon you'll be too old for any under-thirty list. The student newspaper you started at your high school profiled cool, young teachers and you didn't make the cut. You failed a couple of senior essays out of spite.

You have no girl. The One departed a year ago. Because she was lovely, and because you anointed her as The One, you ache for her on cold days when there's a spiteful breeze in the air.

She was something too, something real: stretch marks on a booty which registered the tiniest hiccup of the Eurasian Plate, a Care Bear hug that warmed from the inside out, and toes so cute they reconciled arguments (you could never apologize to people with ugly toes). She chose a restaurant meal quicker than a Jamaican sprinter broke a world record and improved your knowledge of obscure herbs and spices. Your attempts at replicating her tarragon fish long after she'd pulled herself ashore from the maelstrom of your breakup reminded you what a catch she was. You whimpered for her.

Unlike the other *cherries van die* Laeveld, Kloppersdal, or Donkerhoek—who said Jesus, Chuck Taylor, and Jack Purcell were the only men who'd never let them down—your girl wasn't impressed by Imprezas. Girls from those blurry margins between hoods graduated into women in the backs of boys' cars when puberty peaked through their blouses. When she let you take her out on a date ("It must be public—I don't want to be in a place where only you can hear me say no") she didn't negotiate with her dignity. "The price of all of this," she said, "is all of you. All of the time."

When you curled up behind her in bed, all you smelled was shea butter and coconut oil. You squirmed from that thing she did with her finger. Her pussy was hotter than a pan of oil and had possum power—you played dead for an hour after hitting it, leaving your sheets looking like Jackson Pollocks. Get this: you let her handle your *Yu-Gi-Oh!* cards. In your shady womb raider past, you'd dive into vulvas in the back of Volvos *inyama kwa nyama*, but you *never* let anyone touch your cards. She asked if it was a sign you were ready to

11

talk about more than surface things. You said you were, sneak-peeking her trailers of the life to come. She said you were motivated by faith, even if you'd never admit to it—that if you believed in something you didn't shift from the goal. Your conviction, she said, would make you a good father. You couldn't get it up for two weeks after that. You, the man with a dick harder than an end-level boss. (Her words, not yours.)

Why?

You were scared you'd make her a mother and didn't want to get into the habit of losing them. You saw what it did to your father. He shuffled from home to work and work to home, husked out, thinned, colder than zero, lonelier than the loneliest hero.

Fourteen days of your girlfriend asking if everything was okay. Fourteen nights of you telling her everything was fine, afraid if you took her to bed you'd go from Smash Bro to Splash Brother, shooting fatherhood and till death do us part into her ovaries with Curry-esque abandon. On the fifteenth day you managed to squeeze a semi into her.

She thought it was something she did, or something she wasn't doing.

You wondered how to tell her about the hollowness which silenced you in her comforting company; about your belly button, throbbing, aching for that distant First Sundering; or the alien sadness inside you which ripped through your chest and preyed on your world. You remained silent and kept your shields at sixty-five percent—strong enough to keep her questions at bay, weak enough to make her feel like she'd wear them down to zero and receive an answer that wasn't the press release you gave everyone else: okay, cool, no worries, all good, a'ight. You, my friend, were a slow puncture of love. Even when the ride stopped, she got out and pushed a little longer. Then, finally, your mother's absence showed up with the pull of a collapsed star. No light or hope could escape its event horizon.

You sat her down, looking at the start in her; she saw the end in you.

You did that thing where you said you didn't deserve her. She did that Destiny's Child thing where she realized you didn't. She went Sub-Zero cold, fatality-kicked your ass out of her Earth Realm, an exile so catatonic you lost five kilograms. Her next man would listen to her talking about you, wondering how you managed to lose her. You knew all of this because you were *that guy* who sat down with her on Day One of Forever listening to her talk about her fumbling exes. A month ago you saw her at the mall and ducked into a plus-size shop, watching her walk by the store's window while you pretended to peruse the skirts.

She's in Costa Rica now. Her Instagram is full of curved beaches and green trees. She's drenched in sunlight you said you'd see together. You can't see it in her pictures but you have this intestine-twisting feeling the person holding her camera phone is some Alejandro who protects her heart and puts such a furious dicking on her she forgets you ever existed.

That was a year ago.

You're twenty-nine, fam. You have *fokol* paperback to your name.

So, what do you do?

You flick through your diary for the wisdom you'd share with the *The Paris Review: Writing is confession.*

You add another: *Reading is some kind of forgiveness.*

That is your hope, prayer, and anthem.

You summon the courage to record the fall so far:

Okay. Listen. This is how it's going to go, kid: in a week's time you'll be thirty and there's nothing you can do about it.

B-Side

W I C K E D

The first time she touched Salman's hair she felt a sliver of envy. Why would men be blessed with such beautiful hair? They did not need it for job interviews. They did not need it to entice their lovers. Salman laughed when she said that. "Then according to you," he replied, "my daughter will easily find a job and have her fill of men. The first one is okay. The second I'm not sure about."

He said it so casually—*my daughter*. She asked if his daughter had a mother.

"Of course," Salman replied. "My wife."

The first tendrils of wickedness snaked their way through her. He looked at her intently, waiting for a reply. Instead she finished eating, thanked him for the meal, and exited the restaurant quickly. He had called her for a couple of days but she refused to answer.

▶︎❙❙

Salman's black curls were soft, unlike her hair, which was coarse. The chemical treatment she gave it every other month never sunk deep enough to her genes, where it mattered most. Sooner or later the coarseness came back, prompting another enrollment in the hour-long course of gossip and scalp burns at her salon. The first time Salman ran his hands through her straightened hair he said he preferred the natural texture. She refused to wear it the way he wanted. Men had a way of saying they wanted natural things without wanting natural things.

She watched Salman sleep. She wondered what words he had whispered to his wife when they were still young and new, the vows he had made to always protect and provide, the magic words of parenthood they said when they agreed on their daughter's name.

She wondered how Salman felt knowing he had failed to protect them. She could never know how he felt about being unable to unite his family under one roof. It was not something they ever spoke about. More than once she wanted to ask him how he felt about his fruitless search for his family. Perhaps, she thought, the search was a ritual he carried out to maintain his standing and rank as a husband and father. She thought about how much she would miss this moment with this man when she arrived back at her place. She would miss this room which made her feel wicked.

The green walls were pitted in places. The square space in the wall masquerading as a window filtered the late-afternoon sunshine so that yellow and orange rays hit the opposite wall. Faded magazine and newspaper cuttings of George Weah and Jay-Jay Okocha pasted on one wall passed for decoration. An Arabic prayer she could not read hung above the door. The bed on which they lay was metal and old. The springs squealed during their shy sex, the lovers shamed by the noise made by their efforts. They tried to slow down, to be discreet with their needs so the awkward sounds would not sell out their wants. When they slumped on it afterward it looked like a kangaroo's joey-laden pouch. The mattress was covered in floral-patterned sheets, the flowers' colors were faded, probably from being washed too often. Washed away, she thought, along with whatever wicked acts they witnessed. She wondered if she and Salman were the only ones who came to this place, this room with its yellowed plastic fan that creaked as it windmilled wafts of semicool air across the room, its cracked sink where Salman splashed his face with cold water—when the tap was not broken or when the water was flowing—and its cupboard with no hangers. The wooden bedside table held Salman's cassette radio, the only accompaniment they ever had for their romance. No flowers, no chocolates, no expensive perfumes, no lingerie—they had the black radio which squeaked its music into the room. When the Nairobi heat lulled them to sleep, her dreams would seem only half-real with Ismaël Lô's "Tajabone" playing in the background.

Today, Salman had brought a cassette with Yousso N'Dour and Neneh Cherry on it. As "Seven Seconds" floated from the treble-heavy speaker she thought of this moment, this hot afternoon when everything was sweet, when her concerns and struggles seemed far away, when their bodies pushed away worries of him leaving soon to go to Dadaab to search for his family. It also seemed to presage the time when he would not be in this room with her. At the end of the week he would take a rickety Starbus to Garissa and alight at the refugee camp, passing parked Toyota Land Cruisers and miles of wire fencing, to scroll through the lists of fresh arrivals, scanning for Aaminah and Calaaso Ghedi. She imagined the wife would be pretty, with a long,

17

oval face, a high forehead, and jet-black sheaves of hair, hidden beneath a hijab. The daughter would be lanky until womanhood changed her and her fortunes forever.

Salman made the journey to Dadaab once a month. When he left she became heavy, moving like a woman deep in pregnancy, eager to be released of her burden and at the same time afraid of what the future held. She became snappy and anxious. She was lonely. For long periods of time, she was bereft of words, happiness stolen from her. She became all the things she vowed she would never be for or to men, both in their presence and in their absence.

The First Never: dependence. Never again, she vowed, would she be shackled to a man like a dog to a post. She had a job and her own money. She bought her own clothes. In time she would drive her own car and own a house, perhaps in Kilimani or Kileleshwa. She would never be dependent on a man to provide for her, to take care of her when he saw fit, when he needed favors or the comforts of her thighs.

The Second Never banned patience and compromise, the twin gospels men used to trick women into becoming their mothers, sisters, confidantes, lovers, and therapists all in one exhausting combination while they managed to remain themselves, unschooled, underdeveloped, untethered. *Kamwe!* No more trips to jail to bail out a boyfriend. If the next one was arrested, he had made his choice: he wanted the company of other men. The bottom of her stomach fell out when she recalled the three separate evenings she spent traveling between ATMs to make the withdrawal of the necessary shillings to bribe her way into the police station and pay for her ex-boyfriend's bail. She had risked rape and robbery for him. She had been a patient girlfriend. She had been a compromising woman. He had repaid her in frequent, lengthy, and unannounced absences. Never again! The money she spent on him could have bought her a holiday in one of the places she saw on the television: Malaysia-Truly-Asia, I-Love-New-York, or any of the other places in the world she had never visited.

The Third Never outlawed waiting. If time waited for no man, she was certain it did not care for women at all.

She would *never* wait for a man again.

But in the days before Salman departed, she became more than these things to him and for him. When he was gone she felt like she had become less to herself. Salman left her hoping he would find what he sought. At the same time, she hoped he did not. Her prayers were an exercise in contradiction. "Please bring him back," she whispered feverishly into her clasped hands, "safely." *And alone*, she thought to herself.

Sometimes, during their weekends she woke with the sun gone, with Salman sleeping next to her, muscled and pressed against her own darkness. Salman called her his cup of Ketepa black tea when he undressed her, a compliment which eroded her resolve and all her Nevers. When he placed his mouth upon her breasts she was reduced to desirous dependence, eternal patience, and willing compromise.

She was happy to wait.

▶ ‖

She bunched his soft hair in her hands and teased it out in its fine individuality, stretching a curl until it was straight. The feeling would linger long after she had taken her *matatu* back to Rongai and the apartment she shared with her cousin so that whenever she came across anything with fibrous strands she would stroke it to relive the connection. Like her cousin's wig, the cousin she lived with who told her there were many men like Salman, men who needed many half-lives to make them whole. Or the tassels at the end of the rug which knotted themselves of their own volition. Even her mother's knitting wool and the scarves she made drew her fingers to them. Her hands sampled all of these in longing recollection, each texture never coming close to the softness that bewitched her fingertips. Despite the abundance of strings to stroke there was no substitute for the thread that was Salman.

This was going to be a tough week for her. It was filled with the potential for Salman to find his family and the selfish hope he would not.

She felt her heart flutter coldly.

She was being unfair.

She was being wicked.

She wanted Salman to find his family. She wanted him to be whole. She wanted his daughter to grow up with a father. She wanted his wife's ears to hear all the whispered indecencies of lust and all the promises of love Salman lavished upon her. She wanted Salman to find peace at the end of his pilgrimages.

She also wanted him to come back to her, to this room, and to the next moment just like this.

This week she would take detailed minutes and diligently file reports. She would allow her boss to pinch her buttocks when she came to present him with a list of the week's meetings. She would sidle away from his touch politely, never saying no, never saying yes, carefully staying in the middle ground, which did not cost her the job which stayed the cruel control of the First Never.

It helped her situation when her boss's wife had come to work one day and stalked around the office, scrutinizing every female employee, weighing up each woman's beauty, and gauging whether they were a temptation for her husband or not. The boss's wife had floated past her desk without so much as a second glance. She was not pretty enough. But the junior secretary had been thoroughly appraised with a look that acknowledged the presence of competition. The look warned. It also pleaded.

At the end of the week, after dodging her boss's hands, she would not be able to run to Salman's, which knew all the points of pressure and pleasure. There would be no arrangement to meet in this room in Eastleigh, a suburb of spices and fabrics, of color and colorful crowds. Eastleigh, where Salman and anyone who looked like Salman were the target of prejudice and violence after Westgate. No shillings for the man at the counter who thought she was a prostitute. No long walk down the corridor. No key, no turned doorknob, no hesitant hello, no frantic kissing, no fracas of friction, no quick pause, no eager resumption, no tinge of regret, no sadness, and no sleeping Salman's hair to caress.

Her cousin told her there were no rights in love back when Salman was about to become a string of Saturdays to savor. She had walked into the apartment and her cousin, watching a Nollywood film about a family whose fortunes had been squandered by a demon-possessed son, looked at her from the sofa in surprise. She was back too soon from her date. They finished the film together, talking about Salman all the while. Her cousin listened to the promises she had made in her past to safeguard her future self. "Surely," she told her cousin, "Salman's honesty about his wife and child meant something."

"Foolish," her cousin replied. She began to undo her thick braids in preparation for washing her hair. "The first thing my boyfriend told me was that he had a wife and three children. He said he loved his wife and nothing would change." She carried on frankly. "There're no rights in love, my dear. The sooner you know that the better." A thick braid hung undone, unshod of its plaited dignity. She helped her cousin undoing the rest. "Who did my boyfriend give his vows to? His wife. Who does he complain to about her now? Me. I'm for better. She's worse. Who cooks for him? His wife. Who does he whine to about her *ugali* and wet fry he doesn't like? Me. Who gave him children? His wife. Who does he fuck like it's the first time? Me." Her cousin detangled an obstinate knot. "Honesty? It doesn't mean anything."

She had looked at her hands in shame, slick and shiny with the oils her cousin applied to her hair to keep it soft.

"You're hurt by this truth," her cousin said, "but love doesn't have any legislation. No rules. If things work out, they work out. If they don't, well, that's life. You know this. You had a boyfriend. You're not the only one who wasn't someone's somebody. There's no return policy on love, my dear."

"I didn't say I love him."

Her cousin snorted. "You've been walking around touching your hair absentmindedly. Looking at yourself in the mirror for too long. Only a man can make a woman do things like that."

"It isn't love."

"If it isn't, then it isn't. If it is, be careful."

Salman slept as she dressed. She combed her hair and put the brush in her handbag. She put some lipstick on her lips. She opened the door gently and stepped into the corridor.

"*Nakupenda*." She closed the door and felt the joyful release of the truth.

Then she felt sad.

And then she felt wicked.

CRUNCHY GREEN APPLES
(OR, OMO)

Look how the city becomes littered with little location pins marking the places you went with her. The crowded park with its broken swings and sunburned seesaws. The swimming pool with the deep end she warned you against. She snuck food into the cinema: she had paid for the tickets and that was that. The long walking routes where she pointed out ugly houses and criticized people with too much money but no style.

You tread through town carefully, avoiding geocaches of memories. You shy away from the nursery where she adopted flora to fawn over and steer clear of textile shops. No imported Javan wax prints in lieu of *kitenges* with their emotional triggers formed against you shall prosper. You sanitize your life of her presence. It works for a while.

The memories do not respect your borders and steal across your lines in the early morning as you pour cereal into the bowl. They sneak through your fences in the afternoon when you spread the thick layer of peanut butter on a slice of bread. Your walls are scaled in the dead of night as you gargle and floss. You rush to bed, turn off the lights, cocoon yourself in the duvet. The memories run around your apartment unseen like mice in a ceiling. They ambush you. Like when you do your laundry and recall the soapy smell she had on her hands when she scrubbed the collars of your school shirts.

"OMO—*Itakupatia* what you are looking for."

For some inexplicable reason she liked that commercial and muttered the payoff line under her breath when she poured the powder into the basin, frothing it with the whisking motion of her hand. She would say it, peg the clothes to the washing line.

The mere sight of golden apples sets you off. She detested them. She said they cheated her of the crunch they were supposed to make when they were bitten. On the sixth page of your third-grade English textbook the freckled boy had a speech bubble with a binding edict: "Yum! This apple is crunchy. I love crunchy green apples."

It became a bylaw in the house that apples which did not crunch were a crime. Whenever Granny Smith apples were unavailable, orchards in South Africa became agents of dissent. When you were younger, still young enough to be entertained by her repetitive jokes, she would come home after shopping and shout that she had bought apples. You and your brother, avatars of helpfulness and kindness, ran out of your room to the kitchen and helped her unpack the bags. As one, you reached for the apples and said "Yum! These apples are crunchy. We love crunchy green apples!" and become entangled in giggles.

Back then.

Later, when the two of you grew older, when you became members of a tribe called cool, you did not play along when she triumphantly announced she had bought apples.

"It isn't that funny, Mamma." You walked into the kitchen and opened the fridge, scrounging for something to eat.

"Nonsense," she replied. "You liked it when you were young."

"Maybe." You shrugged and sipped juice from the carton, a habit she had tried to discourage for years. "But we aren't young anymore."

"You will always be young to me." She beamed at you, determined to draw some sort of affection from you.

"We find different things funny now."

Those tiny scratches you made against her when you started flexing your claws popped into your head when you thought of her. How many times did you hurt her with your merciless metaphors, your savage similes, your devilish double entendres?

The tally scared you.

What if, you thought one night, lying in bed, what if all the bad things we say to people subtract a second or a minute from their total life span?

—*Mamma, if I wanted your opinion I would've looked in the annals of antiquity!*

—*Are you done? Really, are you quite done? We're running out of Amazon forest to turn carbon dioxide into oxygen and you're busy shouting at me like that.*

—*What did you expect, bro? She's old, man. Old people are . . . excess capacity.*

—*Mamma, Margaret Thatcher wants her jacket back.*

The possibility there was a causal connection between your casual cruelty and her weakening heart muscle scared you.

What if cruelty kills people?

Nah!

What if . . . ?

NO!

What if . . .

Maybe.

What if you killed your mother?

You avoided the fruit section in shops. When you really had to buy some fresh produce you looked over the apples like they did not exist, like you and they did not go all the way back.

Here you are in this shop, wheeling a trolley, collecting sustenance and sundries for your place. Your girlfriend has given you quite the list. You do not make enough from teaching to fill your fridge so, without thinking, you slip into a familiar aisle.

You are right about one thing.

Everything is a matter of time. The present runs past and becomes the past and loops all the way around and then comes back as the future.

You scan the middle and bottom shelves for marked-down things since your money cannot reach all the way up. You spy a can of baked beans and—*whoosh!*—the whirlwind of memories blows down the tin shack of your refuge, taking you back to the times she took you shopping, squeezing mileage out of inches, making twenty dollars stretch to a hundred. Her grocery list appears, Hamlet-like, and leads you through the aisles of memory.

▶ ‖

28

PASTA: Spaghetti, macaroni, elbows, and screws. Everything else which was classified as "fancy" was called pasta. That is how it went in households like yours; things were generic until there was enough money to be specific. Only at university—and by accident—did you look at the names on the Fattis and Monis packets and realize tagliatelle and penne were different things. You paused, embarrassed, wondering what else you did not know about. (Everything that was not Aromat was called spice. Later, your girlfriend schooled you on the uses of cilantro leaves, marjoram, fennel, juniper berries, caraway seeds, cumin, and saffron.)

RICE: When the living became better she bought a rice cooker, upgraded from plain rice to jasmine and basmati rice, the kind of rice that looked special and delicious on the cooking shows she liked so much. Soft, fluffy, flavorful, not the white mush she occasionally burned in her steel pot. The rice cooker brought her friends' envy. All the other mothers had the same model within a month.

MAIZE MEAL: She treated *pap* like the plague and kept it out of the house as much as possible. She missed *ugali* and its textures of home. She mourned the loss of the cassava connect who left the country because of paperwork issues. "People think stricter immigration laws make borders safer, protect the labor pool, and keep criminals out," she said, "but they just make Jollof rice weaker."

WHITE BREAD: She looked for loaves with arched, dark brown crusts. The first and last slices were her favorites. She let them dry and harden and then crunched them with her tea. When she bought brown bread nobody complained about anything because it meant money was running low. Brown bread brought a black mood to the house and everyone knew it was best to leave her alone; even your father let her watch as many cooking shows as she wanted even if Champions League soccer was on.

BAKED BEANS IN TOMATO SAUCE: Beans reminded her of the village. It was all they ate with dry potatoes. She had to fight to fist a handful from the pot she shared with her older brothers. She developed strong hands. "Anyone with weak wrists went to bed hungry," she told you whenever you complained about the suppers she prepared. She really, really hated beans. But there were times when the money Houdinied out of your lives and she would scoop up the cans in their dozens, putting them in her trolley with poorly disguised shame.

TINNED FRUIT JAM: It dyed slices of bread a gory red when it was mixed fruit. The bits of strawberry looked like scabs on bread. You are quite sure the jam glowed in the dark from the colorants and preservatives in it. She longed for days when jam came in jars; reaching for the top shelf was the next family milestone.

SALT: Cerebos, always. You called it the X-Men salt and she never understood the joke. When you think of it now, that was the precise moment your mother fell from your constant praise and favor. It occurred to you there was another world, a world of mutants and magic she could not understand. Hers was the realm of motherhood, a maternal middle ground you had to traverse to get to the other side and emerge cool, independent, free of her. Free of her criticizing your baggy pants and bandanas, and her prohibitions against rock; free, most of all, of the five-second delay before she laughed at something you said.

—*Mamma, if you were any slower you'd get the joke at your funeral.*

(Kid, in *die trappe van vergelyking* you were the fucking worst!)

30

CORN FLAKES: She bought ProNutro once. A small serving swallowed half a carton of milk so she never bought it again. You went back to corn flakes. If the milk ran out you used hot water with sugar.

DISHWASHING LIQUID: Sunlight or Ajax—she diluted the green ooze in the bottle and made it last longer, the hallmark of an excellent drug dealer. She cut the green with water, leaving just enough kick to deal with the grease. Even to this day you can make the last centimeter of liquid last a whole week if you have to.

BLACK TEA: "Rooibos," she said, "is not even tea." Its taste, its aroma, everything was off. Five Roses, that thing everyone in your house still calls "normal tea," was the status quo: 100s, tagged, each bag used twice. Lipton was strictly for guests.

OROS: Another one of her great shames. As soon as her tax bracket changed she bought Hall's granadilla concentrate. Her goal: a fridge of fresh fruit juices, pulp *en alles*, unspoiled by the hand of man.

WILSON'S TOFFEES: Watching your mother look for new places to hide packets of sweets taught you about the tense relationships prison guards have with prisoners. The guard worries about many things: the prisoners' food, their health, and the specter of violence. The guard has to watch *all* the prisoners. But *all* the prisoners worry about *one* thing: the guard. They watch him. They know him better than he knows them. The length of his strides, the beat of his walk. Your mother, bless her, did her best to keep the sweets out of your reach. But those ten-cent delights put holes in your teeth and kept dentists drilling.

ROMANY CREAMS: Strictly for Friday tea: everyone got two biscuits. They were savored and eaten slowly. Fridays were the best days unless guests came over because then a whole packet was sacrificed to the hospitality gods.

ZAM-BUK: The one, the only, *The Real Makoya*!

PETROLEUM JELLY: Blue Seal, a small tub in her handbag, whipped out with alacrity when she saw an ashy elbow or forehead in need of greasing at church.

DRUM MAGAZINE: She loved Credo Mutwa's tales and, embarrassingly, all the stories of *tokoloshes* impregnating women in South African townships.

TOMATOES, ONIONS, AND CARROTS: Bought from the roadside. She bought each good from a separate woman and never haggled over the price. You asked her about this once and she said: "When you see prices in shops do you negotiate with the manager about the price? No. You accept the price of an avocado even when you know it is too expensive. But when people see someone selling fruit on the street they want to see how low they can drive the price. It is embarrassing to negotiate with poor people."

WASHING POWDER: She bought the hand-wash variant, soaking laundry overnight before wringing it in the bathtub, yielding to her efforts. When she bought a washing machine her Saturdays stretched out before her since she did not spend them beating dirt out of clothes. Sometimes, instead of Mamma you called her OMO, thinking it was funny to address her by her labor. The nickname stuck in a way that never washed off. You called her OMO when she washed your clothes but not Kindness when she put plasters on your knees. You did not call her Patience when she put up with you and your anarchical teenage-hood. You did not call her Love when she was around, an unwavering female presence. You never called her all the nice things she was to you. No, she was OMO to you. Her passing was like ripping North from the compass face. The needle of your life spun around recklessly looking for its own purpose, its own anchor, its own driving force, something that was not she and what she did for you.

▶︎II

You have been pushing your trolley around absentmindedly, lost in your recollection. And then there she is:

OMO!

Hand wash, twin tub, top loader, *now with new micro beads.*

But still the same trustworthy OMO from your childhood. The one who made your brown shirts crisp and white again.

Eyes moistening, your chest is constricted by reminiscence.

You need to leave this damn shop.

You must escape.

You escape.

Sit in the car.

Breathe. Breathe. Breathe. Just a trick of memory. Just your eyes catching the sweats. Nothing major. This kind of thing happens all the time to the weaker species. Give the super negro genes time to kick in. They will harden the exterior and relegate this moment of weakness to the past. *Breathe.*

All better, right?

Right.

OMO! *Itakupatia* what you are looking for.

Your ass needs to get searching.

B-Side

THE NEIGHBORHOOD WATCH

MONDAYS: AUASBLICK, OLYMPIA, AND SUIDERHOF

(MAYBE PIONIERSPARK)

Elias roughly shakes everyone awake. For breakfast, a chorus of yawns sprinkled with stretching. There is some grumbling. Then everyone starts folding their blankets and pieces of cardboard. A can of water is passed around. Everyone cups a handful and splashes their faces. Elias goes first, then Lazarus, then Silas, and then Omagano. There is little left when it reaches Martin, the newest and youngest member of the Neighborhood Watch. When the can is empty it is stashed away with the other valuables in a nook under the concrete abutment of the bridge. The bridge's underside is precious real estate. When it rains it remains dry and in winter it wards off some of the cold. More than once it has been defended against a rival posse. It belongs to the Neighborhood Watch now and everyone else tends to leave it alone. The "NW" sprayed onto the bridge's supporting columns has the same effect as musty pee at the edge of a leopard's territory. It promises bloody reprisal if any encroachment is made onto the land. The Neighborhood Watch's hidden stash is as safe as their fierce reputation and basic street common sense permits it to be. Generally, stealing is frowned upon. Stealing is bad because it makes everything a free-for-all and then everyone has to lug their scant possessions around to protect them. More luggage means slower foraging. It also means pushing one's poverty around in broad daylight. Nobody likes a thief.

The light of day is not full-born when they set out. Elias, the oldest and the leader, leads with his lieutenant, Lazarus. Omagano goes with them, trying to straighten the kinks in her hair, using her fingers as comb teeth. They head to town since they have the best clothes and will not stand out too much or draw the ire of the city police patrols or the judging stares of security guards. If they walk slowly enough other pedestrians will not catch their stench. On any given day they have a multitude of things to worry about and shame is one of the first things a person learns to shed on the street. But smelling bad is something they try to avoid as much as possible. People's eyes can accept a man in tattered, browned, and dirty clothing, even in a store or a church. But a smelly man is despised everywhere.

Elias knows most of the kitchen staff in the city's hotels and restaurants. They call him Soldier or Captain. Sometimes the staff leave out produce about to turn for him and his group. Some potatoes with broken skins, mangoes which dimple at the slightest pressure, or wrinkled carrots. When they are feeling especially kind the cooks give him some smushed leftovers from the previous night in Styrofoam containers—half-eaten burgers, fries drowning in sauce, salads picked clean of feta. But that is only sometimes. The kitchen staff have to squirrel away leftovers for their own families, so often there is little left for them to put aside for Elias.

The real prizes are the overflowing bins behind the restaurants. In the early morning, with steam billowing around vents, with the bins laden with last night's throwaways, it is possible to get lucky and find some edible, semifresh morsels. By late morning, the sun turns them into rotting compost heaps. Elias, Lazarus, and Omagano lengthen their strides to get to town in time.

Elias has a racking cough. He pulls the mucus through the back of his mouth and arcs a dollop away where it lands with a plop. The cough becomes worse each day. Sometimes there is blood in the gunk from his chest but he waves everyone's concerns away. Blood is a part of life. Blood is a part of death. He does not argue with his biology. His graying hair is unevenly cut but not so much that it draws attention. Omagano managed to do a decent job with the scissors.

Lazarus walks behind him, alert, leathery limbs toughened and blackened. At first glance his tattoos are invisible. But upon closer inspection the shoddy work of an unsteady needle and a rudimentary grasp of illustration are seen on his forearms and biceps. They look more like scars than artwork. His ferret face scans his surroundings, always on the lookout for a bin, or marks that let them know they are encroaching upon rival territory. In general, town is an open supermarket for everyone. But sometimes young upstarts try to cordon off particularly fruitful blocks or alleys. Sometimes they become brazen and will beat up an old man they find rooting around in a bin. They would be foolish to try that with Lazarus. His presence in a fight drastically changes the bookies' odds.

Omagano brings up the rear, her frame thinned and stripped of fat, collarbones shining beneath her spaghetti-strap top, nipples sometimes showing their topography through the thin material, still as passably pretty as the day she joined them. Small children are the most valuable recruits. They are nimble and loyal and when you get them young enough the possibilities are endless. Women come next. Sometimes the rubbish bins the Neighborhood Watch visits are fenced off. Guards threaten to beat them for trespassing. Sometimes they want a bribe. Ten dollars, twenty when they know the bins have a high yield (if they have not rifled through them themselves already). When Elias has the money, he pays it. When he does not and they really need to find food, Omagano goes behind a dumpster with a guard and does what needs to be done. The three of them are always on food duty.

Silas and Martin look for other essentials. Discarded blankets and mattresses, rent clothing, usable shoes, broken crates, trolleys, toothpaste tubes worth the squeeze, slivers of soap, pipes and pieces of wire, and anything that can burn. They loiter around construction sites and in shopping mall parking lots looking for something to filch. Wheelbarrows are useful, but nothing beats a trolley. When a trolley is unattended outside a store they push it out of sight quickly. If they find someone in need of a trolley they trade it for something useful. If not, they wheel it back to the bridge. So far they have three trolleys, but they are not too eager to add to their collection. Trolleys take up space and their value can embolden thieves.

Silas likes risk. He has a habit of discovering things that have had previous owners. Like cell phones.

"Where did you get that?" Elias will ask.

"Discovered it," Silas will reply. Shrug of the shoulders, curl of the lip.

Elias constantly warns him not to be a Christopher Columbus and Lazarus threatens him, but there is nothing to be done about it. Silas steals. If he finds something worth selling, then they share the proceeds. But if he gets caught stealing and is beaten or arrested, then he had it coming. He is short and skinny but he screams danger to anyone who knows what to look for. A cocksure walk, an impish grin, eyes that never look away, and hands that hover over a certain pocket when the talk around him gets too rough. Martin follows him around, learning the codes of the street, trying to look tough too, which is hard to do when he has to pull up his baggy trousers every couple of steps. The width of the streets, the height of the buildings, and the number of people walking around still amaze him. Silas says he will get used to it all after a while.

The two groups work separately and meet up in the late afternoon. The food crew shares the lunch. Half a loaf of brown bread, some salty mashed potatoes, soft grapes, and some water. The valuables crew has a stack of newspapers, plastic piping, and two battered, floppy poorboy caps. Elias tries on one, Lazarus takes the other.

"Auasblick tonight," Elias says when they finish eating. "Get some sleep."

It is too hot to be on the streets now. Night is a better and more lucrative time for the Neighborhood Watch.

Auasblick is nice. They still know how to throw away things there. If they hit the bins early enough they can score some good things. Broken toasters, blenders, kettles, water bottles, Teflon pots or pans scrubbed raw and rendered common and cheap, giant flat-screen television cardboard boxes, and, maybe, some food. Omagano and Martin will push the trolley. Elias, Lazarus, and Silas will scout ahead, opening bins, perusing the wares, gauging the value of the detritus of suburbia.

The only problem with Auasblick is how far it is. The further the city spreads itself out the further the foragers have to go. And Auasblick is getting fat, it is already spilling over its sides. New plots are going up for sale, tractors gnaw into steep hillsides. The bountiful weekly dustbin harvest there means more and more crews are creeping in. Soon it will be overcrowded. Like Olympia and Suiderhof. Pionierspark used to be worthwhile, but these days it is not. Too many heads peeking through curtains to find the source of disturbances, too many dogs barking, too many patrolling vehicles with angry, shouting men.

"Blerrie kaffirs. Gaan weg!"

The earlier the Neighborhood Watch can get to Auasblick the better. *Auasblick is die beeste vullisblik.*

TUESDAYS AND THURSDAYS, IN DAYS PAST: KATUTURA, HAKAHANA, GOREANGAB, WANAHEDA, AND OKURYANGAVA

Poor people only throw away garbage. And babies. Garbage is disgusting, babies are useless. That is why the Neighborhood Watch have stopped scavenging on the other side of town.

When Elias and Lazarus were just starting out they used to flick through every bin they could find in every suburb they could reach, walking blisters onto their feet and holes into their shoes. They were indiscriminate and desperate and always hungry. Every bin was fair game. Elias had been by himself for a long time before he met Lazarus. Finding enough to eat and all of the other paraphernalia he needed to survive a day on the streets by himself was taxing. When he proposed an alliance, in the light of a burning drum under a bridge in town, Lazarus was hesitant at first. Lazarus was doing just fine by himself. To team up with an old man like Elias was not an ideal situation. But few things are as persuasive as the fangs of winter. It forced them to work together. Two people could cover more ground. Also, if they specialized—one for food, one for other essentials—they could do a lot more in a day. It made sense, and it worked for them. Anyway, Lazarus liked Elias's company. The old man was not big on small talk. Although when he had some beer or cheap brandy in him he could spin a yarn or two.

Elias was not frightened by Lazarus's prison tattoos. He had faced the gunfire of the South African Defence Force in the jungles of Angola and the rolling Casspirs and the *sjamboks* of the *koevoets* in the North. In his sleep he still heard the bombs as they dropped on Cassinga. Sometimes his slumber would be fitful, and he would whimper until Lazarus shook him awake. The two men regarded each other as equals, both outcast by their former allegiances. Lazarus never volunteered information about his prison stint. Elias never asked. Everyone brought a past to the street and the present was always hungry. The street snacked on those who regretted, those who dreamt of a tomorrow that still required today to be survived.

That was the first thing Elias told Lazarus: the street has no future, there is only today. And today you need food. Today you need shelter. Today you need to take care of today.

On garbage days the two would methodically scour every bin they

41

could find in their old territories of Katutura, Hakahana, Goreangab, Wanaheda, and Okuryangava. But poor people's bins are slim pickings, and Elias and Lazarus talk about those days learnedly, trying to pass on what they know to Martin, Silas, and Omagano.

"When we started out, we weren't picky. We had to survive," Elias says.

"When you have to survive you don't get to choose what you have to do," Lazarus trails.

"Everywhere, we went. Everything, we did."

"We had to survive, *julle ken*."

"But you can't survive by being around people who are also trying to survive," Elias continues. "All you'll get is whatever they don't need to survive, you see?"

"You need to go where people have enough to throw away."

"Where there are white people."

Lazarus laughs a little. "Or black people trying to be white people."

"Then you can survive there."

"Remember when we found the baby?" Lazarus asks. This is a common evening tale. "That was when we knew we had to upgrade."

"We are going through the bins. In neighborhoods where we even have cousins, aunts, and uncles. In places where people might know us. But we go through them."

"To survive, *mos*, just to survive."

Elias's voice becomes grave. "Usually in a bin you have to be ready to find shit. Old food, used condoms, women's pads with blood on them, broken furniture. Those are fine. When things don't have a use they get thrown away, *neh*? But this time we are in a big bin by the side of the road. I reach for some newspapers I see so we can start a fire that night. They are wrapped around something and I lift it up. When I open it I scream and I run."

"I think he has found a snake the way he runs," Lazarus chuckles, a haw-haw sound like a saw biting into a thick piece of wood. Then he becomes quiet. "But I see in the newspapers the baby *met sy umbilliese koord toegedraai om sy nek. Jirre jisses!* I also ran."

"Dead dog? It is okay," Elias says. "Dead cat? It is okay. It is witch-craft. Cats is witchcraft." Omagano nods her agreement. "Even dead person is also okay." Martin's face shows his shock and revulsion and that makes Silas laugh. He really is new to the streets. "People die, *laaitie.* Or maybe the dead person thought he was smart and said something foolish and now he is not going to say anything foolish ever again. Dead person is okay. But dead baby? That is something else."

"Dead baby is evil," Lazarus says. Omagano wraps her arms underneath her breasts and rocks herself a little.

"So," Elias says after a while, "we get smart. We move away from poor people. We find a flyer from the municipality with all the rubbish collection dates. We make a timetable and we start watching the neighborhoods even before there is a neighborhood watch."

"On Tuesday and Thursday nights we stop going to poor people's places because poor people have nothing left to throw away but themselves."

WEDNESDAYS, IN DAYS PAST: KHOMASDAL

There are some neighborhoods not worth fighting over. Dorado Park and Khomasdal are crowded with other starving, roving cliques. The neighborhoods are already spoken for. All the places that break the wind have long-term tenants and all the generous churches already have their squabbling regulars. The Neighborhood Watch never enters Khomasdal because people drink too much there. Alcohol is what took Amos. Not really. It was pride.

After a particularly good week, Elias, Lazarus, and Amos decided to water their throats at one of the many bottle stores that siphon husbands away from their wives and families on Friday and Saturday nights. They shared three quarts of Zamalek to start, then a cheap whiskey, then some more beer. If there were two things Amos could never hold it was his tongue and his drink. But it was his tongue that carried more consequences. It was his tongue that cursed people with swear words that could scour the grime and funk off a dirty pavement. It was his tongue that goaded people. It was his tongue that called someone a *ma se poes*. That same tongue refused to apologize for the slight. Amos could never bring himself to back down from anything.

Then there were three things Amos could not hold. His tongue, his drink, and his guts.

The knife flashed quickly. In, out, in, out, and then slashed across.

Amos looked at his bloody hands and tottered on the spot.

Before the fall comes . . .

Amos fell.

Everyone ran.

If there is one thing that is bad for everyone on the streets, friend or foe, temporarily homeless or permanently on the pavement, it is a dead body.

A dead body has to be explained. To the police. Who like their explanations to be delivered quickly. Slow explanations can be sped up by a few baton bashes in the back of a police van. By the time they throw someone in the holding cell half the crime has already been solved. The paperwork is what seems to frustrate them the most.

That is why everyone ran. Even Elias and Lazarus.

Especially Elias and Lazarus.

The first thing the police do is look for the dead body's living pals. They ask questions. Hard, booted questions. If they know someone is innocent, they kick harder. But if someone has the good sense to be guilty, they ease up because nobody wants the magistrate to ask questions about cuts, bruises, and bumps. Sometimes, when there has been a spate of robberies or a murder the police cannot close quickly enough, they come around and ask someone to take the fall. Jail has food and shelter and sometimes that looks like a good deal. If it is a murder that has made headlines they will offer even better conditions. A single cell, maybe more food. Maybe put you in the same block as a friend. Sometimes someone takes the offer. The streets are not for everyone.

Elias and Lazarus ran until their lungs gave out and then they continued on.

When the police finally caught up with Elias and Lazarus they were interrogated roughly at first and then they were questioned politely. Elias said polite questioning was the worst thing he had ever endured. Worse, even, than being beaten for days on end when he was caught by the *boers* during the insurgency years.

They were eventually let go because they refused to change their story. Yes, they were there when Amos was stabbed. They ran because they were afraid. No, they did not do it. No, they would not say that they did it. No, they did not see who did it. No, they could not identify anyone if they were shown pictures.

Could they then, to a reasonable degree—and, of course, a bruised, bleeding degree—be certain that *they* had not, in fact, murdered Amos for two hundred dollars and then run away after ditching the bloody knife that lay on the table in front of them? Yes, they could be.

For their reasonableness they were let go with a warning, swollen eyes, three broken ribs a pair, and limps that took days to heal—a bargain, really, all things considered. Bones heal, cuts stop bleeding. Everything grows over or grows back, except life.

Elias and Lazarus were lucky. But they chose not to go back to Khomasdal in case the man who killed Amos thought they were out for retribution.

FRIDAY AND SATURDAY: HEADQUARTERS

Under the bridge, behind some bushes, away from the others, Omagano lies down. First Elias takes his turn and then when he is finished Lazarus waits for Omagano to call him so he can also take his. Omagano is only for Elias and Lazarus. Silas and Martin are not allowed to touch her under any circumstances. They are told they are too young. Omagano looks at them with scorn when they make indecent proposals to her.

Instead Silas and Martin have to make the spit. Silas shows Martin how.

Martin has to pull down his dirty denims to his ankles and bring his legs together. Silas spits on his thighs and spreads the saliva between them. Then Martin has to lie on his side while Silas lies behind him, thrusting into the friction until he is finished. Martin rolls over and wipes his thighs and asks Silas to do the same. Silas refuses. It is

Martin's job as a new member to make the spit. Silas had to do it when it was just Elias, Lazarus, and him. Then Omagano joined and the two men claimed her. For now, it is Martin's turn to make the spit for Silas, and for Elias and for Lazarus when Omagano is going through her woman phases. Maybe if they find a younger girl to join, then Martin will not have to make the spit. Or maybe Elias and Lazarus will take the younger girl and give them Omagano. She will be old. But an older woman is better than making the spit.

Fridays and Saturdays are generally spent under the bridge at Headquarters. Elias calls it that because he used to be in the Struggle. He calls broken bottles and thorns APMs. When someone has a wound that needs to be looked at he says it is time for a Tampax Tiffie and when they are low on food he says it is time for the rats. Headquarters is a safer place to be on Fridays and Saturdays because those are the days when the police drive around looking for any signs of mischief. They are the days when pride is most likely to manifest itself. Amos died on a Friday night.

Silas cannot resist leaving Headquarters though. He calls to Martin to join him but Lazarus says no. Martin cannot go. If Silas is going he must go by himself. If mischief finds him he must know no one will come to look for him.

Elias, Lazarus, Omagano, and Martin sit at Headquarters and talk about what they saw in the streets that day. They talk about the fools who sit by the roadside in Klein Windhoek and Eros, hoping they can paint a room, fix a window, install a sink, or lay some tiles.

"They are too proud to be like us," Elias says. "But they are the ones going home hungry every day."

"Pride is poor food," Lazarus says.

"But sometimes they can find a job," Martin chirps.

"They can, sometimes," Elias answers. "But they can find a job as often as we can find twenty thousand dollars. How many times have we found twenty thousand dollars?"

Martin's brow furrows as he thinks and that makes Lazarus laugh. "Idiot," he says.

"Maybe things can get better for them," Martin says.

Elias and Lazarus look at him and then at each other. They sense hope, the scent that leads the street to your hiding place. "Maybe is tomorrow, *laaitie*," Lazarus says.

"And there is only today," Elias adds.

"Today you need food. Today you need shelter. Today you need to take care of today."

"And tomorrow?" Martin asks. Omagano harrumphs.

"Every day is today," Elias says.

SUNDAY: AVIS, KLEIN WINDHOEK, AND EROS

Sundays are the best days. Eros and Klein Windhoek have the highest walls, dogs safely penned behind fences, bins lined up on the pavement, and, most important, people who recycle. The paper, cardboard, plastic bottles, tin cans, and aluminum foil are sorted into separate plastic bags. Some people even wash the trash before they throw it away. Everything else that is of no use goes in the big green bins, which is a much more efficient way to forage. It saves time, mitigates disappointment. Those suburbs are also close to Headquarters, so the Neighborhood Watch does not have to stray too far from their home.

The best thing about Eros is old Mrs. Bezuidenhout. She sits on her front porch in the early evening with her son, waiting for the Neighborhood Watch to come by. When she sees them wheeling their trolley down her street she calls to them. They pause by her gate as she goes into her house. They wait while she makes her slow, brittle way to the electric gate, cheeks sucking in and out on her gums, her son watching her every step. Her gate slides open a fraction and she hands them a plastic bag. Some cans of beans and peas, two or three bananas. She gave them the pair of scissors they use to cut their hair. She gave them the circle of mirror that shames their appearance on some days. In winter she collects old clothes and knits jerseys or blankets from an endless supply of wool. She hands them old books, which they burn, and rosaries they read with their fingers in the dead of night when only God and the streets listen.

The Neighborhood Watch has three pillars: Elias's street savoir-faire, Lazarus's contained violence, and Mrs. Bezuidenhout's generosity. For her, the Neighborhood Watch would fight all of the gangs of Windhoek if they had to. Lazarus is not a believer but even he says Mrs. Bezuidenhout is worth praying for, and to. When she sees them she asks them how they are. Elias replies for them. "*Ons is okay, Mevrou Bezuidenhout.*" She asks them if they need anything else. "*Niks, ons het net nodig wat jy vir ons gegee het.*"

Silas once asked Elias why he never asked for toothbrushes, or soap, or medicine, or a space in her garage where they could sleep, if she was being so generous. Elias said it was because Mrs. Bezuidenhout took from them more than she gave. "She gives and she gives and we take and we take. Soon she will not be around to give and give but we will still need to take and take. She gives something from her home to us

49

and takes some of the street away from us. We need all of the street to survive the street. You understand now?"

The Neighborhood Watch starts in Avis as the sun is setting, hunting for the new apartment complexes that bring a fresh crop of bins to the interlocked pavements, shying away from joggers who avert their eyes when they see them and dog walkers who slacken their grips on leashes. Then they traverse the steep hills of Klein Windhoek, where people only put out their bins at the crack of dawn to dissuade the dustbin divers from perambulating through their streets. That is how bad it has become, Lazarus says. The rich have got so rich they have started hoarding their trash. From there they scour Eros, from top to bottom, through all the streets named after mountains they will never climb, the rivers they shall never see, all the precious stones they will never hold: Everest, Atlas, and the Drakensberg; Orange, Kunene, Okavango, and Kuiseb; amethyst, topaz, and tourmaline. They rove and roam across the neighborhood like wildebeest following the rains, the street following them like a hungry predator.

They leave Mrs. Bezuidenhout's street for last, eager for her kindness, afraid of the day when she will no longer be around to give and give, when they will still need to take and take, when there will not be enough street in them to face the street. The day before they hit Eros, the day before they visit Mrs. Bezuidenhout, the Neighborhood Watch breaks their one rule. They start thinking of the day that is not today, they say goodbye to the day that is yesterday, and worse, they start thinking of the day that is tomorrow.

BLACK, COLORED, AND BLUE
(OR, THE GANGSTER'S GIRLFRIEND)

The problem with the Gangster's girlfriend, upon further reflection, was this: it seemed as though every time you put your dick in her vagina he put his fist through her face. True, there was no conclusive proof her smashed ribs had anything to do with you tickling her throat on the regular, but your guilt gushed whenever she showed up at your place looking six kinds of pretty and seven kinds of broken.

You told yourself you had nothing to do with it because the two of you were always discreet. If there's anything this country can do well it's keep a secret—buried, filed away. Sure, the windy corner you call home might have a small carpet, but it sure as hell has a big broom. Whole annals of history can be swept under the rug. Just ask Lothar von Trotha, who used the Herero and Namaqua tribes as genocide practice before the Germans moved on to the big leagues with the Jews. Before Auschwitz and Dachau there was Shark Island, a place of hunger, built for butchery. The severed heads stacked better than

LEGO blocks. The bones were used to research superiority. What couldn't be burned, buried, or scattered to the sea was sold to collections, museums, and universities in the Second Reich. Like Rinzlo's wizened grandmother said one evening at a family party you'd been invited to: "They learned how to kill them by killing us." An entire people massacred or raped into prevalent identity crises. Everything silenced for years.

You figured, heck, if a documented, photographed, and archived attempt at human mass extinction could be so casually hidden from the hot iron of history, you and the Gangster's girlfriend were merely another crease in the fabric of society, too insignificant to be straightened out.

Thanks to your wild years at university, secretive nocturnal meetings were never a problem. A great part of your third year was spent acclimatizing to the sexual schedules of certain lecturers. To this day you feel that one essay was poorly marked because your Austen professor found out the African literature tutor was also showing you ankle. She'd been quite specific about you not messing around with anyone else. Your youth, enthusiasm, and eagerness to please belonged to her. You were a hung trophy for her cabinet, bed, sofa, staircase, kitchen counter, office storage closet, and car alone. But you were young, yet to develop or understand the possessiveness of age. You figured there was enough of you to go around. Your pride bought her prejudice.

—*This writing shows a poor understanding of male-female relations in Austen's era and what women had to do in order to secure male attention and, hopefully, the provision and security essential for survival. While it could pass muster in African literature, where promiscuity is profligate and highly praised, even expected, I'm afraid there's not enough substance in this essay to warrant a higher mark. What this kind of writing needs is more sense; what the writer needs is more sensibility.*

Forty-nine percent for your essay? Man, that woman was mad disrespectful.

Nighttime escapades aside, you realized you were too broke to eat at the restaurants the Gangster's girlfriend and her man would patronize, so you never feared bumping into them. You'd never see each other in any of the city's clubs because you were tired of the scene. You had a strong feeling the Gangster wasn't much of a reader. It wasn't like he'd put in an appearance at your favorite bookstore or the public library looking for you.

Sure, sleeping with the Gangster's girlfriend made your life expectancy swan-dive into the soon-to-be tomorrows, but what kind of late-twenties Casanova hasn't found himself in a secret affair that could conclude with double homicide?

You felt secure about the whole tryst because nobody assumed the Gangster's girlfriend would be foolish enough to cheat on him.

Or to cheat on him with someone like you.

But she did.

And you were fine with it until you started doing the math: whenever she came over to your place she'd be sporting some new hues on her toffee-colored skin. You asked her about it, asked her if you were getting her into trouble, and she shrugged it away. "Maybe," she said. She saw you flinch. "Maybe not."

Fifty-fifty.

There was a fifty percent chance the Gangster's abuse was a direct result of the affair, and a fifty percent chance the Gangster was recreationally rearranging her features because he could. This country being what it is for women, you decided the Gangster's violence was another part of the geography, like the desert and the drought, or the scorching afternoons and pastel-smudge sunsets.

Anyway, you thought, if the Gangster knew you squatted in his girlfriend's womb on the daily, you'd be dead already.

But you weren't.

It sucks to admit it now but there was that one time you feared she was pregnant with your child no matter how much she told you she wasn't. She got so tired of your limp anxiety, the next time she came over she barged straight into your dingy toilet, peed on the stick, and waved it triumphantly in front of your face.

You couldn't pull your gaze away from her face. The Gangster made her cheek look like it was expecting.

How could she be that battered and even giggle when she said, "There. Happy now?"

How could she still insist the two of you carry on with such foolishness as she reached for your belt buckle?

You should've called it off then. Everything in you said you should. But each time you prepared to denounce her you'd get the afternoon shakes and the evening shivers. When she showed up again everything would be okay.

You wanted to end it.

You needed it to stop.

But you didn't.

Never mind that she had two children—a boy from the Gangster, a girl from a nameless man in her past—or that when you first met she wasn't the one who came on to you. You're the one who wheedled her number from a friend of a friend of a frenemy thanks to this shoebox city and its three degrees of separation. You sent the message first, not really expecting a response. She replied.

—*Hi. I remember you.*

You smiled. Back and forth the conversation went for a week or so. The Gangster's girlfriend was cool, all charm and prompt responses. Nothing hectic, nothing racy, nothing to set off your Spidey senses.

"Not even after she told you who her man was?" Franco asked when you told him the story. He looked at you strangely.

"Nah. Not even then."

Never mind that the newspapers front-paged The Gangster for a year straight: dodgy diamond deals in the Congo, housing tender fraud in South Africa, more pyramid schemes in Nigeria than Pharaoh Khufu, and shady ties to politicians and the president back home. ("Dude, the president!" Franco had to walk out of the room to collect himself.) He was rumored to be middlemanning deals with dictators in banana and cassava republics in West Africa. He flew in and out of the country more than Jason Bourne. No passport control, no customs check, no nothing. When the papers caught wind of him they knew they had a new bottom line. They fed him to the printers by the editorial-load. One column went as far as saying "the country would probably have been bounced into Second World status were it not for the Gangster and all he stole." This dude was hated more than Judas Iscariot and that's saying a lot because black people hate the shit out of him for betraying White Jesus.

The Gangster's girlfriend showed up on your doorstep on multiple occasions, bruised purple and blue, and each time you let her inside your overpriced apartment, with its shitty lighting, kitsch furniture, food-starved fridge, slender single bed, and listened to her talk about the depths and scope of the Gangster's exploits. You heard about the horse mackerel fishing quotas handed out to Icelandic consortiums in exchange for bribe money circulated through Cyprus and Mauritius; the oil contract fleecing in Luanda, which pumped millions of dollars out of the country; the antiretroviral scams in Lusaka; the arms deals in Khartoum; the real estate developments in Dubai being built by Bangladeshi slave labor; and the Zurich-based banks that never asked questions. The Gangster's business was so shady he was becoming light-skinned. "It's really a matter of time before he turns white," you said. The Gangster's girlfriend laughed at that. A laugh she cut short to spare herself the abdominal pain.

That's what got you each time. The amalgam of pain and beauty, locked together, sometimes good, sometimes bad, venomous and deadly all the time. First she was beauty and then she became pain. Then, for an instant, she was neither, floating in the middle, disoriented like Alice in front of the Cheshire cat. You didn't know from whence she came, you didn't know where you were going. You'd like to say you were lost but lost implies the possibility of being found. The two of you were just messed up.

Like the do-good knight you thought you were, you tried to slay her dragon. You kissed the broken lips, tasting blood, softening the contact when you saw her wince in pain. You massaged the sensitive flesh with cool aloe vera balm like your mother used to do for you when you came home from a basketball game on the other side of town, where all the public schools fielded teenagers who looked like men. You even thought you could stroke some sense into her. Surely, you thought, if you just angled her this way and then thrust like this she'd see that she could do so much better than the Gangster. Whatever logic you spilled into her didn't take root in her uterus walls, because a couple of days later she'd show up looking like a peach Mike Tyson used for speed practice.

The first time you told her you wanted to stop she looked at you, confused, reaching to unclasp her bra. "What's the matter?" she asked.

"I'm not sure."

"Not having fun anymore?" Her skintight denim peeled off.

"I'm not having fun all of the time."

"Some of the time's better than none of the time." She stood in front of you. Flawless but for the contusion on her navel, the blush you ached to kiss.

"None might be best for you," you said after a while.

She walked toward you, slowly, and asked if the sex was bad. You said it wasn't as she parachuted your top over your head. It was actually the best sex you were having and the block had pretty much been around you. Not since you and your girlfriend had parted ways like the path in that Frost poem had you met a woman who could ride you out of your daydreams, distractions, and slight mood depressions into the here and now with her. The Gangster's girlfriend's fingers trod down your arms, sending your biology into a frenzy. "So what is it then?"

"It just doesn't feel—"

"Right?" Your left nipple vanished into her mouth. She pulled on it gently. "You're really going to give me that?" She released it and then bit it hard. "If it's wrong then what're you going to do about it?" She looked up at you. You closed your eyes, unable to withstand her smirking gaze. She waited for an answer as her hands found the precious inches in your pants. She reached up to kiss you. "Don't bring me problems if you don't have solutions," she said. She paused long enough for you to open your eyes and look at her. "And don't presume to know what's best for me." The finality in her eyes.

"Okay," you whispered.

You used the sex to deal with the guilt. Acknowledged but unaddressed remorse is such comfortable inertia. It's reassuring for guys like you. Guilt means you still feel something. You only cut off the limb when you can't feel anything, right?

Half the time you were together you weren't sure whether you were more afraid of the Gangster or the girl crazy enough to stick with the Gangster. You were smart enough never to talk about it to anyone though. Not even to your boys when the braggadocio was doing the rounds. Your lips were sealed like a classified CIA assassination file from Latin America in the seventies and eighties. Even Franco, your boy, could never wheedle the information out of you when you didn't show up for *braais* or games nights. He felt so betrayed—"I thought I was your boy, man!"—much later, after you told him whom you'd been keeping secret, he calmed down. "Well, damn," he said, looking at you with newfound respect, "I'd also keep that shit under wraps!"

You and the Gangster's girlfriend developed a routine.

She only came over on weeknights. The weekends were for her children and the Gangster. She didn't like sitting around, watching films, or listening to your eclectic music collection. She rustled through your bookcase, asking you what you were reading, looking through your journal before you pulled it from her hands. She asked what you were writing and seemed disappointed when you didn't have a new story to tell her. She never offered to cook, never brought food over, never left any of her possessions over at your place, never asked if you were seeing other people, never asked about your days, and never asked about your family.

You were never permitted to call or text her. Never. Not even if it was to cancel or to reschedule a rendezvous. Whenever she came over, when she was done with you, when you started to reach across to her to pull her close, she got up and started dressing. Then she told you when to expect her again. Tomorrow night. On Friday. "Next week on Wednesday." You asked her what would happen if something came up, or if you were running late, or if you had to let her know she couldn't come around. She looked at you long enough to let you know that nothing could or would ever come up.

Nothing came up. (Unless, of course, she made it.)

The contraception issue never arose. The first time she came over you made a polite stretch for the condoms in the bedside drawer while she hovered above you, the heat and smell of her so close. Just as you managed to grab one of the foil-covered sentries you felt her lower herself onto you, squeezing you into the ancestral plane. It was a wrap after that. From then on your pullout game had the messy grace of an abstract expressionist painting.

The Gangster's girlfriend came around when she said she would. Unless she couldn't. Then it was your appointed task to sit and wait for her, from rosy sunset to blue-balls midnight and sometimes for a couple of hours thereafter. On the nights she didn't show up you were a prisoner in your own apartment, moving aimlessly from books to boredom, from pirated films to frustrated first-person shooters, and, finally, to palm-itching cellphone twiddling. You never called or texted.

You didn't have the minerals to dig deep and break her rules. There's a reason why dogs are man's best friend. They know they're destined to drown in their loyalties forever.

That's life.

Them be the rules—she texted this to you once when she was feeling indulgent. (She was at a state dinner with the Gangster. She said she couldn't come over because she'd have to entertain politicians' wives and listen to tepid gossip after supper.) You had cleared out your whole evening anticipating her arrival, drooling with desire about upcoming delights.

But there's only so much patience a man has before he thinks he's too cute and too fresh to be a sidekick. Your Robin-to-Nightwing moment came when you were at your dad's for his birthday. Somehow the old man looked like he had aged three years in the previous twelve months. Your brother even baked a cake. It was a shit cake but the three of you managed to have fun together for a change—no arguments and no relapses into remembrance about how dope birthdays were when your mother was still alive. You looked at your watch and realized you had twenty minutes to get to your place. She said she'd come through at ten.

Surely, you thought, she could wait a little. It was, after all, your dad's birthday.

Plus, you were tired of having your chain yanked. You waited for your father to blow out his candles before you panicked and made your hasty, empty excuses. Your father was genuinely sad to see you go. It was the first time in many months the three of you had enjoyed each other's company.

As you pulled up to your place you saw her white Range Rover make a furious U-turn up ahead, nearly taking off another car's side mirror. When she sped past you rolled down your window, trying to get her attention, trying to get her to stop just long enough so you could explain that your father's birthday had gone into overtime. She sped away.

You couldn't call and you knew she wouldn't. For three weeks the Gangster's girlfriend had you coming home early, waiting for her, hoping she'd come back so you could explain the situation.

When she finally did arrive she floated into the lounge, blithely, and alighted on the couch like an autumn leaf in a too-still pond. The silence rippled from her, waiting for you to tender your apologies. You didn't get far before she said, "Don't make me wait like that again."

"It was, like, ten minutes."

"Seven."

"You were counting?"

"Don't make me wait again. This isn't how it works."

You thundered and blustered about the wait not being that long and just how the fuck could she not understand there'd be nights when you'd have shit to do. Also, you said, pacing in your lounge like a small tempest, what the fuck did she think she was doing coming over to your place on a random night like that? What if you had shit to do? She looked at you with scorn, arching her finely threaded eyebrows. "If you have something else to do instead of me then you should do it," she said.

You didn't have shit to do and it wasn't a random night. You were waiting for her. You'd been waiting for her for a month. You would've waited some more. You knew it.

Worse, she knew it.

You knew the Gangster was out of town when she showed up with that immaculate skin that was the same even tone all over, when the contours of her face were finite, when she didn't have to cake herself in makeup. She lingered longer on those days. But when the Gangster landed back in the city you'd know by the gingerly movements she made in bed, easing herself into a position that didn't put too much weight on the parts of her he had hurt. Those were the days when you'd be at your most righteous. (Internally, of course.)

This, you told yourself, would be the last time.

No, *this* would be the last time.

Seriously, *this* would be the last time.

You cock-crowed at the lie.

The last time you told her it was the last time it was the last time for about a month. You sat across her in bed and looked at her dead in the face. You told her you'd had enough.

"This has to be the last time," you said. "Unless—"

She threw her legs over the bed and began to dress. She didn't even let you finish your ultimatum: *me or the Gangster.*

She chose, you told yourself.

You waited one week for her to show up without warning, then a second one just for good measure. By the third you figured you'd poisoned the well enough for her to never come back. You filled your time with your friends again. You visited your father and brother more. You tried to get back in the game but no one stacked up.

In your diary you wrote: *There's no last time like the first time you realize it's the last time.*

The Gangster's girlfriend did an unnatural thing after ghosting you for two months: she called you.

She said she wanted to meet up. You said, "I'm not sure that's a good idea." (You were fucking ecstatic!)

She said it didn't have to be for long. (You hoped it would be!)

"Don't worry," she said. "Absolutely nothing's going to happen."

You were disappointed by the conviction in her voice. When the Gangster's girlfriend decided something was a no-no it remained a no-go zone forever. Like the time you tried to suggest getting some takeaway. It was late, most of the restaurant kitchens were nearing closing time, but you felt like cruising the streets looking for something to eat. She waited for you to finish your suggestion. Then she said the flattest no this side of flat-earth conspiracies. You heard the same certainty in her voice over the phone. She said she was on her way.

While you waited for her, you kept busy by cleaning clean dishes and boiling and reboiling some water for tea.

When the Gangster's girlfriend knocked softly on your door you opened it. She walked in and threw her handbag on the sofa. She sat down and removed her dark sunglasses. Then she removed her jacket, the one that probably cost more than everything in your apartment, and you saw her arms. The Gangster was definitely back in town.

You sighed. "Again?"

"Again," she said.

You went to the fridge to see if there was anything you could give her to drink. You knew you didn't have anything but the attempt was still polite. You returned with a glass of chilled water and placed it on the coffee table that had sturdily held your combined weight on nights of Kama Sutra past.

"Coat hanger?" you asked.

"Mmm. Wire."

"When?"

The Gangster's girlfriend fixed you with a look which made you want to crawl back into your question, back into your very being, and out the other side into an alternate reality where you weren't thinking about the shape, texture, and taste of her even as she looked so balefully at you.

You both looked away.

You'd asked her once before but you felt like it was your duty to ask again. Repetition is the father of learning and unlearning as well as zero-sum, dead-end relationships. (You'd write that in your diary later that evening.)

"Why're you here?"

She inhaled deeply and looked around your open-plan lounge, kitchen, and bedroom. You looked with her. The books stacked on the salvage-wood shelves you and your brother made from abandoned pallets; the ring-stained writing desk with its dictionary, thesaurus, and assortment of pens; the sea-green walls; and the one-person kitchen which didn't permit romantic behind-the-back hugs for cooking couples—you know this because you tried this with the Gangster's girlfriend and she left you, walking out of your place, with you trailing her and apologizing for the attempted romance. You came back to find your stir-fry burning in the pan.

"What've you been writing?" she asked.

"Nothing I want to talk about." You saw her eyes become arctic at the edge. You retreated from your retort. "Not much. But you haven't answered my question."

"We're getting married," she announced.

"Really?"

"Yes," she said. "It makes things easier for the children. It'll be stable."

"What about you?"

The Gangster's girlfriend let out a harsh laugh. "What about me?"

"It just seems—"

"Wrong? Really?"

"You know what? Never mind. I was just asking."

The Gangster's girlfriend sat up. "Anyway, I just came by to let you know this can't go on."

"That's why I ended it, in case you forgot." Your chest flared out a little, like a junior bantamweight boxer turning pro.

She smiled, fleetingly. She said the universal "okay" younger brothers use to piss off their older siblings. The "okay" of "Sure, whatever makes you feel better about yourself." The "okay" of "This thing that matters so much to you is of no consequence to me."

The Gangster's girlfriend was in your lounge, sporting cuts on her arms inflicted by her soon-to-be husband, breaking up with you after you broke up with her. ("The unmitigated gall," Franco said when you gave him the rundown.)

Your stomach soured. "Anything else?"

"There's nothing else."

Another period of silence passed by and then the Gangster's girl-friend got up and walked to the door. At the threshold you stood apart. The air between you, for once, didn't crackle with sin and secrets. You shifted your weight onto one leg before forcing yourself to stand up straight and face her. "I think," you said, "you're doing something stupid. You deserve better."

Her smile slitted and her nostrils flared.

You saw her fists clench.

Then she relaxed.

Her shoulders drooped.

Then she said, "I know."

She walked away.

That week, when you sat with your old man and brother at home, watching a Liverpool game, you looked at your phone every once in a while. You knew she wouldn't call. You couldn't beg her back. You couldn't borrow her. You couldn't even steal her. You autopiloted the conversation with your father, which annoyed him. "You know you don't have to be here," he said. "But if you insist on being here, then I insist on you being present." You ate a cheerless supper with him before heading back to your place.

You went to bed angry, lying awake for a while. You looked at your phone, a voyeur of your first messages with the Gangster's girlfriend. What recklessness. What energy.

Where had it gone? Now you waited to be petted, Pavlovian and pitiful.

You realized, sadly, that that was how you'd become with your girlfriend. You'd gone from god—*Shazam!*—to mere mortal through negligence, comfort, routine, and the inexplicable belief that you'd get better because you were *you*. You were that one-in-a-million kind of guy who'd go from bummer to mamba mentality without even trying. You wouldn't have to put in those Kobe hours. Not you, the born-not-made MVP.

You opened your Instagram feed and scrolled through your ex's, scrolling past the videos of her joining the fitness cult, the vegetarian recipes, and the peaceful sunsets with quotes from Neruda and Rumi for captions.

You scrolled all the way down, down, down to the very last picture you remember of her posting when you were still together. It was the week before your birthday, you still shared an apartment with her. You'd come home to find her cooking and dancing in the kitchen to Natalie Imbruglia's "Torn." You looked at her throwing her energy around, inviting you to join her. You shook your head and smiled to hide the abscess that was already too far gone in your soul, the rot of loneliness, the sadness that cloaked you like a secret power. You took her in your arms, kissed her gently, knowing what you'd do to her in a few hours, and told her she deserved better. She'd tapped the wooden spoon on your nose and said she knew. "That's why I have you," she added. She laughed and went back to cooking.

You lay in bed thinking, first about the Gangster's girlfriend, and then your ex-girlfriend.

To the darkness, and to both of them, you said the painful truth: "You deserve better."

And you knew you weren't it.

B-Side

IMPORTANT TERMINOLOGY
FOR MILITARY-AGE MALES

*T*he good old days. That's what everyone calls them. I just remember them as being old. Dry, dead, endless heat. Days hiding from the sun. Nights with only stars for witnesses. Hours of nothingness, waiting outside a village, tracking movements. And minutes filled with whizzing bullets. *Paah-paah* when they left the gun. *Chook-chook* when they hit the sand just in front of me. Or *whoosh-whoosh* as they zoomed into the trees and bushes behind me, stripping them of foliage—it's easy to remember the sound of bullets when they don't hit you.

There! A target.

Take aim, breathe—fire!

Terrorist down.

Do it again. And again.

"The good old days, eh?" Pietermaritzburg reminisced as we sat on his farm's *stoep*. Intel. Enemy movements. Missions. Targets. Clear and defined.

"*Ja*," I replied, "the old days."

Looking at dirt paths, trying to see if the earth had been disturbed by mine planting. The evenings, humid, sticky, full of malaria and the harrumphing of hippos when we were near the Okavango. The mornings of creaking muscles—the nerves, stretched, steeled, and sharpened. The monk-like blanking of the mind, the vacating of the soul. No wants or desires beyond the day's hunt: insurgents, guerrillas, rebels, freedom fighters, terrorists—kaffirs.

The old days.

I remember Pietermaritzburg's barking briefings, Kaapstad's jokes, Kimberley's religious dogma, East London's short-lived advice, and Knysna's naivete. I remember my conscription, my diligent training, the awakening of my bloodlust, my belief and faith—my soldierly qualities. My reassignment: "South West Africa—you're the kind of man we need up there." I remember being told I was a closed file already, a corpse that would never be claimed. "Nobody is supposed to know we have covert units there."

I remember meeting the others. "We'll call you Johannesburg," Pietermaritzburg said, "save the other details for a pretty date."

Kaapstad laughed at my introduction, formal, with a sharp paper cut of a salute. "Do you know what we do in this unit, Joburg?" he asked.

Counterinsurgency: monitoring, tracking, and reporting.

They laughed.

"Not all wrong," Pietermaritzburg said. "We observe the kaffirs. We monitor the kaffirs. We track the kaffirs. But we're not David Livingstone or Henry Morton Stanley—we don't record the lives of kaffirs, Joburg. We end them. Do you understand?" I said I did. "We shall see." Pietermaritzburg winked at Kaapstad. "How is your military alphabet?" Alpha, Bravo, Charlie, Delta, Echo—I was cut off by more laughing and hooting. "It's shit." Pietermaritzburg smiled. "Don't worry, we'll help you improve it. The first thing you need to know is this: *G* is for gift. We have a welcoming present for you. Follow me."

The good old days.

Just days to me.

Old, old days.

▶ ‖

ANGOLA

as in Republic of; as in República de Angola and Republika ya Ngola; as in "one of the kaffir countries playacting independence," Kimberley said, by way of welcome, "your new home"; as in mottled shades of green and a silence not found in nature—not even in the desert; as in "Keep your eyes open because the kaffirs are out there," Pietermaritz-burg said, always wary, giving everything two and then three pass-overs with his eyes. "This whole country is camouflage—it puts on its best colors just for you and dulls your senses with nature while it hides the kaffirs. Stay alert, Joburg"; as in ambush, with bullets spraying from anonymous clumps of bush; as in "Step exactly where João steps be-cause these fucking kaffirs have mined the whole place," East London instructed, "you don't want to stray off the path and—"

or, *apartheid*—as in racial segregation; as in God's Law; as in "God

71

made white people and put them in Europe. Then He made kaffirs and put them in Africa. The yellow Chinaman He put in Asia. And the red people He put in America. Think about it," Kimberley said, certain, "putting them all on separate continents was a sign the races were never intended to mix. We only came to Africa to manage the bloody kaffirs because they couldn't do it by themselves!"

BANTU

as in the Ntu peoples; as in migration from West and Central Africa heading south; as in "They're not even from here originally," Kaapstad said, laughing at the incredulity of land claims while we were on the march.

or, *Benguela*—as in oceanic current; as in the *poes kou water* in Swakopmund or the lonely Skeleton Coast when I visited recently; as in the city by the sea where the kaffirs put some wild blood in the Portuguese women over there; as in Eriel Leila Dos Santos, who said she'd take care of *it* by herself if she had to, not knowing she'd have to; as in "She's just another woman," Kaapstad counseled. "Beautiful, but still a half-kaffir. That child's going to be whiter than her—that's an improvement in her general fortunes, I think."

or, *bushman*—as in San; as in desert pygmy; as in "The best trackers alive," Pietermaritzburg said, remembering one who'd served with him. "He could smell which direction kaffirs farted from a kilometer away and tell you their tribe just by looking at their shit. Decent guy"; as in "What happened to him?" asked Knysna, always curious; as in "Had to put him down after he got drunk on the job and nearly got us ambushed. Once you get alcohol in these kaffirs they're pretty useless. But that *boesman* was a hell of a tracker."

CASSINGA

as in Operation Reindeer; as in there is no difference between civilians and soldiers when it comes to the kaffirs: "There are only targets and all that matters is whether they're moving or still," Pietermaritzburg said when the news reached us.

or, *Che*—as in Ernesto Guevara; as in the Argentine Karlo-Marlo terrorist; as in "the Communist Jesus Christ whose lies the kaffirs have ingested whole," Kimberley said.

or, *colonialism*—as in the Scramble for Africa; as in "the best thing to ever happen to the kaffirs and the last time anything civil ever happened on the whole bloody continent," Kimberley added, older, sipping his beer, raising his voice in the bar, certain of securing agreement from the other patronage; as in "These kaffirs complain too much. Didn't we bring them roads, schools, advanced medicine, and electricity?" he added to vociferous cheering from everyone else.

DE BEERS

as in the diamond company; as in a draft dodger: "Do you know where diamonds from South Africa wind up?" Kaapstad asked. "Somewhere else!"; as in "Then why am I still here?" Kimberley asked; as in "Because you're not a diamond," Kaapstad replied, "you're a *doos*!"

ENGLISH

as in "The *fokken souties* who took this country from us," Kimberley said; as in "Everyone who discovered tea and crumpet roots and fled to that miserable little island to escape the draft," Pietermaritzburg added.

or, *East London*; as in never really knew him before he died; as in "The army always has vacancies," Kaapstad said later that night, eyes dark with hatred after shooting João ("He should've known better!" he shouted after Pietermaritzburg asked him why he'd killed our guide), "job openings that need to be filled by soon-to-be dead men. You, Joburg, do you know what we call a pension in the army? A general."

FIDEL

as in Alejandro Castro Ruz; as in the Communist Godfather; as in the Cuban kaffir who flooded Angola with soldiers we had to work hard to avoid; as in "The fucker outlasted ten presidents, eh," Pietermaritzburg chuckled, aging, cancer shooting through him. "Maybe there's something in that Communism shit, eh?"

GIFT

as in the first kill; as in "Right, as you can see, we're a small unit. We don't have the resources to keep prisoners," Pietermaritzburg said.

"This one here says he isn't a PLAN soldier but I don't believe him. And because I don't believe him it means he's lying. I don't like liars, especially kaffir liars. You see this knife? You're going to fetch me his eyes, tongue, and ears. If you don't do it, I will shoot you. You die in real life just like you died on paper when you joined my command. Understand?"; as in I understood very well.

HAVANA

as in Cuba; as in the capital city of Communism; as in "the first gate to Hell," Kimberley said, "the safest thing to do is blow that whole island up."

or, *Hendrik*—as in Kaptein Witbooi; as in "Why you shouldn't teach the kaffirs how to use a rifle," Pietermaritzburg said, angry, looking at Malmesbury—another short-lived member of our unit—lying prone, bullet hole through his head after we'd flanked the lost PLAN unit and destroyed it completely.

INSPIRATION

as in electrical shock; as in castration; as in hanging; as in firing squad; as in "Giving the kaffir a reason to answer questions forthrightly," Pietermaritzburg said, looking at Knysna's wide eyes when he realized why the captured men were drawing lots. "The one with the short stick gets the long end of the rifle."

or, *interview*—as in interrogation; as in when kaffirs are given the opportunity to answer questions forthrightly "as best as they can to see if they get a job among the living or the dead," Kaapstad said, laughing.

JOCK

as in *of the Bushveld* by Sir Percy FitzPatrick; as in "I named him after the one in the book," Kimberley said, lovingly petting his Staffordshire bull terrier when I visited him at his seaside cottage overlooking the Indian Ocean—"I never want to see anything the Atlantic touches ever again," he'd said earlier in a moment of reminiscence, hands gripping the armrest of his chair.

or, *Johannesburg*—as in the city of gold; as in home; as in me when Pietermaritzburg phones me and says, "No doubt you've heard about what Knysna is trying to do. Well, we've got to stop him. Just like the good old days, eh?"; as in another long trip far from home.

KAFFIR

as in *aapie, blackie, darkie, bobbejaan*; as in the Bantu; as in "all the hard-heeled motherfuckers we fought against to get this land," Kimberley said, taking aim; as in "Ten rands that kaffir makes it to the tree line," Pietermaritzburg wagered, gauging the distance, knowing Kimberley was not a good shot; as in "You hit him clean in the brains!" Kaapstad exclaimed; as in "Kaffirs don't have brains,"

Kimberley replied, "just spaces between their ears where we put our judgment."

or, *Kaapstad*—as in the comedian from Cape Town; "He's a *soutie*, but a good one," Pietermaritzburg said by way of introduction; as in the best shooter in the unit; as in killed in action in Owambo-land; as in "Leave him," Pietermaritzburg shouted, running toward some rocks for shelter, with gunfire sniffing at our heels; as in "Poor bastard," Kimberley said, wiping his eyes, taking a sip of his whiskey in the bar, "he could always make a joke. Gave those kaffirs real hell up there!"

or, *Kimberley*—as in the Big Holy; as in "beloved father, brother, uncle, son, and soldier"; as in died of diabetic complications; as in survived by his widow, his son, my godson of military age, and his daughter; as in "I understand why Knysna felt the way he did, and why he pursued that course of action, but I'm not sure what happened next was correct, Joburg," he said, years later, looking out at the waves tumbling over themselves in their glee. "I'm not going to shy away from my part in it, but I'm not sure we did the right thing"; as in "Diabetes? That's a *kak* way to go, eh," Pietermaritzburg said, drunk, emotional, scared of the mutiny in his own body. "Imagine surviving Suid-Wes only to be killed by fucking sugar. I'm telling you, it's not right for soldiers like us to die from civilian causes. Let me face all the kaffirs in the world again, but cancer—"

or, *Knysna*—as in a boy in a man's body trapped in a devil's war; as in the youngest member of our unit, sent to East London; as in the one who always asked if there was no other way; as in "No, there's no other way, Knysna," Pietermaritzburg said. "This is the only way in this unit. Now, you either open your gift or I take this knife and unwrap you. Do you understand?"; as in the one who had the worst disease civilian life could conjure up, worse than cancer: the conscience; as in a resort town on the Garden Route; as in a hotel room; as in a restaurant near the marina where we shared drinks—me, Pietermaritzburg, Kimberley, and Knysna, with tense, forced-out laughter, and furtive looks to the left and to the right; as in "Remember the good old days?" Pietermaritzburg asked; as in "There were no good old days," Knysna replied, "just days, and our evil part in them"; as in "Stop that kind of talk," Pietermaritzburg said, "it's the kind of talk that could get you into serious trouble"; as in "Is that why you're here?" Knysna asked; as in "No, Knysna, we're just on holiday," Pietermaritzburg replied, "just a short trip to visit an old friend."

LUSAKA

as in the capital city of Zambia, formerly Northern Rhodesia; as in the Lusaka Accords; as in the signed lies of ceasefire Castro laughed at; as in the useless pieces of paper that had no hope of ending the Border War.

MANDATE

as in granted to the Union of South Africa by the League of Nations after the Germans lost the First World War; as in administration, not annexation; as in "There was no way the kaffirs could form their own republic," East London, who considered himself to be a keen political mind, said, "so of course we had to take it over and run it as another province."

or, *menopause*—as in a ceasefire; as in a temporary pause on the bloodletting during the Lusaka Accords.

or, *missionary*—as in to lie flat on the ground when under fire.

NAMIBIA

as in the Republic of; as in the former South West Africa; as in the country born from the South African Border War—an illegitimate child of the Cold War; as in the place where military-age males were required to serve; as in the land of savannas, sunsets, the Fish River Canyon, Sossusvlei and its red sand dunes that look like they lapped up all the blood spilled in birthing the country, and the Skeleton Coast in the oldest desert in the world, where the ghosts of dead freedom fighters lurk, whisper, and cry; as in I visited it last year, retracing my steps in a country born from guerrilla warfare and Communism, now a capitalist utopia like the very best of the fallen Soviet and Cuban disciples.

OWAMBOLAND

as in Northern Namibia; as in the blanket and all-encompassing heat; as in the land of the most populous kaffirs in South West Africa; as in entire villages stripped of men and run by women; as in dry patches of sand that turn into miniature lakes in the rainy season.

PIETERMARITZBURG

as in unit leader; as in another "beloved father, brother, uncle, son, and soldier"—I used the same monikers from Kimberley's funeral since I couldn't think of anything else to say about the man; as in survived by his daughters; as in "That's the coldest kaffir-killing bastard around," Kaapstad told me after my gift was unwrapped, "an odd sort, a soldier's soldier—you stick with him and you'll be okay"; as in the man who saved me from certain death countless times; as in the man who could not be reasoned with; as in "Listen, Joburg," he said over the phone, angry, "Knysna's conscience has declared itself to be our enemy. Finish *en klaar.* I'll see you in the morning."

or, *PLAN*—as in People's Liberation Army of Namibia (formerly SWALA); as in the military wing of SWAPO; as in saboteurs and guerrillas; as in "the nearly invisible monkeys that cannot come out and fight like men," Pietermaritzburg said; as in the kaffirs who received material assistance from the Communist republics of the world; as in "the devil's foot soldiers," Kimberley said. "These devils will fight tooth and nail for this patch of sand beyond reason and hope. They're up against a superior enemy, but still they fight—if that's not kaffir black magic I don't know what is."

QUININE

as in antimalarial drug; as in "I can't think of other things beginning with *q*," Kaapstad said; as in "That's a hard one," Pietermaritzburg agreed, scanning the landscape, stopping the day's march and bringing a pause to our game of military alphabet. "We stop here for the night. Looks quiet—there's one for you, Kaapstad: quiet."

ROOIBOS

as in tea from the red bush, as in a sunset in the south when summer is at its peak; as in "a virgin girl," Kaapstad said, "because after twelve it's teatime. What? You've never had yourself some rooibos? You should try it. Calms the nerves, it does."

or, *Robert*—as in Mangaliso Sobukwe; as in the founder of the Pan Africanist Congress; as in one of the few kaffirs who knew the only way for the kaffirs to fight against his inevitable fate—past, present, and future—was together; as in solitary confinement; as in "You know," Pietermaritzburg said, fighting a new domestic war, struggling to settle into a life without combat, "I've been reading some of the writings and ideas from all the kaffirs on Robben Island. Dangerous stuff, I tell you. If all the kaffirs woke up to such things this damned continent would be quite different"; as in "Isolate the kaffir and the kaffir can't spread their lies," Kimberley replied, changing gears, driving toward Knysna's house, "or our truth."

SWAPO

as in South West Africa People's Organisation, as in the former OPO—Owambo People's Organisation; as in led by Samuel Shafishuna

Nujoma—"The *Bobbejaan Koning*," Pietermaritzburg said, "you take that kaffir out and you cut off the head of the snake!"; as in "Give it time," Kimberley said, "all that socialism bullshit he's preaching is light cologne. It can't work in that heat. Eventually, the capitalist sweat of the kaffirs will come through."

TANZANIA

as in the United Republic of; as in Dar es Salaam, the halfway home for SWAPO exiles; as in "the training grounds for many of these damned terrorists!" Pietermaritzburg raged one night, flea-bitten, ragged from the march, low on rations. "I don't understand why we don't just wipe out the whole damn lot, from the Cape to Cairo, and be done with these kaffirs once and for all."

or, *transition*—as in the strange state between war and civilian life filled with alcohol, nights of sweat-soaked sleep thinking of the ghosts of kaffirs and knowing the war was justified, and "A soldier serves, he doesn't ask questions," Kimberley said, gazing at the sea once more, "we did what we had to do"; as in the years spent learning how to shake hands with kaffirs, learning how to be employed by them, how to sit next to them in church and smile and offer them the sign of peace.

or, *truth*—as in Reconciliation Commission; as in Knysna wanted to appear, testify, and ask for forgiveness; as in "To get amnesty you'd have to tell the whole truth, Knysna," Pietermaritzburg said, "and many people would be implicated"; as in "The truth will out," Knysna said; as in "Yes, but not from you," Pietermaritzburg replied; as in "What happened to brotherhood? We kill our own now?" Knysna asked; as in "You are the last mission," Pietermaritzburg replied, picking up the gun; as in *the truth shall set you free*; as in "A man is a poor vessel for secrets," Knysna said once, hollow, after we'd finished inspiring and interrogating some kaffirs we'd captured—it took the whole day, "we weren't made to live with lies"; as in spending time compiling important terminology for military-age males, or a truthful account of the old days—still a work in progress, but one step toward the truth in some small way.

UNITA

as in National Union for the Total Independence of Angola; as in the Angolan kaffirs we are bound to help as an excuse to continue fighting the South West African kaffirs.

VASBYT

as in perseverance, as in "Hang in there, Joburg," Pietermaritzburg said, staunching the wound, "it's just a scratch. Hold on. *Vasbyt.*"

WEATHER

as in vane; as in "How do you figure out the direction of the wind?" Kaapstad asked; as in "Simple," Kimberley replied, "you round up some kaffirs and ask them where their PLAN relatives are"; as in "Then you get some rope," Pietermaritzburg enjoined, "and find a good tree and rope the whole lot and use the direction of the swaying to figure out whether it's a southwesterly."

XHOSA

as in tribe; as in Maqoma, a chief of the kaffirs; as in raider and torcher of homesteads; as in "Round up all the kaffirs and send them to Robben Island is what I say. And drown the remainder," Kimberley said.

YES, *BAAS*!

as in "the only good words to come out of a kaffir's mouth," Kimberley said, swatting at bugs, loaded down with equipment; "I think heaven is a place where all you hear is *Yes, baas!* all the time."

ZULU

as in Shaka; as in killed by Dingane and Mhlangana—"The *kaffirs* don't even have basic brotherhood," Pietermaritzburg said. "But not here, Joburg. Here we're brothers. It's the only way we'll make it through this. Do you understand? You do what I tell you, follow instructions, and maybe, just maybe, you might make it out alive. There will be no songs about us. No medals. So forget all that glory shit. All we have is each other and our targets. We take out our targets before they take us out. Understand? Good. Pass me my knife—you did an outstanding job with unwrapping your gift—neat, no fuss. Now you've started on a proper military alphabet. Time to get going on your ABCs."

Yog'hurt
(or, Just Breathe)

MOUNTAIN

—"This pose teaches you to stand with steadiness and strength, like a mountain."

The instructor says it might feel as though all you are doing is standing but, really, there is so much more happening in your body. You do not believe her. How could you? Ye of little faith in anything slow or spiritual. You trust in speed, in shifting quantifiable weight: "If it isn't heavy, it's light; if it's light, it ain't right." She talks about "being one with your body"—isn't everyone already, you think—"feeling yourself fill out every bit of it, being whole." You are convinced she is saying random shit to fill up the hour. You cannot believe this is what you took time out of your day to be a part of. You even paid for this class. She talks about centers. You snort loudly. Your girlfriend, on the mat next to yours, throws you a look. You know that look. You have been seeing it more and more these days. You compose your face into something that looks like earnestness to show her you are here for it all, and for her.

—"Stand with your feet close together. Press down through all your toes . . ."

You are told to engage unknown muscles in equally unknown ways—you lift, sure, but this is altogether some different kind of sorcery, you know only the sermons of steel and sweat. Anything else, you have decided from the jump, is a lie. You figure half of making it through the session is pretending. There is no way everyone in this class understands what is happening. It feels like being back in post-modernism lectures with everyone saying they understand Derrida.

—"You have to imagine a string at the top of your head all the way up to the ceiling which pulls you straight. Good, and breathe deeply for eight breaths. One, two, three . . ."

TREE

—"This will help to ground you . . ."

As though you need help with that. You are stuck. You and your girlfriend are stuck. That is why you came to this class in the first place. This is her thing, not yours. She said you do not do enough things together. Things that are not each other. Things that are not *your* things. You mentioned that thing at the art gallery. "Your friend was exhibiting," she said. Your thing. The camping trip at the lake? "All your friends were going with their girlfriends and you didn't want to be left out," she replied at a smooth trot. "And you hate camping." Your thing too. What about the Tarantino marathon? You distinctly recall that being fun. She looked at you in a way which let you know it was also *your* thing.

You like your girlfriend. Perhaps you even love her. Maybe that's why you told her you were down to do whatever she likes. You want to be a supportive boyfriend. You want to be *present.* She distinctly used the term when she listed the things she would like you to be for her—"participative and present." The first seemed clear enough. The second, not so. Being present, to you, means doing some of the things she likes. When you had the deep conversation—initiated by her, about her interests, hobbies, and drives—you discovered there were differences among the three: interests are what pique her curiosity; hobbies are the relaxing activities that filled her spare time; drives were things that kept her going, especially when she was not feeling all there. You were miffed when you were not listed in any of the categories. But just because you wanted to be present did not mean you would hand-wrap your balls and dignity and give them to her. You quickly ruled out church, running, and watching period dramas just so she did not get any funny ideas. Also, you added quickly, you would not try part-time vegetarianism. Not even for her. You said you were cool with everything else though.

Hence this yoga class and your disinterested presence in it. She said it might be a good idea. Couple goals and all that. You figured it was time anyway. Yoga is the one thing she stuck with, the one part of her routines she has not changed since you started dating. Now that you think of it, everything else really has been your stuff. She even bought a PlayStation controller so you could shoot zombies together. She is becoming pretty decent at *FIFA*.

Yeah, you had to take this yoga class with her.

—"Put your right foot on your inner left thigh, as high as you can go. Then bring your hands together in prayer . . . and breathe deeply . . ."

This is nonsense. You sigh too loudly. Your girlfriend looks at you again.

You said you would not complain.

You said you would do *her* thing.

DOWNWARD-FACING DOG

—". . . try to keep the legs straight, stretch out those hamstrings, good, good . . . move your hands forward on the mat to give yourself more length . . ."

You laugh. Give yourself more length. Your girl looks at you again. *What is wrong with you?*

What? That was funny. Come on.

—"And hold for eight breaths. Good . . . four, five, six . . ."

PLANK INTO CHATURANGA

—"And then down, nice and steady, don't drop all at once!"

This is more like it. Your core tickles a little as it ignites—this kind of thing is fodder for your physique since you started practicing calisthenics. It is the closest you have come to being alone in your body, repping out sit-ups, pull-ups, bench dips, and all of the other movements that do not require additional weight. "Your body is enough," the trainer said in the first session. You also did not believe him for a while. "In a while you will realize your body can be too much." Oh, you found out, all right.

But this . . .

—"and breathe, nice and deep breaths . . ."

All this crap about breathing is annoying—who needs to be reminded to breathe? Someone in the back is puffing like Thomas the Tank Engine. You sneak a glance back at the Little Chubby Engine That Couldn't.

COBRA

—"Push the pubic bone into the floor . . ."

You laugh again. Someone else does too. Your girlfriend rolls her eyes.

This is not so hard. What was the hype? Any minute now she is going to say—

—"Breathe, breathe. In, out, feel the air move in your nose, and breathe, feel it exit through your mouth . . ."

It's just air, you think. Oxygen moving in and out of the lungs, a life characteristic hardwired into the being. You take in air when you need it, you expel it when you don't. You shelve the incessant calls to breathe with detox and juicing fads. You did mention to your girlfriend that you were fine with taking this class provided there was "none of that Om Shanti shit because that is just too much." You want the practice, not the performance; you came seeking deliverance but not the deity.

That isn't how this works. To get to the Pearlies you have to know Peter. And having a girlfriend means being a boyfriend. In that regard there is nothing which can become reflexive, everything needs to be done anew each time—morning text messages, lunch dates, lounging on the couch, the holding of hands, the silence of closeness—nothing can become air or simple biology, everything in love needs to become a craft.

Presence, not mere attendance.

You should focus and breathe.

WARRIOR ONE

This pose is just a lunge that went to private school. The other students are so into it though. The studio looks like a cult worship ceremony with everyone reaching up for the rapture. If only your friends could see you now. (Much later you will realize the crippling nature of this hypothetical gaze. But until then you will live in fear of it, and you shall act in accordance with its dictates. It will ruin you, but that's not for a long while.)

But this matters to her. And she matters to you. You shall restrain yourself. You shall endure. For her. For who she is to you. For what she has done for you. These, you decide, are good enough reasons for pretense. Surely, others have sacrificed more for less.

You just wish yoga had more . . . *oomph*.

And always with the damn—

—"Breathe."

WARRIOR TWO

This is nothing but stretching with a view. Your girlfriend has the best ass—wiggling at her will, jiggling under gravity's. She has a head of curls which makes you preach the curly-girl gospel. Depending on how she styles it she can be five different women. Thanks to her changing hairstyles you even know what a pineapple bun is and you bought her a kente cloth head wrap that one time. The best is when she has her mane out, fierce as fuck. Sometimes you help her to detangle it—with you on the couch and her seated on the floor, gently picking your way through the soft knots with a knitting needle, with the Lijadu Sisters or Jennifer Lara on repeat—like you're the perfect melanin couple in a neo-soul music video.

There is another girl two mats over who is worth a sly peek or two. The other women are okay-ish. Some of the poses push their figures into interesting shapes though.

There are two other guys in the class. One, you decide, is definitely gay. His eyelids do not even flutter a bit when homegal two mats over has her breasts bearing down on him like a car with its brights on. The other guy, sinewy and lithe, looks like he was coerced into this as well. You give him a *well, what're you gonna do* kind of shrug and he smiles back. Maybe you are not the only boyfriend in search of yogic redemption. In this you are correct: there are legions of guys like you taking cooking, pottery, dancing, painting, gardening, or yoga classes as last-ditch efforts for relevance in your girlfriends' lives. There is a pattern to you guys too—what attracted you to your girlfriends is what you reach for right at the desperate end. You just need this class to end so you can finally use all the hashtags you could not use before.

#relationshipgoals #doyoueven #theadventuresofyogabear #my favoriteposeisbae

TRIANGLE INTO EXTENDED TRIANGLE
INTO REVOLVED TRIANGLE

Whoa! Whoa! Things just scaled up. Triangle was okay, but what the hell is this?

You are facing your girlfriend. You can feel a vein growing in your forehead. The vein you get when a bad curry calls your midnight hotline. Your girlfriend looks serene. You try to keep it together so she does not see you struggle. If there is one thing you are determined never to show her it is weakness, especially in a damn yoga class. There are many ways to go out—like a punk bitch ain't one of them.

—"Keep your right hand on the ground and your left reaching up. Imagine trying to touch the ceiling."

You're bellowing like a piston, shallow, quickly, panicking. You should slow down, take your time, probably stop chasing waterfalls and stick to the planks and push-ups that you're used to. But you're going to have it your way or nothing at all—you're moving too fast, too soon. Ain't that the way love goes?

What you need to do is breathe. Let the air flow around you, into you, and through you. Let it wash away the strain and stress of muscle against muscle. Become one with this new practice, take your part in this novel performance where you are neither star, sidekick, nor understudy—just you. There is a reason yoga is taught in a group format; everyone has a part to play. Their strengths and yours are not the only desirable attributes; the weakness, too, have their time and place. That is why everyone is encouraged to breathe—it is the one thing everyone can do.

"Just breathe."

"Be present."

"Be here."

Now.

REVOLVED SIDE ANGLE

—"Keep your back heel down in this pose!"

This shit is getting ridiculous. Parts of your body have to meet other parts of your body they were never made to meet. Homegal two mats over stumbles a bit but she regains her footing. The Little Chubby Engine That Couldn't is huffing and puffing like the Big Bad Wolf. The other guys do not seem to be struggling. Even the boyfriend-looking one. He was supposed to be on your side. You were supposed to struggle together but he looks like he has been here before. Are you the only person who has not been accompanying their girlfriend to yoga classes? What new boyfriend level have you not unlocked?

—"And stretch forward like you're trying to touch something just out of reach . . ."

You will come back to this moment and think it is where everything went wrong. That isn't true. This class, this mat, the tightening of tendons, and the stretching of sinews are merely tremors being felt from an epicenter you do not know exists. You see, this yoga class has been coming at you for some time, like a distant asteroid outside of your selfish solar system on a crash-course trajectory with your ego. Because everything in your relationship has been all about you—what you like, what you do not, what you fear, and what you shy away from—a void where her things should be has opened up. Note this: horror vacui—nature abhors a vacuum. This empty space is about to be filled by harsh reality.

CROW

—"Bring your shins into your armpits . . ."

Nah! This bitch is tripping!

—". . . and then lift up onto the balls of your feet . . ."

You grunt.

—"Find your balance."

Your girlfriend is silent.

—"If you're finding this one hard . . ."

The whole class is silent.

The edges of your vision close in.

Thump!

—"Breathe! Come on, nice deep breaths! There we go. Breathe. Give him space. You're going to be all right. Just breathe."

CAR

You cannot bull through the lull in your relationship like your work-outs. Nonetheless you will try. Many times.

You look out of the window as the storefronts zoom past the car.

You sulk.

And you miss the lesson: the possibility of improving upon one's shortcomings can only be done bit by bit, one slow and controlled pose after another.

Maybe this is why she brought you to her yoga class. To just breathe and realize there are no other times but these. To be present with her, even with your weaknesses.

To be here.

And now.

This is what your muscles tried to teach you earlier. Love is an art form and romance is its craft, practiced one participative, present moment at a time. You have not realized that yet. But you will.

You frown.

You do not talk to your girl all the way home.

ANNUS HORRIBILIS

At the end of what they called the terrible year, the annus horribilis—after the fizz and tingle of the first kiss (more like cheap vodka on his breath and something lemony with gin on hers, but we allow lovers greater latitude when it comes to memory) on a chilly, spring-shy September night that teased gooseflesh onto arms (when the meteorologists had predicted biblical deluges and fields were furrowed in agricultural anticipation) at the dusty, asthma-unfriendly country fair which didn't look like anything from the movies (because this wasn't the movies, this was Real Life, Namibia, a place no films were made of, a city no poets serenaded with verse, a place of small, unrecorded tragedies where one of the options for a first date was to ogle sheep and watch farmers haggling over prize cows at the annual agricultural show), with his amusing obligatory attempt to win her the plush teddy bear (he didn't), and the foot-long hot dog which spilled tomato sauce on her top, the ride on the creaky, death-trap Ferris wheel (despite the unspoken fear of heights from both parties because love truly is for morons), the fingers inching toward each other at the top of the vertigo-inducing cycle, the disjointed kiss of elbows, the static, stinging exchange of attraction (yes, even a place like Real Life is allowed its clichés every once in a while), and the moment when they finally (finally!) kissed; after the "whirlwind of love," which is what she called it at the start of a cloudless October (filled with exactly zero millimeters of rainfall and four prevaricating weathermen) when she told Brennadine, her best friend, who (being from the Bahamas, she had more experience with the wrath wreaked by winds in the Caribbean) merely raised an eyebrow (because windy metaphors were some of her least favorite things, along with *The Tempest*, which she'd suffered through in the twelfth grade) and wisely kept quiet (since the L-word had been invoked—the use of earthier, less breezy terms like *patience* or phrases like *damn girl, take it easy* would've been mistaken for jealousy because bitterness and bile from Brennadine's ex-boyfriend pinged on her cellphone at an average rate of three messages per hour); after the "I don't know, man, it's whatever . . ." which is how he explained it to his friend Zaylan at the tail end of October (when dam levels ran low) when the homies noted he'd been spending what they called *a matrimonial amount of time* with the girl; after the ceasefire of daytime flirting in text messages, the nighttime engagement in hostilities of passion, which came to a halt on a hot November night when at the eleventh hour of the eleventh day of the eleventh month, on his bed, with the mosquitoes kamikaze-ing their naked bodies (nobody knew where the damn mosquitoes were spawning since there was no rain and, therefore, no exposed surface water for the pesky things to breed), with Salif Keita and Cesária Évora's "Yamore" playing (a strange choice, but the mood was so, so right), she sang along to high notes reserved for West African singers with platinum-selling albums, she said *I might not have the Rover, but I've got the range!* and he conceded the point, kissed her, and said they had to be *serious*, like serious-serious, not like all the other couples who weren't (apparently unaware that, eventually, everyone becomes what they judge), he whispered, disguising his fear in humor while signing the proclamation of love: *Imma love you from the skinny cock's crow until the fat lady sings!* (a promise so tight anyone could see it was a self-imposed Carthaginian peace), and she hastily moved to ratify the declaration of dependence with the ministrations of her body; after the motions of commitment commenced in December (when the land started balding of grass in earnest, when grazing was scarce and feed stores ran low) by way of onerous restaurant reparations for late replies, reluctant cession of slices of selfish, solitary time to the other, cautiously de-male-iterizing after taking part in the War of the Singles (Adam and Eve–present) and taking the road trip to the coastal towns (smaller, holiday-crowded, and racist versions of Real Life, but with German heritage stretching all the way to 18-*voetsek*), the New Year's Eve party in the dunes, dancing over endangered desert lichen, an oasis shaded by trees from Lesotho's finest (cough, cough, pass) and drowned in the perennial waters of the Reinheitsgebot (*Deutschland uber alles!*), and the midnight kissing: *Happy New Year, babe! Happy New Year! Hope it's gonna be a good one!*; after the abortion (that getaway trip to Cape Town) in January (when the government, fearing national panic, said there was no drought, only *acute and localized rainfall shortage* since, to be fair, there was rainfall everywhere else, it wasn't like the whole world had run out of it), when they had many tear-soaked debates about damnation (she was a believer), the cost of childcare (he was pragmatic), and assurances that later, when things were a little further along, they would try again; after the hell-hot and hollow February days which made armpits squelch with uncomfortable moisture became filled with vacant staring at computer screens (on her part), the drudgery of adoration (on his), the government banning farmers from taking photos of dehydrated and dying cows (the newspapers could still print pictures of dead black people though, so there was some give-and-take), and evenings of ratings-busting, game-show trivia such as *Are you hungry* (fifty-fifty, ask the audience, or phone a friend) and *Not really but I could eat, what are you having?* (ham and salami pizza for a hundred points, basil pesto and tomato for fifty), or *What do you want to watch?* and settling, instead, for pretending to fall asleep halfway through the film so they could go to bed and feign even more sleep; after panic-level March when dams started emptying (they had, of course, been doing this for a while but the harsh reality crept up on the nation like a languid low tide), when water restrictions kicked in (except in the affluent suburbs, where pool parties continued undisturbed), when they made valiant attempts to get back to love, gingerly at first, and then with more rhythm, a soldier's grim sense of duty (for queen and country, innit), but with some warmth, like ashy embers, not the prurience of the past which could have irrigated the south of the country when they used to be in top form; after the fierce quietness and early nose-drip chills of autumnal April (choking, tap-sputtering water restrictions became the norm), when the days shortened, ending the workday too soon, and the nights with nothing but each other's proximity for entertainment stretched on too long, when their mutual busyness became that seemingly immeasurable word *space* (SI unit: silence) and space became that measurable thing called *distance* (SI unit: other people); after the casual cruelties of jealousy in the brumal month of May (rinsing one's mouth after brushing ran the risk of a municipal lawsuit for excessive water consumption), when the distance between them could only be measured in lie years (and three people each); after June, a *bliksem* month of flu and colds sorely and solely warmed by the fire of arguments (him: *I just wish you wouldn't be so rectitudinous!*, her: *I don't know what the fuck rectitudinous means!*, him: *Sanctimonious, holier-than-thou—*, her: *Well, if you're the bar, it isn't that hard to get over*, him: *What the fuck does that mean?*, her: *It means exactly what it means. But I'm sure you know a German word for "you're-lying-and-blaming-me-for-catching-you-with-some-other-bitch!,"* him: *I don't, actually. But I know Clive is English for "you-were-fucking-around-too!"* (it actually isn't, Clive is normal-speak for *colleague*, the word he's looking for is *Zaylan*); after unforgiving, hyperborean, tap-freezing July, when they lived together but apart, self-isolating and physically distancing because forgiveness is a contact contagion they avoided (Oh—almost forgot: the drought was *finally* declared); after August, slowly warming, with the certainty of hay fever in the air but no moisture (the weathermen were, understandably, quite reserved with their rainfall predictions), and Remo Giazotto's Adagio in G Minor becoming the leitmotif for this *thing*, whatever it was, when they held hands and smiled at dinners (becoming what they'd judged, yearning not to be, but too afraid to say so); after coming back to another September, the anniversary of the boarding of this train to nowhere (we, of course, knew where it was going), a once favorably fated month in which the confluence of forces and inexplicable eddies in the space-time continuum (translation for the layman: Brennadine hosted a house party) saw her sitting alone for exactly forty-three seconds before he approached her, his cap tipped to two o'clock in the reggaeton-thrumming night, his sneakers smiling with each step as they made their whiter-than-white way toward her, and his saying *Hallo*, a word she hadn't heard from the opposite sex in a while (*Yo, Bren, who's your fine ass friend?* was the going rate), the way she looked up at him, her vinaceous lips and threaded eyebrows settling into that exasperated did-you-really-leave-your-boys-and-talking-about-handing-out-two-hours-of-whoop-ass-in-*FIFA 19*-to-come-over-here-and-ask-me-why-I'm-sitting-alone expression which can only be achieved with the proper application of the latest Fenty Beauty shades (brought in by a friend from Dubai), an Instagram makeup tutorial, a get-ready playlist stuffed with Lizzo and SZA, and forty-three seconds of Brennadine's absence when she went to the bathroom, how his hands came up like he was preparing for a police frisk: *I carry nothing but myself . . .* , how, for some reason, he looked off-balance in her presence and she said *A good start . . .* , and that made him laugh and sit down in Brennadine's chair (which she didn't mind because he had a laugh that sounded like good company, plus he'd said hallo), how he said he wanted to just talk and they talked about random things like the party and the music, what they didn't do for a living (which was a lot, they had plenty in common when it came to unfulfilled childhood dreams), places they'd visited (which she'd done more of, the most recent place being Italy, which gave her the right to share this gem about the *Venus de Milo*: *I wish she had arms so she could choose whether to cover up her titties or not. I mean, hey, David has his arms. It's his choice to have his dick in the wind like that. But I know Venus would pull up her dress given a choice!* to which he said he didn't agree and she countered with *Of course you don't. You're not the one with your tits on display for centuries!*), before they looked up at the sky and both

104

of them said it looked like rain—all they will think about is the start, and how when they walk away they'll carry nothing but themselves.

Except her. In October, when it finally does rain for the first time in a year, she'll have another abortion, a secret, a consensus of one. You should've seen this coming: the fruits of the past only bloom in the future, and life always makes a start, even if love comes to an end.

This we—and now you—know.

LOVE IS A NEGLECTED THING
(OR, CORINTHIANS)

The way love felt last night was too familiar. The same steady rhythms, the same motions, the regular and replicated highs. The same sighing conclusion. Love closed its eyes for a bit, catching its breath, and then it fell asleep. You, however, remained awake, alert into the late hours of the night, thinking about what you were going to do, how you were going to do it, and when you'd do it.

Today? Tomorrow? On Thursday? How about now?

No! Not now.

▶ ‖

Love lies there in the morning when the day is new. It rolls over as you look at it. It stretches, resplendent. "How'd you sleep?"

You shuffle quickly to the bathroom to brush your teeth. "Fine," you say.

▶ ‖

Love is there in the memes and videos that used to make you laugh but irk you now and in the voice notes quoting corny rap lyrics that you mute.

That's how you read its messages: blindly—without bias to past feelings or moments, or the things you used to do together, all the plans you made. All of Love's words wind up in the slush pile.

You close Love's messages and turn back to your English class with fresh energy in your voice. Some kid asks why they have to read *The Adventures of Huckleberry Finn*. To be fair, it's boring and not right for their reading level. But the wrinkled copies are all the language department can afford right now. It's all that it could afford last year and the year before that as well.

▶ ‖

At lunch, Love is there in the sandwiches which have been cut more cleanly than a mirror's edge, stuffed with pastrami, tomato slices redder than passion, a thick white cheddar slice, and fresh watercress leaves. One of the other guys, Mr. Petersen, the math teacher, says you must be putting in the midnight work if you're getting lunch like that. Another one, Mr. Loubser, the geography teacher, ruefully looks at two brown slices mortared by peanut butter and says, "Love, don't let go of it, my young apprentice."

When your phone buzzes in your pocket you ignore it until your thigh stops quivering.

—Hey, how's your day going?

Love is kind.

▶ ||

When you show up at Franco's flat that evening his face registers surprise for an instant before he nods you over to the couch. You flicker between channels, undecided. Champions League commercials. A mumble rap video. Catastrophic Brexit negotiations. Nature documentaries—you ask him to pause on the leopard dismembering the impala.

"All good?" Franco asks.

"Mmm."

You finish the documentary and get the updates on your boy's philandering.

Back home you mention you stopped off at Franco's for a bit. Love just smiles and says, "Cool. Hope you boys had fun."

Love is not jealous.

You almost wish it was.

▶ ||

The way Love holds your hand when you walk to the shop, or when you go for a stroll in the sighing dusk, just so, with the slightest bit of moisture greasing your palms. You want to let go of the hand you thought you'd hold on to forever.

"Is everything okay?"

You give Love a wan smile. "Yeah. Of course."

You lengthen your stride. The hands pull apart.

▶ǁ

Love has inside jokes which no longer tickle your ribs. Now the humor punches like a sour left hook. Love winks at you at a dinner party and you backhand silence to it, swinging its emotions left and right, running it ragged. Its closeness seems too close. Its fragrance no longer sends you reeling. Its movements seem clumsy and careless. And there are crumbs everywhere on the kitchen counter. Like, everywhere.

—*All the time, Franco. How the fuck are there crumbs everywhere? Women are filthy creatures.*

—*You're the only guy I know bitching about that, dude.*

You turn away from the phone. Franco's no help at all.

"You're awfully quiet," Love says.

"Mmm."

"I deserve more than that." Love comes and wraps its hands around your waist and looks up at you.

"Mmmm."

"That's better." Love reaches up to kiss you. You hold out until the last second of rudeness before you bend your neck to meet its lips. Your mouth autopilots through the saliva exchange.

Love is patient.

▶ǁ

You remember the first hello, a greeting of such power you couldn't contemplate ever saying goodbye. You were calling to take out Love on what felt like the umpteenth date. (It was the third, thank you very much!)

"Hello."

"Hi," Love said.

"I'm—"

"I know who you are." You both made small talk and then you asked if you could meet up. "Look," Love said, "I already know who you are to everyone else. But who or what do you want to be to me?"

"Forever," you said.

The pause. You could hear it breathing into the phone.

"Yours," Love said shyly.

That night at the restaurant all it did was look at you. Long. With the gaze which could separate you into boy, man, flesh, words, lies, hopes, and fears. In the past you would've fidgeted and sweated. But you were cool. This was what you wanted. You were certain.

When the bill came you said you'd get it. Love said the two of you should split it and you said, nah, you could split the mortgage and the child-rearing duties when the time came. You said you'd start lobbying for longer paternal-leave days. Love looked at you straight. You didn't look away. It read you the Miranda rights: "Careful, anything you say can and will be held against you."

"I say you, then," you said.

Love laughed.

Back then.

Way, way back.

▶ ‖

How the present fails to live up to memory. Now look how the laughter ebbs away, and the knowing silence gnaws away at the thing that could never die without either one of you first dying. Even though you're both still alive, your love's already left for the hereafter. You're just sleep-kissing and sleep-loving through its wake.

Look how Love tries; how it puts in the time, time, time, time, and how it tries to burn, burn, burn but time does not catch a fire. Time flies instead.

Look how Hooke's law applies here, how deliberately careless you are, knowing if you pull it and stretch it, Love will come back to you again and again.

And again.

And again.

Love loses its luster when you belittle it with your trial.

Love will always show up, always willingly.

▶ ‖

A morning comes. The sun's rays turn the burglar bars into jailhouse shadows on the walls. Love rolls over and sits up. It sees you at the end of the bed. You have your back to it but you can feel its hands stretching out to you, just about to make contact with your shoulders, then Love pulls back. You wish it had touched you. Maybe it would've changed things.

It did the first time way, way back when.

You sigh and straighten your back.

"Careful, anything you say can and will be used against you," Love says before you can even say anything.

You turn to face her.

Look at her. How she bites and reigns in the pleading words. But the eyes, they adjure, they beseech. Nothing wants to die—everything fights to cling to life when the dark beyond starts blocking the light. You think about that impala at Franco's house. The way it thrashed around madly even though its eyes knew the leopard's jaws were as strong as finality.

You look at her. She looks back at you. She doesn't say anything.

You wash your face in the bathroom. You brush your teeth. You comb your tough hair. When you come back into the bedroom she's sitting up in bed. You look at each other again.

You don't have to say anything. She knows.

Love always knows.

Later that day you start moving your things out of the apartment. By the next day everything's been cleared out. She's not around when you finally turn the key in the lock for the last time. You leave it beneath the dead chili plant and walk away.

B-Side

The Giver of Nicknames

PRELUDE.

When we were clowns, children, and things—before we sprouted per-
sonalities, individual hopes, and collective guilt; before we reconciled
all aspects of our conflicting beings—there were four Donovans at
our school: Donovan "Donnie Blanco" Mitchell, the rapist; Donovan
"Donnie Darko" Manyika, the fastest kid in our alma mater; the short-
lived Donovan Latrell, who, hoping to be called DL when he realized
there weren't enough Donnies to go around, was called Fatty; and
Mr. Donovan, our English teacher—Mr. D for short.

1.

Donnie Blanco was this white kid with colonial money all the way
to Diogo Çao's arrival in Namibia. His parents had mining interests

deeper than Dante's Inferno, sat on numerous companies' boards, and owned game farms as big as provinces, panoramic swathes of land with wild sunsets lacking only in the absence of Meryl Streep and Robert Redford to give them their *Out of Africa* romance. Because they paid some of their taxes instead of caching them in Caribbean mulct havens, the Mitchells—Los Blancos—were considered Namibian model citizens. They were allowed to add their billionaire's two cents to any damn topic: Sir Ken Robinson's TED talks; border security and the movement of people, pandemics, and dreams; social media, climate change, or the nutritional requirements of the modern corporate go-getter. Los Blancos even prescribed parenting methods for raising future moguls. Their money had bestowed upon them prophetic status; I was a nonbeliever. To me, all Blanco's parents had was money—they knew how to play the rigged capitalist game the same way my uncle always made himself the banker whenever we played Monopoly. In everything else, especially in their son, whom I still refer to as the rapist to this day because he is, I found them woefully inadequate.

I despised the Blancos because of their privilege. But I especially loathed them for their ability to co-opt my poverty into Donnie Blanco's cover-up.

▶ ‖

In addition to his presence at our school—the top one in Namibia—Blanco's parents believed traveling was the best education. Our parents, mostly middle-class folk who stressfully and strenuously financed our stints in private school, believed education was the best education. Unlike Blanco, we were parvenus trying to acclimatize to the rich air of lush lawns, changing rooms with hot-water showers, and a computer lab with more Apples than the Garden of Eden. We weren't collecting passport stamps like the philatelic travelers with diplomatic passports who made up the rest of the student corps—we were academic work-horses with one job: to keep the test scores high and, in so doing, our parents happy and gloating with their sacrifices. Blanco and his ilk provided the necessary posh veneer which permitted the fees to rise and spike each year. While we were clocking into and coining out of the lone video game arcade or shuttling between onerous weddings and sweaty funerals in towns so small Google Earth never bothered to give them coordinates, Blanco was hitting up twenty countries before he turned fourteen. He'd smelled the hot rubber of the Monaco Grand Prix and posed with *Christ the Redeemer* in Rio de Janeiro. Our English teacher, Mrs. Braithwaite, who gloated over Blanco's globe-trotting essays, always marked down our writings, using her socially distanced red pen to tell us we needed *more traveling in them, broader horizons, higher skies,* and, *a keener sense of adventure.* Basic Bs and discourag-ing Cs were what you'd get if you hadn't been on a first-class British Airways flight to Amsterdam or Basel. Blanco had A-plussed his way through English because he'd seen the Alps, the Andes, the Rockies, the Hindu Kush, and the Himalayas. We were told our *compositions barely rose above sleep level.* All we wrote about was the calefaction of days in the north, the sand in the south, and the repetitive stories our *oumas en oupas* told us when we were condemned to stay with them in the long December holidays.

The year I dubbed Donovan Mitchell Donnie Blanco, his family had taken a tour of the Spanish-speaking world. They'd passed through South America and finished off in Spain. He went on about the *guapa* girls of Ar-*hen*-tina and Chi-*leh*, the Colombian *culo,* and did a lot of *hombre*-ing and *muchacho*-ing about all the friends he'd made in Me-*hi*-co. He returned from Spain with signed soccer jerseys from Madrid's and Catalonia's top teams—the souvenirs we envied most (we really didn't give a shit about the landscapes in his descriptive essays, which Mrs. Braithwaite insisted on reading aloud)—and kept telling the rest of us untraveled *campesinos* to pronounce Bar-*the*-lona properly. Understandably, we were annoyed by this fucking *pendejo.* I, being a much sought-after merchant of humiliating sobriquets, the fast-mouthed comeback kid who could roast the devil over his own coals, was assigned to Blanco's case. I took my duty to follow in Carl Linnaeus's scientific steps, to formalize teenage taxonomy in such a way that class, neighborhood, physical deformities, or crippling insecurities were easily denoted, quite seriously. If my previous work in getting Naomi "Naai-Homie" Nakwafilu (it was one moment of indiscretion, but one too many), Daniel "Lying Den" Shikongo (that one explains itself), Layla "Refu-G-Unit" Madioka (shame, she wasn't a refugee, but we didn't know anything else about Congolese people), and Gottlieb "Gone-Arears" Hendricks (poor kid was always out of school because of late school fees) to become popular nomenclature was any indication—even teachers used Pirra, Peeta, and Blackimon, to differentiate between the Canadian, Namibian, and Ugandan Peters—then Donovan Mitchell would've been an easy case.

Only, it wasn't. Blanco's parents directly or indirectly employed most of ours. And we knew it. We didn't want our mammas being called into HR offices and our families being put on the streets because we'd taken liberties with playground banter. We didn't know if corporate retribution played out that way in the real world, but we didn't want to fuck around with our families' well-being. I wisely settled on Donnie Blanco. He thought it was because he was white. It wasn't. It was the safest and slyest thing we could call him. Because the Gini coefficient allowed us to outnumber Blanco ten-to-one, and because we were so mad at this boy who had enough money to insult us in foreign languages, Donnie Blanco stuck.

It was petty but sweet revenge.

For all his money, private tutors, and his mother's unchallenged and unconstitutional tenure on our school's PTFA, Blanco was *el imbécil supremo*. He'd been passed through every grade because his parents signed extravagant fundraiser checks. Our heavily endowed Catholic school which ran from pre-primary all the way to the twelfth grade, true to form with its finances shadier than a clerical scandal, wasn't immune to Blanco money. After the not-so-small matter of Donnie Blanco forcing himself on Aliyanna, and our school's principal, my mother, his parents, and Aliyanna's agreeing to keep quiet about it, I Sherlocked the web of Mitchellian patronage: there was a correlation between Blanco nearly failing the seventh grade and our library's newly minted computer wing; the spiffy senior chemistry lab equipment capable of Nobel Prize–level testing followed his entry into the eighth grade; the patchy, sun-smacked grass on our soccer field gave way to expensive and evergreen Astroturf in the ninth grade; and in the tenth, after the rape, Mitchell Education Foundation (MEF) scholarships were handed out to every overachieving student like Communist pamphlets in the Soviet republics. Our first- *and* second-string basketball, hockey, netball, and soccer teams attended once rare out-of-country sports tours to Botswana, Zambia, Zimbabwe, South Africa, and Mozambique thanks to the Mitchell sponsorship and PR machines for the rest of his tenure at our school. In class, everyone's test scores were read out in ascending order—to keep us competitive, we were told—but Blanco's tests were placed face-down on his desk, top secret, classified, and way above everyone's pay grade. While the rest of us did our best to earn the grades needed to discourage our parents from looking for cheaper schools, we watched Blanco grade-surf each year. We found some comfort in knowing Donnie Blanco was white as snow, rich like whoa, but dumber than *daaayuum*.

Only later would the full gravitas of the name I'd given him become apparent and abhorrent. Even now, I wonder if the person who names the monster shares the blame with the one who flips the switch to release the lightning-charged current. I still feel like if I'd been braver and called him Why Boy (because we couldn't fathom a reason for his existence) or Needle Dick (since he was such a prick), things would've turned out differently.

Maybe not.

It's my experience that money alters destinies forever. Kismet for chaos is for broke people. The rich just send karma back to the kitchen if it comes out under- or overcooked.

In the principal's office, I'd explained what had happened after basketball practice to the convocation of parents. I thought I was on the road to being an A-grade whistleblower like Daniel Ellsberg or a conscientious objector with a million-dollar-grossing biopic from Steven Spielberg soon to be declared.

I told them what I'd seen: *Donnie Blanco raped Aliyanna in the boys' changing room.*

You'd think SETI, with its satellite ears scanning the sound of silence from the outermost reaches of the solar system, would've detected the hush which descended on the room following my testimony. You'd be wrong. There was no reticence.

Money talks.

—*Hmm. Did she try to push him away?*

—*And was it a firm no or a coy no?*

—*Are you sure it was my son and not someone else?*

—*Are you certain? A boy could go to jail here. Do you understand that? You must be absolutely sure.*

Yes, Mr. Bla—I mean, Mitchell—she tried to push him off.

It wasn't coy, Mrs. Mitchell—it was pretty robust. (I hate to admit it but I was rather pleased that I knew what *coy* meant.)

It was Donnie Blanco—sorry, Donovan Michael Earl Mitchell, sir.

I'm telling you the truth, Mrs. Mitchell. It was your son.

Then came a question I couldn't answer.

—*What were you doing while all of this was going on?*

Everyone leaned forward in their chairs.

—*Am I to understand you saw all of this and did nothing?*

—*You certainly sound like a man of action. Omission or negligence would surely offend or implicate someone like you.*

I turned to my mother. She looked at me, frightened by this new line of inquiry from the Blancos, who shared a look I couldn't fathom. Mr. Van Rooyen, the principal, slitted his eyes while Aliyanna's parents' eyes scoured my face for any evidence of complicity.

I . . . err . . . I . . .

—*Yes?*

I didn't do anything, Mrs. Mitchell.

—*Really?*

(Since then I've equated Mrs. Mitchell's uncrossing and recrossing of legs—without any Sharon Stone shenanigans—as the quintessential sign of moral indignation and disbelief.)

Err, Mrs. Mitchell, I was, err, too shocked.

—But you're sure the girl was being raped?

Err, yes, sir.

—You don't sound too sure now.

I'm sure, ma'am.

I looked at my mother. Her dotted dress held her gaze in its lap.

—But you didn't do anything.

No, sir. I was too surprised.

—Seems highly improbable to me someone can be aware that such a crime was happening but do nothing about it.

I . . . I . . . I'm doing something about it now, ma'am. Mom?

She kept quiet.

I wonder if there's a statute of limitations for shame. I've never forgiven her.

I'd walked into the boy's changing room after being dismissed from practice by our coach. I'd dissented when he prescribed suicides for every missed layup. (*This isn't* Remember the Titans, *Coach. You're not Denzel!*) In one of the showers, Blanco's buttocks peeked over his red shorts (he'd been excused from the team's fitness training for fatigue) as he thrusted into Aliyanna's pulled-up skirt. I, coming across this scene, this after-school activity which made everyone blush in the sexual intercourse module during school hours, had been thoroughly startled.

What the—!

They turned at the sound of my intrusion. I pivoted quicker than Michael Jackson on a concert stage and walked out. I went back to the court's bench, shamed and scared of being a witness. Ten or fifteen minutes later, Blanco came out of the changing rooms and strutted toward the school's gate. He climbed into the shiny Audi waiting for him. Maybe five minutes later Aliyanna exited the bathrooms, smoothing down her hair, wiping her face. She looked around the basketball court. In the cursory contact of our eyes I understood the difference between an instant and a moment, something Mrs. Braithwaite struggled to explain to us in our literature class: an instant is blinked away, forgotten so quickly it's barely registered, but a moment spills past its temporal occurrence—*a moment has consequences*. Aliyanna walked toward the gate and waited for her parents to pick her up in their significantly less shiny Toyota Corolla.

Only later, as I sat outside the school's gate waiting for my mother, did I realize that a moment can be slowed down, panned around like a three-sixty-degree bullet-time shot to reveal nanoscopic details you miss in an instant: the biology and physics of penetration had been explained to us, but what had happened between Blanco and Aliyanna lacked the chemistry of consent.

I recalled his hands wrestling her wrists, her legs looking for purchase on the floor, her pelvis trying to push him off, his telling her it was *okay* and that *we agreed*.

I remembered her saying *no, no, no*.

Mr. and Mrs. Blanco were wrong. I had done something: I'd walked to Mr. Van Rooyen's office and barged past his receptionist to report Blanco.

Within the hour, I, my mom, Aliyanna and her parents, and all the Blancos were outside the principal's office. The parents went inside. Aliyanna, Blanco, and I were to be seated apart and wait to adduce our evidence. The gruff and confused receptionist kept muttering about having *a family to attend to even if no one else does and, really, this is above and beyond my duties.* Blanco pressed buttons on his razor-thin flip phone while Aliyanna's knees rubbed against each other with nervous friction. She avoided looking at me.

Aliyanna was called upon first. Blanco and I defiantly stared at each other before he broke the deadlock with a dismissive shrug of his shoulders and returned to his phone. My spine steeled. Blanco was going down.

He was called in as Aliyanna walked out. The two of us sat opposite each other, avoiding all the moments our eyes would make. The recently vacuumed carpet, with its circular whorls of fibers sucked against their grain, seemed a point of interest for her.

I went in last.

—*You said you heard my son saying they'd agreed to do "it." Is that correct?*

Err, yes, Mrs. Mitchell, but I'm not sure what they agreed to do.

—*It certainly wouldn't be the first time teenagers have regretted their choices halfway through something.*

I understand, Mr. Mitchell. But she said no.

Mr. Van Rooyen inhaled in what seemed like a businesslike manner and thanked me for my emphatic assertion. I waited outside as Aliyanna and Blanco were called back in. With night slipping under evening's covers, the receptionist grumbled some more. The door opened twice, once when the boxy printer and copier churned out a sheaf of documents the principal collected quickly before returning to his office, and the second time when Aliyanna's family walked out, followed by my mother, the Blancos, and Mr. Van Rooyen.

Everyone, except the receptionist had a moment.

Mr. Van Rooyen broke the pall by saying he was glad *that bit of confusion was ironed out hehehe these things happen you know with all these teenagers together hihihi bound to happen hahaha yes always bound to happen hohoho.*

Aliyanna's parents nodded to everyone; her head remained bowed. Blanco stood with his boredom weighed on one leg, the other foot-tapped his impatience. Mr. and Mrs. Blanco shook everyone's hand. When it came to me, Blanco's father squeezed my hand too hard while his mother, whose hand was soft, said it was wonderful to hear of my academic, cultural, and sporting talents from the principal.

—*He's a fine boy.*

My mother looked from Mrs. Mitchell to me and concurred.

—*By the way, I'm sure it's just playground nonsense, but why do you call Donovan "Donnie Blanco"?*

(I've never heard anyone physically use air quotes with their voice while their hands remained crossed in front of them, Cartier carats counting the seconds.)

It's just a nickname, Mrs. Mitchell.

—*Hmm. Of course.*

The principal ahem-ed and said such tomfoolery would surely stop and ahem-ed some more as he ushered all of us out, into the parking lot and into our cars. Aliyanna's family drove away first, out toward the flat suburbs of flattened incomes, where we were also bound. The Blancos made for the hills.

On our way home, I asked my mother what had happened.

—*It's been sorted.*

She kept her eyes on the road.

What does that mean, Mom?

—It means it's been dealt with.

A whetted tone sliced through her voice, signaling that *something* was res judicata—decided, settled, and final, certainly not something she wanted to discuss with her sixteen-year-old. The only time she used her silencing voice on me was when I asked about my father: "Your father is just that, your father. Not my husband and not a parent. There isn't much I can say about him." I could never get more out of her. Whoever he was, wherever he was, whatever he did—all of these were secrets my mother held firmly within herself.

Dealt with how?

—There's no need to bring this up again.

She didn't look at me. She said it to the road in front of us, driving us away from a past she didn't want discussed again.

Bring what up? That Blanco's a rapist?

—I don't want you saying such things in public. Is that clear? I said it's been sorted.

Mom.

—Listen, you have to understand that I work for these people. They've offered to pay your fees. And hers.

Mom!

—Yes?

She said no.

My mother turned to me. In the instant between her engaging the indicator to turn right her mask slipped for a moment. I saw Aliyanna in her face. I saw my father's absence.

—I know.

126

2.

Before Donovan Mitchell became *un archivo en blanco*, Donovan Manyika joined our school in the ninth grade. He immediately became the top student on our competitive campus. He was Zimbabwean and everything Blanco wasn't: smart, quiet, and the poverty scholarship kid financed by the Mitchell Education Foundation. Manyika knew every African country's capital city, currency, and lingua franca, excelling at everything on the sports field and in the classroom. He Tenzing Norgay–ed our school's reputation to the top of every math and science olympiad and general knowledge quiz, and ran the home stretch of the relay in athletics meetings, making up for everyone else's lost time, dishing out disappointment and embarrassment to all he passed en route to the finish line. Whenever Manyika's name was announced at our annual prize-giving ceremony everyone applauded loudly. His success was our success, and given how hard he had it, nobody envied his achievements. The price of his brilliance was unrelenting hardship—he single-handedly looked after his three brothers and two sisters (also MEF scholars) who were then making their way through primary school, filling in their older brother's footsteps and collecting every bronze, silver, and gold star in the teacher's cupboards. Even though Manyika had our collective respect, I called him Donnie Darko to let him know gravity was a bitch and affected all men equally.

Donnie Darko stole something important from me, my athletics title: Onion Marks.

When I arrived in the third grade, I didn't make friends easily. I couldn't speak English, Afrikaans, or German. I was shunned. The first couple of weeks were hellish. No Kinyarwanda, no Swahili, not even a smattering of French—in each class I was surrounded by incomprehensible noise. I was a tropical orchid in welwitschia country. Slowly, and with much laughing from the other children at my pronunciation, my larynx picked up some of the common tongues. The only period I enjoyed was physical education. The other kids might not have understood my words, but they knew exactly what my body said whenever we lined up for races:

"Onion marks! Get set! Go!"

—*I'm too fast for you.* (Bang!)

—*You can't catch me.* (Five meters!)

—*I can let you catch up now.* (Twenty meters!)

—*I can let you gain a yard.* (Forty-five meters!)

—*I can even let you think you're going to win this.* (Sixty meters!)

—*But I'm just too fast for you.* (Finish line!)

I earned their respect because children, like most people, are drawn to visceral elemental forces like earth, wind, water, fire, strength, beauty, violence, and kindness. They admire and fear speed.

My speed made friends slowly and enemies much quicker.

From the moment I crossed the finish line in first place I felt Blanco's hate on my heels in second place. Thus far, he'd been the fastest third grader around. After me, he was another obsolete white boy. I didn't fully understand what I'd snatched away from Blanco until it was taken away from me by Darko. Being Onion Marks made you top dog of the *ludus*, a reputation recorded in the ledgers of the school's history. The fastest runners in each grade were awarded silver onion-shaped pins which sparkled on blazers, letting ordinary plebeians know they weren't governed by the normal laws of the Pax

Slowmana. You bragged like few others could. *No need to cry, man—it's just Onion Marks, bro.* With Blanco's head already struggling to stick with the pace of third-grade math and reading, I stole the sense of selfhood he'd made for himself with his feet. He became slow in more ways than one.

There's no honor among thieves, and this is how the story of black-on-black crime goes: you're the blur of speed at local and regional level, unable to compete at nationals because you aren't a citizen. You focus on destroying the track at provincial meetings, letting everyone else who goes on to represent their country at international competitions know the immigration laws granted them an unfair head start. At the hundred-meter dash in the ninth grade you and Blanco stretch in the fast fourth and fifth lanes, eyeing each other. His new running spikes claw the track's surface; your worn-out ones pinch your toes. You take your starting position and inhale once, twice, three times. A vision of yourself crossing the finish line in thunderous glory jumps the gun ahead of you. All you've got to do now is chase your dream down the track. Your name is chanted in the stands.

Onion Marks!

Get set . . .

His name is Donovan Eloterius Manyika.

He runs barefoot.

All you know about him thus far is that he's the new kid. His heels wink up and down as he sprints in the eighth lane, with you straining to catch him. You're rugged from the sprint and breathless with disappointment.

You watch as Manyika has his skinny arm lifted in the air.

"Onion Marks!"

You catch Blanco's eye.

A moment.

Only one of you has lost the race: he's still Donovan Mitchell. Donnie Blanco. Rich. Slower than you.

But you aren't Onion Marks anymore, the title that made you untouchable.

You're just a second-place shit-talker.

Blanco smiles at you.

3.

Fatty insisted on being called African American instead of black. He got faux mad when we called Namibian Coloreds *Colored*. He couldn't accept things were different on the continent, that whatever black people called themselves in Chicago, Oakland, or Detroit was none of our stick, but here, at home, *in the motherland*—which is what he called it—we had the right to discriminate and differentiate among ourselves as we saw fit. There were blacks, whites, Afrikaners, Coloreds, Basters, Indians, Chinese, Asians, and foreigners (basically, Zimbabweans and Angolans). No amount of Martin Luther King–ing us into disinterested boredom would make us judge people by the content of their hidden and undisclosed characters when the color of their skin made it quite clear who they were and weren't.

I shouldn't have called him Fatty. But I only realized this later after he committed suicide.

We didn't know casual hazing was a leading cause of death in American teenagers. We assumed a return to Africa would bequeath him a thick skin, a hide so tough it couldn't be penetrated by our tick bites of bad humor.

—*Hey, Fatty, your country needs to leave the Middle East the way you need to leave* vetkoeks *the fuck alone.*

—*Yeah, Fatty, we know—you're African American in the Useless of A, and maybe that's a badge of honor where you come from, but around here you're just American.*

—*For shizzy. Around here you're just another Fatty from the Block. Keep quiet.*

Fatty had arrived at our school in the middle of the eleventh grade, taking Aliyanna's vacant seat in our classes. The previous year, Aliyanna's parents had decided to move her to another school, not as good, but far away from the scandal they feared might've erupted if she stayed on. They needn't have worried, because my mother had promised me everything had been worked out by the adults, everyone was happy with the solution, and everyone, Aliyanna included, thought it was for the best she transfer to another school. My fees had been paid up until the end of the twelfth year of my school career. Our fridge at home filled with food from SPAR instead of ShopRite. My mom bought herself a new car and copped me the freshest ANDı kicks. Maybe, I thought, skipping onto the basketball court and shimmy-shaking to applause from the rest of the team, it really was for the best. I was still young. Guilt clung to me as briefly as my Axe body spray—I was sweating hormones all the time, erupting into young adulthood, and reveling in my status as the tormentor of the uncool and unpopular.

—*Now lookahere, Fatty, I've got a philosophical question: if a Big Mac disappeared from a restaurant plate in Atlanta but you weren't in the country, did you eat it?*

Besides our losing Aliyanna, our old English teacher, Mrs. Braithwaite, had decided to move back to England for fish and chips and to avoid *the crime in this country I swear to God this whole continent has gone to the dogs I should have moved when Zimbabwe happened.* (Back home, she found tikka chicken to be the new national meal because how about them Indians?) Mrs. Braithwaite was an okay English teacher: heavy-handed with the Dickens; oblivious to the fact English wasn't many people's first, second, or third language; decided the range of your linguistic ability based on the first essay of the year regardless of subsequent improvement; and reluctantly conceded Darko wrote better essays than Blanco even if the former hadn't been to the Taj Mahal or the Sydney Opera House. When she told us she was leaving, I hoped our workhouse days were over. Fatty hoped we'd get an American teacher—a viable hope, since part of our school's success was having a roster of teachers whose diversity was only rivaled by the UN General Assembly. We didn't have an American, though, so Fatty, with his fanatical belief that whatever came out of the United States was better—even though we knew this to be untrue since we had him as proof—hoped we'd get some Frank McCourt–esque English teacher.

—*Fatty, as the abdominous fifty-second state in the United Slaves of America, and the preeminent negro on all things emancipatory, dietary, and otherwise, do you think our new English teacher will prescribe* Huckleberry Finn *as our course reader?*

Huckleberry Finn was prescribed. But our teacher wasn't American; Mr. Donovan was from Liberia—or "Little USA," as Mr. Chikoti, our Malawian physics teacher, called it in one of our classes, chuckling at his own little joke. "Okay, now Fat—Latrell—please calculate the force needed to . . ."

As Mr. Donovan read out roll call in his first class his eyebrows lifted.

—*Three Donovans in one class?*

Donnie Blanco, Donnie Darko, and Fatty.

Mr. Donovan fixed me with a disinterested look which said he'd met a thousand versions of me before.

—*Right.*

He finished ticking names off the register, acquainting them with their corresponding raised hands and faces.

Here.

Present, sir.

Yo!

He put the list down.

—*Okay. Let's begin with some housekeeping rules. First, if you're a clown and you believe your job is to make us laugh with foolish shenanigans, then by all means, feel free to leave this classroom. I don't like clowns. I think they're a waste of good makeup and an unnecessary source of fear. If you're a child, and you think you need more maturing, I suggest you go home and take that issue up with your parents. My classroom isn't a daycare for spoiled children.*

We all sat up, hushed, curious. This was a peculiar introductory soliloquy. Mr. Donovan looked at me directly.

—*And if you consider yourself to be an object, incapable of being respectful toward me, yourself, or your fellow classmates, then beware: things exist to be used, once their utility has expired they're put in the bin. If it's your high duty and supreme destiny to be used and binned, please save me the trouble of crumpling you and tossing you into the wastepaper basket.*

Mr. Donovan and I stared at each other, both of us seeing who'd blink uncle.

I looked away, seething, vowing to find some way to crush this man who embarrassed me in front of the whole classroom.

—*Good. So, we'll only have, let's see, Mitchell, Manyika, and Latrell, and all the other government names on this list. You can call me Mr. D for short if you want. But that's it. Does anyone see a problem with this arrangement?*

No one did.

—*And you, the giver of nicknames, any problem?*
No. No problem, sir.

If there's one thing Mr. D got wrong in that classroom it was to make it a safe haven for Fatty. While I might have been stripped of my power during our nigger-infested readings of *Huck Finn*, Fatty's life was a misery before and after the bell rang. He was Fatty from the moment he stepped out of his father's Mercedes-Benz in the morning until he was fetched in the afternoon. That one hour with Mr. D was the only time Donovan Latrell was addressed with dignity.

You know what?

I plead the First, Second, Third, Fourth, Fifth, and every other amendment under the sun for everything we said to Fatty. We didn't know any other way to be. We were masters of all things group-y: group-think, group-speech, group-walk, group-slouch, group-exclusion. If I thought something, the hive vibrated with the same idea, and if we were unconscious about Fatty's depression, then I sure as heck wasn't woke to whatever he felt and how it affected him.

He shot himself one Friday evening. His younger sister found him in his bedroom.

When we were told the news on Monday morning in our register period, we all looked at Fatty's empty desk, wondering if we were implicated in his death as accessories to cruelty. There were no jokes that day. No wisecracks. No roasting in recesses. Group recrimination pushed us apart to our individual thoughts and actions, fracturing and sundering us to our own paths and ways of being.

When the card of condolences was passed around our classroom, I alone had no message to write. I just signed my name and passed it on.

Our English classroom was especially grave. Mr. D had liked Fatty—he read a very convincing Jim and had scathing opinions about Huck Finn and people who distanced themselves from wrongs by claiming refuge in groups. (Honestly, when I think about it all, Fatty was subtexting us the whole time.) Mr. D didn't teach that day. He seemed deflated. He put us in groups of three and sent us to the library to research *King Lear*, which was our next set work for literature. I was with, yep, Blanco and Darko.

In the library, the three of us didn't talk to one another. Blanco and I had never shared space so closely since that day in the principal's office. He quit the basketball team, which meant I didn't have to in order to avoid him. With his not being the Joker to my Batman in our hateful duo, we never had to wonder what we'd be doing every night: I'd do my best to complete my homework and he'd continue snacking on the world. In this way we'd coexisted—he with his friends, and I with mine. The only time I had to deal with Blanco was when he handed me the baton after running the back stretch in the relay so I could round the corner and give it to Darko, our unbeaten Onion Marks, who then blitzed the shame stretch and brought us the gold. Besides our collaborative efforts to share the podium with Darko,

Blanco and I had no other interaction. I'd been cautioned by my mother not to upset him or do anything which disturbed the bedrock of our newfound easy living. To dispense with any need to talk to him, I mumbled my willingness to look up succession controversies in England. Darko said he'd look into mental illnesses. Blanco chose what I deemed to be the easiest topic on the list Mr. D had given us: costumes and dresses of the Elizabethan era.

—*Should be easy to wrap myself around that.*

What can I say? We were foolish clowns in the circus of life, our teenage-hood was a ringmaster who whipped us through hoops and hopes. In another year we'd have to choose what we would be for the rest of our lives even though in the preceding seventeen we had no idea what anything was about. I interpreted Blanco's words as a slight against me, as an accusation for my part in Fatty's suicide. My stomach boiled. My words bristled. I easily substituted the weight of Donovan Latrell's suicide for the tangible, assailable mass presented by Donovan Mitchell.

Or easy for you to get under, Blanco. You know, with you being a rapist and all.

—*What are you talking about?*

We were petulant children. We needed to be raised. For many of us that wasn't happening at home, so we discovered ourselves in the wildness of our wit, our ids served our egos, shielding us with reflexive name-calling and character assassinations which we considered to be part of our basic programming. Later, of course, these things would be knocked out of us. We'd learn about ourselves, about each other, about other people.

But not yet.

I looked at Blanco, desperate to hurt him, to let him know that I knew he wasn't blameless and could never be.

Aliyanna.

Blanco's eyes narrowed.

—What about her?

We were still away from being people. We were things.

We moved through the world, guided by our own utility.

What we didn't respect, we binned.

She said no.

Darko was confused. His eyes ping-ponged between us as we swatted the onus of guilt between each other.

Blanco laughed loudly.

The whole library looked up at us. We were shushed by the librarian.

Blanco took his time dialing down his volume.

He leaned in conspiratorially.

—So did Fatty.

A-Side

LITTLE BROTHER
(OR, THREE IN THE MORNING)

"Hallo?" I say, voice still sleep-drunk. I sit up in bed.

"It's me."

My brother.

I don't know why he's calling me from an unknown number. My anger rouses itself and beats me to the mouthpiece. "I know. It's three in the morning. What the fuck, dude?"

My brother has a knack for being a younger brother and I have the curse of being his elder. That means he's always looked up to me and I've always found him annoying and inconvenient. On his first day of school, after my father dropped us off, I had to take him to his classroom because he didn't, understandably in hindsight, know where it was. He tried to hold my hand but I was in the fourth grade and much too cool for sissy shit like that. He looked scared as we walked toward the school building, with my dad standing next to his car, yelling at me to look after him like I hadn't been playing

139

guardian angel since my mother's womb popped him out, squealing, small, ugly, but fawned over by my parents. When they brought him home I couldn't understand the fuss. He couldn't speak, couldn't stop crying, and couldn't stop shitting himself. He was a brown bundle of screams aunts and uncles constantly praised. His eyes, apparently, were my—*our*—mother's. When he was silent he had *our* father's stern visage—this is the kind of nonsense people said about my brother when he was nothing more than a wriggling parcel of *Mamma, why does everything have to be about him?*

When my brother grew older, my parents made us share a room. Even though I was older, we had to share it equally. I couldn't understand why someone five years younger than me needed all that space, or why he had to crowd me out of the room with his imaginary friends—there were so many of them, and all of them were indulged by my parents.

"You aren't playing with him," my mother said. "So let him have his make-believe friends. You can go and play outside."

I had to live in a room with Gummi Bears cutouts during the dude's toddler years because I couldn't hang up my *X-Men* and *Spawn* posters. My mother said they'd give him nightmares.

Nightmares? From comic book posters?

I don't quite know how my brother managed to make my parents become so white, but he did it. My parents had been the generic strict black parents with me. While expensive baby food was spooned into his mouth only to be spat out, I think I ate solids from three months. The dude had diapers. I ran around naked like Adam and Eve, shameless, carefree, until I was three or four. My mother stopped working to look after him. I have memories of being bundled off to work, and my cheeks being pinched by colleagues. I remember being told to be quiet while my mother typed in her office. I remember causing her embarrassment when I wet myself on the office's carpeted floor. She jokes the stain must still be there. My brother wet his bed until he was eleven and she's never used him as material for her comedy specials. All the things I had to do—take an afternoon nap even though I didn't want one, eat apples until I was bored of them, watch one hour of television a day, and go to bed early even though I wasn't tired ("Mamma, I already slept in the afternoon!")—he was exempted from. I wonder what it is about younger siblings that makes parents realize corporal punishment is cruel and inhumane treatment. I don't know when the blackness runs out. I just know when my younger brother came along, all the rules were suddenly changed for him.

On that first day at school, I really hoped he wouldn't cry. He did. Three doors down from his homeroom. Why he couldn't have held in his tears until I'd left him in his class to be his teacher's responsibility, I don't know. We stood in the hallway, the two of us, with his saying he wanted to go home. I asked him to stop crying. Then I begged him. Then I pinched him hard. He wailed and stopped. "The other kids are watching us," I said, embarrassed for him, ashamed for myself. I'd been making a name for myself as a schoolyard scrapper. Nobody messed with me or my friends. I couldn't be related to this crying mass of cowardice. My brother slowly sniffed himself to silence. "Stop being a baby," I said. "We're in school now. And you're *my* brother. Grow up." He began crying again. Thankfully, his homeroom teacher was on her way to her classroom, so I shed him off to her.

Later that week, that month, that year, and every couple of years thereafter, he decided to get himself bullied. Guess who had to undecide that for him. Good ol' Big Brother was suspended from school every so often for fucking up the kids who cornered him to give him the most injudicious wedgies or steal his lunch. The other kids couldn't come for me, you see. Anyone I couldn't Sonic-zoom away from got the Knuckles treatment. My brother, being the weaker, slower, and perpetually surprised proxy, was a prime target for juvenile retaliation. My parents would greet each detention or suspension with disgust and threats to remove me from our expensive school. My brother would try to explain that I'd gotten into trouble protecting him, but I'd always tell him to keep quiet. Heroes love their unrequited thanks, from the gritty streets of Gotham to New York City's skyscrapers, from Windhoek's primary school playgrounds to the back of the gym building where kids who screwed with my brother were straightened out.

Wherever I went, my brother followed—primary school, high school, university. If I got something, he wanted the same thing too. The *Biker Mice from Mars* figurines: "Come on, we don't need two Modos. Why can't you get Throttle or Vinnie?"; the FUBU cap: "Really, dude?"; and the Puma Buccaneers soccer boots—in high school, my brother had the audacity to try out for the same position on the team: right wing. I changed from soccer to basketball and tennis to avoid being on the same team he was. His athleticism only took him so far, so I had the hoops and the courts to myself.

When we moved to our new house I could finally have my own room. I'd thought that'd be some sort of divorce for us, with each of us free to make our own way in the world, but I was still tethered to him in more infuriating ways. He insisted on coming into my room unannounced. He took and used my shit without asking. He jacked my whole style. I mean, come on, how was it possible for him to like the *same* white Reebok Classics? If my friends and I were road-testing some new slang, he'd cop our lingo and make it sound uncool. If we were thinking about sneaking out to a party, he'd try to include himself in our teenage subterfuge—we'd give up the whole operation because we didn't want to wind up worrying about him. Plus, he was my younger brother, man. He was a poor clone of cool—like Bizarro, a mockery of Superman. If there was a weaker pussy-pulling magnet than my brother I hadn't found it yet, and I'm the dude who knew random trivia about American history in case some Midwest country gal or southern belle needed to be wooed out of her clothes with subtext-heavy references to the Washington Memorial or Mount Rushmore.

At least in high school he started getting the message and hung around his own people. They were an unusual tribe of role-playing game fanatics. They obsessed about the minutiae of elfin and goblin armor. I mean, damn, I had *Yu-Gi-Oh!* cards, but these dudes took shit to another level. They called each other by their game names: *War Master, Shadow Caster, Nine-Tailed Fox, Doc Orc.* Yeah, they called each other this shit *in real life!* Like, at the mall with other people around. Whenever they were together I'd hear talk of "acquiring more HP," "upgrading my satchel," or "I'll hold the hill until you summon your dragon!" from my bedroom. Look, my brother and his friends were plain weird. They all had older siblings too.

Because of me he was able to tick the university application box that asked whether any family members had previously attended or were attending our university. We weren't exactly legacy kids, but I'm certain that shit helped him glide through the admissions process. While we were at varsity he was, thankfully, in a different residence, but from time to time I had to go and check up on him to make sure he was okay. I'd make sure he had food and that his lectures were going well. Our exchanges were always taut, tense with things unsaid, judgment on my part about his room, which had become the de facto Last Homely House for anyone hell-bent on not losing their virginity, and silence on his part because he really didn't know what to talk to me about. These room calls were mandatory. My mother would never have let me hear the end of it if something had happened to him. Personally, I felt like I'd done my bit. I'd cut out and marked the trail for him since he was born.

When I was twelve, I once asked my mother why they'd had another child. We were in the kitchen. I'd come to look for something to eat. My brother, predictably, had shadowed me. He said he was hungry too. (*Right . . .*)

"Mamma, why wasn't I enough?" I called my brother The Extra, The Side, The Spare, The Other Kid. "Why d'you have to have him too?" I was supposed to be The First and Only, their Son in whom they were pleased.

My mother, who'd been washing some dishes in the kitchen sink, became still. She looked up out of the window for a while, toward something I couldn't see. She absentmindedly rubbed her still-wet hands against her belly. And then she said, almost inaudibly, that I wasn't the first.

"What?" I asked. My eyes narrowed.

"Nothing," my mother said. "Never mind." Before she walked out of the room quickly, she told me to make my brother a sandwich. I heard her bedroom door close.

I looked at my brother, who smiled at me. He was about to receive the *bestest sandwich a big brother could make.* I thought about the extra pair of sneakers I could've gotten if my parents didn't have to budget for him too. I sighed and asked him to pass me the bread.

Now he's phoning me at three in the fucking morning. I ask my brother what he wants.

"It's—"

I'm about to say something but stop. There was something peculiar about the way he said *It's me* the first time. I notice it now. "Dude, why're you crying?"

"It's Mamma."

My breath catches. "What?"

"Papa says you should come to the hospital."

B-Side

The Other Guy

I tell her I've forgiven her.

It's in the past. Soon it will be forgotten.

I say it slowly, pace it just right so it doesn't feel rushed, like I'm saying it to get it over and done with. I make eye contact with her as she sits across from me at the kitchen counter. I say that I too have made mistakes (even if in this I'm completely blameless). I don't sit with my back straight; I bend the vertebrae slightly so it appears the weight of what I'm saying presses down upon me. I've been told forgiveness is a heavy burden. So I make my shoulders look like the cross bites into my shoulders—I pull them down and in, but not too much. Although I'm prepared to carry her absolution toward our Calvarific hill, where we seem destined to crucify ourselves for the love we say we have for each other, she needs to know she'll have to do her share of lifting. *We can move on from this.* I stress the togetherness of our future joint efforts. *We. You and me.* "In time," I tell her, "we can put this behind us."

The thing remains unnamed, seemingly diminished, the pain of its hurt reduced by lack of specific nomenclature which would resurrect in talk of fault, its resultant liability, and the reluctant reparations.

She searches my face for pretense. She finds none. Even when I was younger it was hard for my parents and friends to tell when I was being sincere and when I wasn't. The trick to hiding subterfuge is to adopt a blanket policy of silence—I was a quiet kid, so it was never hard for me to keep my volume button dialed right down to mute. It made my parents believe I was smart, that I was thinking deep, mysterious, and complex thoughts. My school friends found it creepy at first, my reserved demeanor. But when they discovered that my lack of abrasive jocularity, boyhood boasting, and toxic taunting provided them with bigger stages for their own raucous performances, they welcomed my silence. I realized, growing up, that noisy people have a strange way of exposing parts of themselves without being aware they're doing so. Sound has an uncanny way of magnifying a voice's faltering octaves when it's falsely praising someone's achievements, amplifying the crack in the timbre when it's donning ill-fitting bravery, and resonating and reverberating the cut of a sneer. It is impossible to hide in noise; the silent and patient listener will always pick up the flaws clamoring to be heard. Silence radiates nothingness—not anger, not joy, not jealousy, not fatigue, not guilt. It conceals and caches many things: like envy, hurt, loss, and disagreement. It scares me to think of what the universe hides behind its great unyielding and unending hush.

She looks at me the same way stargazers look at the night sky, hoping to find something, anything—any noise—in my face. I cover it with indecipherable frequencies, like the treatment masks she put on before going to bed, focusing on the hollows and edges of the eyes, where most feelings hide; the corners of the mouth that can Judas-kiss and betray the slightest untruth of an utterance with a mere tic; and the cheeks and ears that could inadvertently break cover, giving away the location of a hidden sentiment.

I watch her, the nostrils which flair slightly as she breathes, the arched eyebrows that test everything I say for deceit, and the throat whose peristaltic movements nervously swallow what I've just told her.

I forgive you.

The light in her eyes changes. She smiles, but not with happiness. She's accepting her bondage to my pardon; she's bound and condemned to do better, knowing whatever she does will never be enough.

▶ ||

I tell her friends the same thing: *I've forgiven her.* I say it matter-of-factly, and follow it up with the quietude of those who've transcended possessiveness, pettiness, and resentment. They cross-examine me—*Are you sure? Is this what you want? Are you doing this to prove a point? How do you know it won't happen again?* In their prattling they reveal themselves to me: they wanted the bitterness and drama. They were holding out for the calling of chits, determination of alliances, and the ensuing divvying up of friends and spaces.

There's none of that. There's only what I've said: *I've forgiven her.*

They're disappointed. Peace is a poor conversation starter. It's the conclusion, not the climax; peace is never the story, it's the black screen and the end credits. To lighten they talk about nothing and everything before, once more, I have to tell them that everything will be fine. They hug me, and when we part they say she's lucky to have me.

I tell them no: "I'm the lucky man."

▶️⏸

My friends ask me if I've really forgiven her. *Like for real-real. Not on some be the bigger man type of shit because that shit is for losers, yo—what she did was unforgivable.* And I say, "Yes, I have." They shake their heads. One of them walks out of the room, disgusted. I tell them life isn't black and white, that things aren't always clear even when you think they are. Nothing is ever solved by looking at the present alone. There's history. And the unknown future to think about. Even with this, I tell them, there's something to be salvaged. They laugh. They jeer. They make jokes about the suckers they've made out of other men—"Every single one who's forgiven shit like this thought they were the king of hearts and turned out to be jokers." I tell them since I've forgiven, they should forget. Most shake their heads. Only one supports me. He tells me to do whatever I need to feel the way I need to feel. *That's all that matters, man. Just make sure you're leaving the past in the past.* I tell him that I am. He wishes me luck because forgiveness is foreign territory to him, to me, to us.

▶️⏸

When we meet for lunch she says she's glad we can do this again: be *us*. She always loved our small moments the most. The walks. Watching trash series together. Knocking back reps together at the gym in perfect syncopation with everyone staring at us. She's happy she has me back in her life, that we're easing back into familiar routines—like leaving our offices to get lunch together. She reaches across the table and holds my hand. My palm sweats so I let her go.

She says: "I love you. I'm sorry I ever made you doubt that."

I tell her I never did, not for a second, minute, hour, day, week, or month of the past year. I tell her: "If I did I'd have moved on." I say it confidently, like I've always had the chips stacked in my corner, aware my river card was on its way. I pick up my sandwich. "These things happen. People are tested. Some fail."

She flinches. I tell her I didn't mean it like that.

"I know," she says. "But still."

▶ ||

When we walk I pull her close to me so the world knows I've forgiven her. I laugh loudly at her jokes and slip into the ghost of our past. I encourage, I cheer, I support—I play my familiar role. Yes, she should change her job if she can. Yes, I think it would be good to move in together. But later, not now. *Not so soon after . . . everything.* She says she understands. I tell her I still see the same future with her. *No, a better one.* I tell her this many times until she believes it too.

▶ ||

Later, in bed, she says she missed me, that she missed *this*—exactly this. She says I'm all she wants, all she needs. She breathes into my ear that I've always been hers and she'll always be mine. She cries. I kiss her and tell her we'll be new. *Just like before.* She puts her arms around my neck and pulls me to her heat, and deeper into her body. When I peak I've no choice but to come down into her. She holds me, forcing me to leave parts of myself inside her. I think she thinks that completes her atonement.

When I'm lying next to her, catching my breath, I notice how much she's changed. She lies on the bed as inviting and unashamed as Goya's *La maja desnuda*—confident, with a fresh strip of womanhood she'd never had the courage to sport before, something new for her, something frightening for me. In our old days—before forgiveness— she'd be demure, a dim shadow in the soft lights of our rooms. Now she's as careless as a reclining nude, full of provocative angles which reveal her newfound freedom, perhaps something she couldn't realize with me. Her kissing has changed—forceful, hungry, bruising. She moves her body in perfect sine waves when she is on top. She directs me where to go, and what to do. And when we we're finished, she is undignified. She doesn't shower me with the usual thousand whispers of kindness. Like a piglet after a big meal she rolls over, sighs into the pillow, and yields to sleep without any romance.

▶︎❙❙

On the street, I see him—The Man with No Face, The Stranger with No Name—in every man. The Other Guy who turned me into *the other guy.* I avert my eyes from passersby; I yield the right of way on the pavement to shorter men. Do they cast curious glances my way?

My jaw clenches. My fists close. My breath quickens. I pick up my pace to get away from every man I pass.

I almost run.

▶‖

In the morning The Other Guy is a foot flitting around the kitchen's door as I leave her eating her breakfast. He's a shadow in the corridor's slanting late-afternoon light. At night, in our room, he's an invisible weight at the edge of the bed, an unknown assailant I can't crush or kill. I imagine his cologne, his rough beard, his fingerprints unlocking parts of her I didn't even know existed.

And when I'm inside her I can still feel him.

I've told her I've forgiven her.

But I haven't.

Tornado
(or, The Only Poem You Ever Wrote)

tornado

(noun)

/tawr-ney-doh/

A violently destructive windstorm characterized by a rotating column of air in contact with the surface of the Earth.

Scrambling out of bed dressing quickly and running out of the apartment forgetting to lock up and running down the stairs fumbling the car keys the car coughing like it's about to die and oh my god do not think of death Jesus take the wheel fuck you are not even a believer but death the drive to the hospital skipping red lights and swerving the car into the parking lot and then forgetting to put on the handbrake and the car bumping into the wall behind it and then you are running into the reception calling that simple childish word that

echoes for all eternity *Mamma! Mamma! Mamma!* And the person at
the reception does not know and then you are told that she must be
in the ER and then you are running running through the brightly lit
halls and then the corner where you bump into the nurse and then
the swearing because you are trying to find the corridor that leads to
the room where they save lives and surely this is the place where they
save lives otherwise what the fuck are hospitals for and this is just
the worst fucking thing that has ever happened and then there is the
room and there is the bed and oh my god oh my god oh my god
and oh my god and oh my god and you pull back the curtain
and it is the wrong bed and then there is your father
peeking from behind a curtain and your brother
as well and then the walk that stumbles and the
man is crying and the boy is also crying but
you are not crying just yet but this is about
to change and here you are and there it is
the bed the real bed this time not the
wrong bed but you wish it was not
the real bed but fuck this is the
real bed and here you are and
there she is and no this cannot
be her it is not her it is not it
is not it is not her it is not
her it is not her it is not
her it is not her it is
not her it is not her
it is not her it is not

her it is not her
it is not her it
is not her it
is not her
it is not
her it
is

B-Side

SEVEN SILENCES OF THE HEART

You blink rapidly. You don't know where you are. I do. Recollection returns: you're in a church.

You're at a funeral.

The crow-black suits some of the men sorrowfully sport are crowded out by the colors clinging to the women. Your people never succumbed to death's attempts to deprive life of its numberless shades and hues. I could take their words, temporarily steal their rhythm, but they wouldn't let that steal their color. The women are decked out in dresses cut from prismatic prints: checkered squares of red and canary yellow; whorls of indigo and aquamarine; splashes of teal and turquoise; tiger, zebra, and okapi stripes, leopard spots, fluorescent mandrill dyes—all things bright, garish, and beautiful have come to mock death with their defiant pigments. But for the somber pall this gathering could be a baptism or a confirmation. The routine of religion is the same. Your limbs and mouth remember the motions. You're swept up in the spiritual current and go with the flow: you sit;

you stand; you sit again; and stand once more; you cross yourself and mutter the necessary words. *And also with you.* You don't jump onto the Old Testament when it rolls by as an aunt labors through her reading, creaking verse by clinking verse. The New Testament flies over you. An uncle, still weary from jet lag, delivers a tepid reading. You wonder what it was like for him to fly through four time zones with death as a destination. How do you pack for a burial? What do you tell the immigration officer at the airport?

"Please state the purpose of your entry."

"My sister's funeral."

You stand. The call and response: *It is right to give thanks and praise.*

This is the Gospel of the Lord.

Thanks be to God.

You sit.

The priest begins his sermon. You can't hear what he says. Your senses have been faulty the whole day. Your sight works but it can't find a focus. Sound lapses occasionally. Smell is on a sabbatical after too many sticky hugs spiced with strong perfume and sweaty condolences. You can't remember how many hands you've shaken, how many relatives brushed their faces against yours, once on each side, with their powdered cheeks leaving traces of foundation on your cheeks or their sharp stubble pricking you. The priest's mouth moves, guided by the Spirit or the praxis of last rites. He looks at your father. He looks at you. He says something which makes the mourners murmur. In your peripheral vision you see someone put what they surely think is a reassuring hand on your shoulder. You can't feel whether they squeeze or not.

You stand. Then you kneel. You shuffle forward for Communion. When the wafer alights on your tongue you taste it for the promised healing. Deliverance. Anything. When you kneel to pray your mind is blank. You sit back.

Behind the priest, the choir stands up. Your ears return to the world. The conductor blows lightly on a harmonica; the singers hum themselves into tune.

Your heart beats slowly.

Thump-thump. Thump-thump.

The choir begins singing.

1.

"*Ukuthula . . .*"

Your family sent for kin as best as they could. Many relatives didn't have enough money to make a living let alone travel to honor the dead. Still, enough people arrived to fill the house with their jarring dialects and stories of the place you barely know as home. Your father translated their gentle messages of sympathy for you, since they spoke too fast and peppered their conversations with idioms you couldn't understand. *We came to bury your mother, our sister. We came to help you weep. We came to break apart and put ourselves together.* Your native language had been on its way out for years—you did your best to reply. All you could do was say, "Thank you for coming all this way." They looked affronted. You were speaking from the grammar and politeness of English classes, from a learned reservation they did not understand. They were speaking from their hearts, from culture, from a tradition alien to you in diaspora. *Distance means nothing in death. Not here, not on the moon. We came to show you how not to be alone.* When you cried they understood: grief was a new tongue you needed to learn. *Come, we will teach you.* Uncles and aunts assumed their cultural roles and made the requisite preparations, always consulting with you as your father's spokesperson, his firstborn.

Supposedly.

They should've asked me about the readings, about who'd be called upon to share their eulogies, and the kinds of food platters that should've been ordered for the memorial sessions held at the house. It's my shoulder they should've patted gently as they said, "It's time for you to be strong now—for your father."

They kept the kind words for you instead.

As usual, nothing was said to me.

". . . *kulo mhlaba wezono.*"

The choir prays for peace upon this sinful world.

All told, there weren't enough of your own people to sing the traditional hymns. So you asked the church choir to put something together, unable to decide between "Amazing Grace" and "Nearer, My God, to Thee."

"*Aleluya.*"

How weak you are.

I'd have told them the right song to choose and the appropriate costumes. I'd have conducted them with orchestral aplomb. Instead you let them settle on imported, foreign forgiveness.

"*Igazi likaJesu linyenyez' ukuthula.*"

The blood of Jesus, the choir sings, shouts for peace.

The conductor told you, gently, that sometimes it was easier to choose the song the deceased liked the most. "It would make for a fitting send-off. It's always better when a song comes from the heart."

You consulted your cardiac muscle, but it was mute.

So the choir chose for you.

2.

"*Usindiso . . .*"

You had a girlfriend once, what people would call "a nice girl." She said the two of you had the power to stop and start the world over as many times as you liked. She said you shone, glowed, and glittered.

You broke up with her in the worst way possible. You sent her a message from Franco's phone: *We aren't right for each other.*

I'd never felt love, never had it offered to me so freely—I was only a witness to its presence, not a worthy recipient. I don't know what it's like to have someone's heart pick up the frequencies of your own, to beat in tandem like drummers flirting with each other in a dance circle. I was bitter when you turned down her love so easily.

"*. . . kulo mhlaba wezono.*"

When your girlfriend heard the news about your mother—Cicero might've told her—she sent you a message offering you strength for the times ahead. She'd lost someone too. She knew what you were in for. "It's going to be bad," she said, "for a long time. But you're going to be okay."

"Aleluya."

You told her you wanted to meet up. She became wary and asked what for.

"You know, to apologize for—"

"Thanks, but no," she said. "You never asked to be forgiven and I've already forgotten."

What was done was done. She'd moved on. It was time you did the same.

"Igazi likaJesu linyenyez' usindiso."

The choir prays for redemption and salvation as you think back to that phone call and how closure was a fool's hope, another way of asking to be taken back.

I was glad that you, the squanderer of love—this thing that made you walk through the world with assuredness, so comfortable with your faults—had been held to account. I watched you draw the curtains in another room of your heart, cover the furniture, pinch the candlewicks, and close the door. The hush which descended upon you as you dimmed your soul was a feast for carrion such as I.

Thump-thump. Thump-thump. Thump-thump.

3.

"Ukubonga . . ."

I remember your intrusion into my peaceful world.

The body your parents had made for me was too weak to hold on to life even though I did my best to make it habitable, to fill its corners with their excitement. They made my form using parts of themselves. But it failed.

My body was removed from your mother. It was a frail thing, unable to contain the energy of my being and the dreams your parents had for me.

I should've left with it. But I was too scared to leave the comfort of the chamber of my conception. I couldn't face the world without a body. What if I floated away or disintegrated into ash? I did not want to die before I had lived.

I broke the rules of life and the grand game of death: I chose to stay hidden in the empty recesses of your mother's being, a fugitive, a deeply felt loss, a tenant who paid rent by afflicting her with borderless silences your father could not comprehend. On days filled with sunshine a dark cloud would loom over her face. She would place her hand on her stomach and rub it gently. I would crawl as close to her touch as I could, trying to let her know I was there, that she was not alone. Instead, she would be wracked by inconsolable crying.

Your father promising her everything would be all right couldn't offer any solace. He vowed they'd make a better, stronger body. I remember how eager I was for a second chance. I'd be the child they'd always hoped for. For once, I felt light. The easing of the dense mass lying beneath your mother's stomach was echoed by her energetic return to work, and her renewed, enthusiastic lovemaking.

Love, hope, and biology collided to create life: a bundle of cells that multiplied relentlessly, sprouting arms and legs. I watched the little heart pumping blood around it, vibrating with a fierce rhythm, pushing red life lines around the gossamer veins. Even then I could tell it would become a powerful vessel.

"*. . . kulo mhlaba wezono.*"

I tried to enter it and become who I was always supposed to be. I felt you inside.

I was horrified.

Your parents had promised to make "another one"—another me. Your father had used those exact words.

Instead, they made you.

It wasn't fair. Your parents' betrayal cut and scarred me, reduced me to a misshapen thing, even as your spirit grew and glowed, pulsating like a twinkling star in the warmth of the womb.

"*Aleluya.*"

You and I wrestled in the dark. Our struggles made your mother clutch her stomach and look for somewhere to sit down, her forehead beaded with pain. Your father dropped whatever he was doing to attend to her. She waved him off and said the violence in her womb was a sign: "This one is a fighter."

"*Igazi likaJesu linyenyez' ukubonga.*"

They beamed at each other, grateful for the second chance that was you. They walked through the world, perpetually thankful, their high favor rippling like the gentle chorus from the choir.

They forgot about me.

Thump-thump.

They boxed the world they said I'd inherit, wrapped it, and presented it to you.

Thump-thump.

Once, late at night, with your father's arm wrapped around your mother for protection, I heard your mother whisper: "Please, let this one live." Your father held her tighter and kissed her neck. He whispered back and said, "This one is strong. He won't leave like the last one."

I was ashamed. And I was angry.

4.

"*Ukukholwa!*"

I staged a last bid for the body, wrapping myself around you, trying to push you out of it. You fought, blocking my efforts to seize your brain, your bellowing heart, and the muscles that would shape the world around you. We wrestled until your mother felt a wetness on her thighs. She called your father. *It is time!*

At the hospital, we continued our war of attrition. Your mother screamed the screams of death. She cried. She bit. She spat. She begged for the pain to stop.

I couldn't stop.

I wouldn't stop.

I needed my body. I desired what I was promised. I craved what I was owed: my chance at life.

We fought until they pulled you out of her, with me inside you, two in one body, silent, unmoving. If I could not have this body, neither would you.

Your father begged the doctor to do something.

"*Kulo mhlaba wezono.*"

I felt your spirit tiring, slackening its hold on the body. I had won. I would evict you from the flesh, take control of the magnificent form, reignite its fires, and awake triumphant, baptized in birth-blood.

But your mother did a most evil thing: she whispered your name.

"*Aleluya.*"

She commanded you to live.

"*Igazi likaJesu linyenyez' ukukholwa.*"

Her power heated dead forges, warming the slow gold, boiling the iron used to cast your form.

You spirit stirred.

Thump.

I felt the quickening pulse, the power surging through you, crackling and hissing. A wave of energy built inside you, rolling, barreling toward me. I lost my purchase on the limbs I'd been about to claim. You opened your mouth and screamed and screamed and screamed, cursing me out like the holiest of exorcisms.

Thump-thump.

Your body smoked, steamed, and wriggled from the exertion. I smoldered from defeat like dead ash with only the memory of heat.

Thump-thump! Thump-thump! Thump-thump! Thump-thump!

The spoils of birth were yours. Your body was *yours*. Our father became *your* father. Our mother became *your* mother.

You became the firstborn.

I was no one.

I was weaker outside the womb. I tried to crawl back into your mother but could find no weaknesses in her being through which to enter. She was shielded from me by your presence. I could see myself being forgotten whenever she looked at you proudly, when you looked back at her with your curious eyes, reminding her you were the one who'd lived. You turned me into a memory, waning each passing day, fading each year. How I cried at the thought of being less than I already was.

I was bound to you, the cursed price of not having left your mother when I had the chance, a watcher condemned to be your witness and to record your passage through this world. Your gurgles were like a glove slap taunting me to do the same if I dared. I couldn't. I had no body. I crawled behind you and was dragged in your wake as you ran. The rushing wind nibbled at my fragile essence, leaving me frayed and ragged. You learned to read, to write, to play, to sing, and to dance. I watched you make friends so easily. I listened to you talk about the dreariness of living.

But, little by little, I grew stronger, nourished by my grievances against the world, against you. The happier you were, the more miserable I became. As you shone I found homes in terrible crevices and sunless places, in your dark moods, in your selfishness and your rage. From these low countries of the soul and corners of the heart I watched you, measured your weaknesses, and noted your follies. You reached for me when kindness ran out. You summoned me when you were lonely. In these scattered times I could move your mouth and utter a few terrible words. I could arrest your motion for a moment and allow the world and all of its pleasures to pass you by. I looked forward to your sourness, knowing that for a moment I could make my presence known to the world. I prayed and then planned for when you would fall, when you would give in to despair and have no option but to call for me and ask me to be what you could not: me, the rightful heir of the world you ruled as a false king. Heavy would lie the crown, light would be my ascendance.

You were too busy to notice how my form changed, how longer and stronger I grew, how dark my hide became. There were moments I was tempted to show you my power, to strike out and dislodge you from your aerie. Instead, I built up my strength in secret.

My time would come.

Thump-thump.

5.

Now it has.

"UKUBONGA . . ."

Victory is mine!

Love, the many-feathered thing that's kept you shielded from me, flutters off when it hears my scales scraping against the church floor's tiles. I slither down the aisles. I pass the stained glass saints and saviors, patrons of causes, guides, and guardians. They can't protect you from me now.

I've finally come for you.

I slide through the shields the congregation tries to raise against me with their spiritual mumbling. The priest launches a volley of prayers. They ricochet off me harmlessly. As I make my way toward you I strike at random, displaying my might. A distant cousin cries. An uncle's face has the fresh sheen of tears. An aunt's throat chokes with emotion. Even the choir's members succumb to my presence. Some voices break.

The triumphant chorus is misplaced. It isn't for you. It's for me. I've come for you.

For the past week you've been dodging and ducking me. You've copied, pasted, and sent the same message to your friends: you told Franco you were okay; lied to Rinzlo and said you were cool; *All good, Lindo*, you texted; Cicero didn't let up even after you told him not to worry. "Seriously, dude," you said, "I'm a'ight." You've only succeeded in ensnaring yourself in my trap.

Now here, with your family and friends, you've cornered yourself at the front of the church. There's nowhere to hide.

I wrap myself around you with more strength than I've ever possessed. I sink my teeth into your neck and feel my essence flow into you.

Your eyes water. Your lips quiver. Your breath comes short. You tremble. Your heart is finally going to stop once and for all.

"... *KULO MLABA WEZONO!*"

The sadness in my venom breaks down the barriers between you and the body that should've been mine. You shrink within yourself. I seep into the gaps, stealing through the cracks in your once impervious shell. I find you undefended, on your knees, crying like a child. I make as though I've come to console you, and you, being the feeble fool you are, open your arms to me. I embrace you as a brother and stab you in the heart.

You lose your strength and fall.

Thump-thump. Thump-thump. Thump-thump.

Finally, you see me in all my glory.

Thump-thump. Thump-thump.

I am the real firstborn.

I am no one.

I am the unnamed grief from your mother's womb.

Thump-thump.

You cry.

Thump.

I laugh and dance.

"ALELUYA!"

My poison courses through you, going for the softest memories of your mother. It hardens the hurts against her. This is how grief works: it mines your being for guilt and makes it bubble and froth to the fore. It mutates cells, weakens bone, and deforms character. In time you will learn my speech fluently, you will speak without hope. You will hurt without apology. Already you are beginning to look more like me.

So this is what it feels like to have fingers. These are knees. These are elbows. This is what it's like to run your tongue on the roof of your mouth.

I make your face smile through its tears.

Is this how you do it? Is this how you win love? Am I doing it right?

"IGAZI LIKAJESU LINYENYEZ' UKUNQOBA!"

I reach for your larynx and find your voice, always self-assured and in possession of some clever pronouncement. It's mine now, just like everything else attached to you. Your body is finally mine—

6.

"Induduzo . . ."

I am hit.

I blink to refocus your eyes. I shake your head to clear it of the grogginess. Your eyes adjust. I turn your neck to the left and to the right, seeking the source of a disorienting and invisible blow.

I'm struck again and nearly ejected from your body.

Again and again and again, I'm hit by blows from an unseen assailant.

I hiss, retreat from you, coiling around myself.

I prepare a mortal blow.

A fiery light flashes before me, shielding you from me.

"Enough," it whispers. A familiar voice. It grates my ears.

I try to circle it to get to you but it blocks my path.

"Enough!" The authority in its voice dislodges some of my scales. I shriek in pain and back away.

My poison is failing to erase you from your body. We are as we were when you were born: two in one body. I feel your thoughts. Through your eyes I see myself cowering away from the light. It shames me to be seen like this. My deadly coil prepares itself to spring at you.

Then I hear it and you do too.

It's more than the choir singing now. The congregation has joined in.

". . . *kuloooooo*—"

". . . *mhlaba*—"

". . . *wezonooooo.*"

Some notes lack the purity of practice. Those who know the words sing them, those who don't hum along.

You rise back to your feet even though my toxin should've paralyzed you.

You sing along too.

"*Aaaaaleluyaaaaa!*"

The light increases in intensity. My poison seeps from your body, drawn from it. But there's too much of it to be completely expelled. The corruption remains. I try to shrink away but I am pinned down by another whispered command: "Let me show you."

I see you, Cicero, and another woman talking on a Chesterfield couch. I see you and Franco sitting in his apartment, talking. I see you and Lindo on an apartment balcony, detached from a loud party inside. I see you and Rinzlo in a taxi, finally on your way to being the best version of yourself.

"This," the light says, "is the future of grief."

The visions come more quickly now.

I see you stronger than you are now. You walk in this future world with more care. You're with someone—a person I don't know. She's smiling at you and you're smiling at her. I see you and your father sitting and laughing together at a dinner table.

In these pictures of the future—near or far, I don't know—I'm not there.

I scan for myself. I must be there. My mark upon you will surely survive the passage of time. I refuse to be robbed of retribution.

There.

I'm merely a memory, not the force of nature I'd hoped to be. I'm looked upon with not pity but empathy, remembered as an equal despite the havoc my remaining presence will wreak on you, your family, and your friends.

In one of these visions you do a strange thing: you lend me your body so I can run away from the unpleasantness that's defined me since I came into existence. When I stop, lungs aflame, you hold my hand and we fly into the wide, flat blueness of the sky until it becomes a black sheet dotted with stars. In those air-thin heights you tell me it's time for me to go.

You tell me I've been a hard teacher, a necessary one. You brush away my sorries. You try to disconnect. I cling to your hand. I'm scared of falling. You tell me not to fear, unclasp my hand gently. As I float away, I start glowing.

You look at me, laugh, and say, "This is where you've always belonged."

Despite the brightness of my light, it can't banish the blackness of space. The nearest pinprick is far, far away.

I'm not ready to be alone.

And you say: "You won't be. Just hold the light—help and hope are on the way."

"*Igazi likaJesu linyenyez' induduzo.*"

You sing for me to get the comfort I've never known or had. As I drift further and further away I notice something: I have a heartbeat where a cold silence used to be.

I sparkle. *Thump-thump.* I twinkle. *Thump-thump.* Then I shine. *Thump-thump. Thump-thump. Thump-thump.*

The visions stop. The light dims itself a little and shows its face.

I gasp. I see myself.

It flashes and goes away.

7.

"*Ukuthula . . .*"

You blink rapidly. You don't know where you are, but I do.

175

You're in a church. You're at a funeral. You're at your mother's funeral.

"Ours," you say gently when you see me.

Our father is leaning on you. He wears dark sunglasses, the rivulets sneak past the tint. You tell him it'll be okay. You say, "Papa, don't worry. It'll be okay."

I'm saddened by what I've seen in the days to come, ashamed of my part in them.

"... *kulo mhlaba wezono.*"

I feel myself still pumping through your heart, slowing its rhythm, dampening its strength. I try pulling the grief out. You tell me to stop. "The grief will burn itself away," you say, "and in its place will be hope."

"*Igazi likaJesu linyenyez' ukuthula.*"

I ask you how you know, how you can be so sure it won't become something else, something much worse.

You smile as the cold space inside you grows. "I'm not. But I have you, the one who stayed behind when you should have left."

You sing and pray for my peace.

The future of grief commences.

Thump-thump.

I wait for the day when it turns to hope.

Thump.

THE SAGE OF THE SIX PATHS
(OR, THE LIFE AND TIMES OF THE FIVE Os)

THE WINDHOEK PUBLIC LIBRARY AND THE PATH OF
YOUTH AND FOOLISHNESS

When we were younger there was nothing in this Wild Wild Worst town to do but fight. Me, Rinzlo, Cicero, Lindo, and Franco—the Five Os. We were from the same side of town: torn Millé and Hi-Tec sneakers unworthy of hot-stepping in, out-of-fashion T-shirts from the PEP store with girl-pulling gravity set to zero, and not even a coin between us to spend at the arcade. We'd pool our poverty at the mall on weekends waiting for rich kids from Olympia and Ludwigsdorf to give us shifty looks so we could corner them in the parking lot and pound on them.

Anything could set us off.

Some Jordan-wearing dude looking at our cheap kicks funny? Fight.

Rinzlo getting bullied? Fight.

Some random-ass guy coughing into the west wind while we were coming up from the east?

—"It's so late for you! It's five o'clock!"

Kids in our neighborhoods used to alert each other the Five Os were coming like we were Omar from *The Wire.*

—"It's a quarter to, my guy, we gotta go home."

—"Five-Os! Five-Os!"

I guess if there was a park with green grass and walking trails like Central Park, we'd have gone there for picnics, concerts, and tai chi classes, or just to watch white people walk their dogs or something. We didn't have that. All we had was the waste of water in the city center called Zoo Park which had grass patchier than the Masai Mara in the dry season. In the park's early days there was a gushing fountain with koi fish in it. But guys from the hood got hungry and fished them out. Then the drought came and the municipality cut the water. After the swings were broken and never repaired, we went back to kicking ass. It's what we'd been doing best since we were nine or ten.

We didn't have Sega Saturns or PlayStation Ones. Lindo's 9,999-in-1 cartridges never worked, and even when they did there was only so much *Battle Tanks* we could play before we realized the other 9,998 games were variations of the same game. We made our own entertainment: turning our neighborhood into Vietnam for any pigeon within range of our *ketties* or BB guns.

When we weren't beating down on dudes who disrespected us, we snuck into cinemas to watch Wesley Snipes *skop, skiet, en donner* vampires into dust. We slyly opened *Hustler* magazines in the CNA in town to gloat at college girls and spread-eagles before the security guard chased us out. We always managed to escape with a few comic books hidden beneath our oversized T-shirts. Lindo—God bless the useless Robin Hood—used to steal the most boring ones.

"Lindo," Franco said, "why'd you get this issue of *Green Lantern?* We've read this shit already!"

"It was the closest one, bra," Lindo replied, ashamed.

"Fuck, look before you jack some shit, man." Cicero shook his head.

"What'd you get?" Rinzlo asked.

"*Uncanny X-Men,*" I replied proudly.

"Number twenty? Bro, we haven't read the previous nineteen issues."

"Yeah, well, just use your imagination."

Franco, our captain, was what we called a "Starring," the big action hero whose name was displayed first in the *Die Hard* and *Universal Soldier* VHS cassettes we rotated among ourselves. He was older than us by a year and had the most shit for us to do at his house. There was a paved yard with a rusty hoop at one end that was good for some close quarters two-on-two and stacks of Jean-Claude Van Damme videos to watch. Rinzlo lived three houses down from me with his mom, younger brothers, and his older cousin, who always had a revolving door of girlfriends for us to crush on. Dark- and light-skinned girls of all shapes and sizes with boobs, booty, blind loyalty, and trust galore. Rinzlo was the poorest of us, which meant he lied the most, inventing stories like a minstrel trying to earn an evening meal. Every Monday he'd come to school and tell us about the mad weekend he had. No one ever had the heart to point out there was no way he'd managed to kiss one of his cousin's girlfriends and also score mad hoops at a b-ball game in Eros because he'd spent the majority of the weekend bored with us. Rinzlo also had the fastest mouth, provoking fights like it was a CV-able skill. Lindo was the muscle. He was this agile, beefy black dude who would've had a promising career in South African rugby if he'd had the good fortune to be born across the border. He wasn't, though, so he had to settle for being our enforcer. Cicero was all heart, all loyalty, zero defense, and no attacking abilities—we always had to fight with our spirit power doubled and tripled to make up for his weakness. He was our medic because his mother was a nurse with a never-ending supply of bandages and Band-Aids she stole from the clinic where she worked.

Me? I was the Doer of Homework and the Decider of Disputes, second in line for the throne after Franco, the quiet foreign kid who could throw down when required. You can find one in every crew. They're always the ones called Pope or Priest or Monk. I avoided those lame nicknames by silently KO'ing dudes when shit popped off. They never saw or heard me coming. Everyone always gunned for Rinzlo first (because he'd started the shit), then Cicero (who was the smallest target), then Franco (eventually everyone comes for the king) or Lindo (because everyone thought they could be a giant-killer) after the first salvo of trash-talking concluded the rules of engagement—"Don't say it with your mouth, say it with your chest!"—in the melee I'd shoulder-tap a dude on the left and kidney-punch him on the right. I was the only one without an *o* in my name, so for branding purposes, and because of my overabundance of stealth, I was called Rambo.

At the height of our boredom, at the Catholic private school our parents hoped would provide the springboard into Windhoek's thin middle- and upper-middle-class crusts, Franco suggested we start a fight club. Word eventually leaked we were giving white kids black

eyes behind the boys' toilets. Our parents were hauled into a principal's meeting. Either we straightened out after five weeks of detention,
community service, and regular confession or we'd be kicked out. We
Our Fathered our way through our purgatorial sentence and went back
to beating German kids after they put that frustrating Beckenbauer
defense on us in soccer tournaments, or getting into scrapes after
basketball matches with public schools from the *kasi*.

We were a walking, rumbling, tumbling Punnett square of super
negro genes. We called ourselves The Five Negroes at first. After some
focus groups that involved ingesting copious amounts of Wu-Tang
Klan and too many B-grade westerns, we settled on the Five Os: Franco
Five-Fists, Rollin' Rinzlo, Lion Lindo, Doc Cicero, and Rambo the
Sage.

The Five Os fighting together forever.

We grew out of fighting. I was the first to put childish things away.

In the middle of our teens a rival crew called the Romans—there
were three kids in it called Roman, one Julius, a Titus, a Titus-Julius,
and a Maximus among others (I shit you not!)—gave us a gladiatorial
beatdown after a b-ball match that made me cross the Rubicon into
semimature young adulthood.

The Romans had tried to foul Franco, our best player, the entire
game and the referee penalized us with bullshit calls. Nonetheless,
Franco dodged elbows and uppercuts like Piccolo fielding too-slow
punches from a trainee Gohan. Whenever Franco fadeaway j'd a basket over a Roman, he'd yell "Render unto Caesar!" as the ball broke
through the net's chain.

Swoosh—chuuk! Swoosh—chuuk!

Franco singlehandedly Iversoned and watched over the demise

of their basketball empire. When the final whistle blew I knew the barbarians would be at the gate. The Romans found us waiting for Rinzlo's cousin to pick us up, sprinting toward us, thumbs-down, shouting, "*Ave*, ma'fuckers! *Ave!*"

From the first jab to the last suplex we were pounded like yam, beaten like thieves in a market in Nairobi. When Rinzlo's cousin finally showed up, we were too sore to even swear at him as he laughed at us. The rest of the ride home he told us to leave fighting behind and take up girls as a pastime instead. "What you gents need is pussy. You need to be fucked calm," he said. He'd arrived late to fetch us because he'd been busy finessing one of his girlfriends.

"*Yoh!* They fucked us up," Cicero whimpered as he climbed out of the car. "My mother's gonna have to take a look at me." He tenderly massaged his ribs.

"Yeah, but we're gonna get them back!" Franco, whose head had more knobs on it than a DUPLO block, was riding shotgun, beating his left fist into the palm of his right hand.

"No," I said. He turned in his seat. I looked at him with Michael Corleone coolness and said I was tired of fighting. If he was going to continue, he'd have to do it without me. He laughed and said I was too chickenshit to throw some hands. I told him I was no *moffie* but I was tired of Ryu-ing my life away in a never-ending game of *Street Fighter.* "Every week there's a set of bigger and badder guys inserting coins and pressing the player-two button, man." I chucked the deuces. I was getting out for real, for real.

I had other reasons for stopping the cockfighting though.

My mother had recently given me the Immigrant Speech, the one where the precariousness of "our position in this country" was laid out to me, the one where a black boy is given expectations and bonded to his responsibilities while being given the rundown on life. There was no land for me to inherit. We had money but it wasn't skip-a-generation kind of money. There was no going back to the village. The fear of regression was stamped into my soul.

"All you have," my mother said, "is that big brain of yours. If you lose that, we've lost it all."

That shit weighed heavily on me.

The pounding headache from the recent niggadämmerung from the Romans made my mother's words thump around my skull much harder. I told the other Os not to holler at me if shit went down. I was going to save my brain cells for chemistry and the soporific history classes that only became interesting during the First World War section when white people were killing each other. I said there was a massive literature project from our English teacher who was lost in bardolatry that we needed to do—correction, that *I* needed to do for all of us. ("What the fuck's bardolatry?" Rinzlo asked.) Since my mother had sat me down and learned me some immigrant truths I'd looked around this town filled with Tupac-drunk and Biggie-high dudes obsessed with choosing sides, who wanted nothing more than a fight story to talk about on a Monday morning at school, and decided I wanted out. I didn't want to graduate to impregnating girls and then carrying my own third-trimester beer belly.

"My guys," I said, "this can't be our life." The other Os looked at me in disbelief and joked among themselves that I was joking.

It took them being victims of more four-on-ten pavement poundings and twenty-three-hit unstoppable combos for them to realize I was serious about putting up my gloves.

One Sunday, after they got jumped, Franco called me at home and asked where the fuck I'd been the previous day.

"At the library," I said. "We have the literature project to work on."

"The Dolam Boys are pissing on the Five O reputation and you're at the library? Yo, Rambo—"

"That's not my name."

"Okay, I see you. Fuck you."

"Fuck you too, Franco. And don't copy my work anymore."

They didn't call me for fights anymore but occasionally I'd take pity on them and let them sneak peeks at my homework in the morning during register period.

▶||

The Windhoek Public Library: the homework haven for kids who didn't have Microsoft's interactive *Encarta* encyclopedia at home. It welcomed me with its generous street-postal-address-telephone-number-spell-your-surname-please-okay-just-write-it-for-me arms. My first library card astounded me with its easy access and acceptance. It was a citizenship which took in all colors, classes, and creeds. For the first time since my family had moved to this dry-ass country from the Small Country I felt like I'd found a place I could belong.

Okay, okay—I have to be honest: I was hanging out at the library because of a girl, but, hey, that was as good a reason as any other.

The Girl—let's just call her that for now so that happy homes in Avis aren't destroyed by women trying to rekindle unrequited teenage crushes—was wispy, with straight black tresses hanging down to the middle of her back, the kind of simple, low-wattage Michelle Branch prettiness guys from my part of town secretly aspired to date or marry so they could talk bad about the sisters. We were in the same class. She had these dimples you wanted to put your tongue in whenever she smiled. By leaning back in my chair further than a Terror Squad chorus, I overheard her telling one of her girlfriends she was doing research for the literature project at the library. Taking a hiatus from high jinks was enough for me to choose hoes over Os. Anyway, I knew in a couple of days Franco, Rinzlo, Lindo, Cicero, and I would be boys again. They'd need homework and we'd black boy–need each other to survive high school.

I'd see The Girl writing her notes in the bookish hush of the library and I'd try to figure out how the heck I'd approach her. That we'd been in the same class for two years never seemed to be a good enough opener. She wafted in and out of my library hours. I was always aware of where she was and where she wasn't the same way a Chinese kung fu master can sense attackers sneaking on the roof as he pours his tea, ready to throat-punch them into the end credits of their lives.

One day I decided I was going to say hello to her. She'd just turned into the ornithology aisle. I focused my center before turning right to follow her. I found her kissing some pasty boy with angry pimples on his face. His hands were fumbling beneath her tank top. They saw me and I pretended to look for a book to my immediate left and let out an Archimedean "Hah!" when I pulled *Bird Species of Southern Africa* off the shelf. I carefully pretended to consult it when I sat back down in my nook in case they were watching me. I learned about African hoopoes while hope headed south from the winter in my heart. Despite

The Girl moving on from the library later—maybe her parents finally inherited some white privilege and got her a computer—I kept coming to this hidden kingdom of books.

Even the building's entrance, recessed from the squalor of the street and shaded by tall trees, gave it the quality of being a well-kept secret. The subdued voices and rustling paper made it seem like all inside were hiding from an evil peril just waiting outside.

I loved it. The library was cheaper than the cinema and closer than the basketball courts, and bookish kids were also polite. Never starting nothing whenever I bumped into them in the aisles by accident (or on purpose), and they borrowed and returned shit on time—especially the *Asterix* and *Tintin* comics, hot property back then. In the poorly lit crannies I didn't have to put on the chafing armor I had to wear outside—the Watch Where I'm Walking, Chief!™ breastplate, and the Wat Kyk Jy?™ visor, and the You Stepped On My White All-Stars, Boss!™ shoes that Hermes-flapped you into a fight quicker than you could say sorry.

In the library, I found there were other ways of being. George, James, Charlie, and, Danny—I envied all the Dahl boys and their antics. Gerald Durrell's *My Family and Other Animals* transported me beyond the edge of my limited map. Jules Verne, H. G. Wells, Isaac Asimov, and Alexandre Dumas—I was in them like a high school teen pregnancy statistic. I dreamed about being a woodcutter's son with hidden royal lineage or being the underdog pilot of a starship cruiser. I raided the fantasy fiction shelves often and without mercy. My brain caught a fire, scorching through all the Dorling Kindersley reference books like a terrible spark in an Alexandrian library a long, long time ago. One day, I dreamed, I'd write poetry in the halls of the

Alhambra or read high literature on a cold English beach, with seagulls wheeling overhead.

A boy could dream.

The demure assistant librarian even started recommending and keeping books aside for me. Once, she asked me where I was from and when I told her she replied with a long "Aaaah."

"What?"

"Nothing," she said. I think what she wanted to say was: "Because guys like you don't read."

The assistant librarian is the reason I discovered Terry Pratchett. From him I developed the annoying habit of subtly offending people.

And from her I learned the layout of the labia.

The library was closing, a bell tinkled the minutes down. Thirty, fifteen, ten, and then five—I desperately tried to finish *The Hitchhiker's Guide to the Galaxy* so I could borrow something else. I didn't want to waste my library card on thirty pages. She came around to my cubicle and said it was time to go. I asked for more time. She smiled and said I could finish up while she did her rounds ensuring windows were closed. I found her sitting on one of the reading couches near the checkout counter. She asked to see which books I was taking out. She approved of Le Guin and Atwood. She scoffed at Hickman and Weiss.

"They're cool," I said. "Maybe a bit formulaic, but they write decent filler fantasy when you need a fix."

All she was said was "Hmm," with a strange smile on her face.

She told me to sit down on the floor in front of her. ("Err, okay.") She asked if I liked coming to the library and I said if it was open on a Sunday I'd skip church and come through. She asked about my school, about my family, and about girls. "What? No girl? A boy like you?"

I shrugged my shoulders. "Books are easier to read than girls."

The assistant librarian laughed, light, lilting, a sound that vanished into the stacked and vigilant shelves. Then she told me to sit still. "Stay absolutely still no matter what happens next."

"Sure."

She hiked up her skirt and slid off her gray cotton briefs. (Franco: "No way!"). I was startled. She told me to stay still. She spread her legs. (Rinzlo: "Get the fuck outta here!"). Then she pressed (Cicero: "Fam!"), pulled (Lindo: "FAAAAAAM!"), and prodded her way to pleasure. (Franco: "And you just sat there?") I just sat there, breathing hard, a little scared, but also amazed.

So that's what it looked like.

I'd seen *it* in magazines before. And I'd lied to the Os that I'd seen one in real life from some girl down my street. Now, up close, I was fascinated by the wrinkles, the variegated colors of skin, the wisps of hair, and the tendrils of moisture. It had a lot of personality.

I stared at the spot of recently sated curiosity while she toyed with herself a little and asked me what I thought. ("Interesting? That's all you could say?" Franco asked. "What the fuck's the point of being well-read if all you can say when cooch is in your face is *interesting*?") She asked for my hand and placed it in the moisture. It felt as though my body's power was diverted toward my fingertips. I recall it feeling a delicious kind of warm, the way a small puppy felt when you picked it up, warm and hungry to live. She rubbed my hand up and down a bit, gently, looking at me all the time. She took my hand and licked my fingers, one at a time. ("*Dude!*" Rinzlo nearly passed out.) Then she stood up, pulled up her underwear, and took my books to the counter, stamped them—("Just like that?" Lindo looked like he was

188

about to burst a vessel)—and let me out of the library so I could take a taxi home. Before she closed the door she said, "Thank you."

Too afraid to show my greed for another show, I avoided the library for three weeks. When I went back, she took my books, asked for the overdue fine, and went about her business like she and I hadn't made a pact stronger than the shit Enid Blyton wrote about. No pricks of blood to seal boyhood friendship, I had my fingers in the jelly-roll juice, which made us husband and wife forever. I loitered around at closing time again, pretending to read some Bradbury, but she came and told me it was time to go home. I lingered by the door, hoping for a recall. None came. Not in any day, week, or month of that year.

Why, you might wonder, wouldn't she do it again?

I mean, sexual assault at a young age is a common theme for creatives and I was being given some A-grade material for a memoir: "*. . . in the library with the demure assistant librarian I had come to trust because she seemed invested in my literary development . . .*"

A second incident would've cemented permanent tenure in Oprah's Book Club.

There was no follow-up peep show because for that to happen there'd have to have been a first, and there simply wasn't. There was no sexy alluring assistant librarian who left the Tolkien black guy in the library with a basic instinct for lust and literature. This was Windhoek for fuck's sake, not a tired interracial trope on Pornhub.

I needed a story to get back in with the Os and if there was one thing that could bring us together, I knew it was the joint pursuit of pussy. You should see guys when they smell blood in the water. They sign peace treaties and work on bilateral disarmament agreements. Even in *Braveheart* it wasn't Scottish freedom that really got Wallace and his clan ticked off. It was the English king declaring *prima nocta* and impounding every newly married fud. I swear the Cold War could've ended much sooner if American and Soviet women had the wherewithal to ration the *pizda*.

The day after I told the other Os about the librarian the library's membership swelled by four and the streets were shy a few soldiers.

The Five Os were reunited by the false lie there'd be opening of opuses and thumbing of tomes come closing time in the library. The assistant librarian quizzically looked at the Os enthusiastically borrowing *Watership Down* and Brian Jacques books over and over again. ("I thought the rabbits were suitable and subtle subtext," Rinzlo said when I asked him about it many years later. "Plus, that Martin of Redwall mouse dude was cold as fuck.")

Even after my deceit was discovered the other Os didn't cuss or cast me out. By then they were too invested in the *Wheel of Time* series. I wished they'd read something that wasn't "Book Two of the [insert dragon, elf, dwarf, sorcerer, sword name here] Cycle" so we could have something else to talk about besides dark lords and evil mages, but I was just happy we weren't out fighting anymore.

"That was some real sage shit," Franco said one day when we were at his place. "You straight finessed the streets out of us."

THE RELUCTANT TEACHER AND THE PATH OF WRATH

If I'd been one of the High Elves of Middle-Earth my temper could've smithed a sword capable of Swiss-cheesing Balrogs without ever blunting.

Wrath—and its ensuing folly—is the second path.

The year I spent without work after screaming at my boss doused my furious spark real good. I was doing my first tour in advertising, having washed up back home after four carefree years pursuing literature in Cape Town. I wound up writing copy at a startup advertising agency, pretending I was at the cutting edge of creativity. I lied to myself that being home would allow me to be closer to my family and friends. Sadly, when I moved back it was the same one-horse town with the same old town road. All it had was more money and that's the most cliché thing to have anywhere.

I kept telling myself that sooner or later I'd be able to find purpose in selling loans and credit cards. My boss, though, said my copywriting was average. It was. I said the clients were subpar. They were. I was told to deliver simple concepts that satisfied the briefs—highbrow humor, my boss said, was my hamartia. I tried to follow his instructions for a while, but I got bored once I figured out even being good enough in the industry was exceeding expectations. People just wanted "win-a-*bakkie* competitions and lucky fucking draws." The boss said if I wasn't happy at the agency the door was open. My temper flared like a furnace. I threw my advertising career out the window.

I was staying with my parents then, I had to because there was no money coming in. I woke up late, binge-watched Tarantino, reread the *Discworld* series, played video games, and helped my mother with her gardening. I avoided the Os as much as possible, not eating out, not clubbing, trying to avoid anything which needed money. Cicero got married. Lindo got a promotion at his IT company and cruised the Mediterranean. Rinzlo crunched numbers as an auditor somewhere in the corporate world. Franco fell into some of the shady tenderpreneur money floating around Windhoek. I watched BBC Earth and

Ken Burns documentaries by the Blu-Ray disc–load. My parents kept nagging me for a game plan.

The advertising agency called and said they'd take me back but I knew I couldn't return to that life. Also, cocaine was becoming a thing among the art directors and copywriters and I needed my nose to keep me out of trouble, not get me into it. So I joined the segment of society who said they were between gigs, always bubbling with false enthusiasm about finding something soon.

It was like I'd forgotten I lived in a desert: drought is the default, rain is the luxury. It's not like people were stuck in their jobs for shits and giggles. There was nowhere else for them to go. Up was blocked by the struggle veterans, Squealers and Napoleons who weren't struggling anymore. Down was clogged with the poor. Everyone in the middle was digging employment trenches and preparing to wait out the job satisfaction, pay raises, and promises made to them by boomer babies, capitalism, university, and national independence. Everyone had a *vat-en-sit* mentality.

My mother said something would come along. She said God had a plan and I said God's plan sucked. She sighed and shook her head.

Lindo's the one who got me into teaching. His sister had just left her position at the School for Rich Kids Who Didn't Get into the School for Really Smart Children. They needed someone to English-sit the ninth graders for a term. "It'll be easy," he said. "What teenager wouldn't like your cynical outlook on life? Just swear every once in a while, and they'll think you're cool."

I walked into class on my first day, jittery as shit, shaking from the PTSD of unemployment. I remember the line which let the class know we could get along: "Negroes and negrettes, please, please, please don't be yourselves."

It took time for me to relax, to trust the faith my colleagues and parents put in me, to believe in the laughter my students gave my humor, and to not doubt I was doing a good job.

After the first month I'd learned to turn my failures into lesson plans and comically dark, motivating speeches. My wrath had been knocked out of me, and seeing the eager faces around my classroom looking to me to guide them through a poorly chosen and canonical English syllabus, I decided to shelve my folly.

LUST, THE THIRD PATH

For my lust credits I took the fuck-boy elective. It was not a necessary course, but because I was trying to make it onto the dean's list I did all the prescribed fucking and unprescribed fucking around.

What's there to be said about lust that hasn't been testified to by single-parent households with a son destined to be the first-round draft pick in the NBA or NFL? It's well-known that single moms make future hall-of-famers and daddy issues are the foundations of a five-film superhero franchise. Come on, even *Star Wars* is about one family with an absent father fucking up a whole galaxy—far, far away, yes, but also close to home.

In the mixtape that's a black man's life before he becomes a fully-fledged album, lust is the interlude and hook for creeps that's put on three-peat.

All I can say without shame is that I lost myself in women the way Alice got lost in Wonderland. I had entire Google Calendar notifications telling me whom I was supposed to be meeting up with, where, when, and noting relevant details about them so I wouldn't fumble foreplay. If only I'd diverted all my scheming, lying, and impeccable time management productively, I could've been a Fortune 500 CEO. At the very least I would've been a millionaire motivational speaker or an American preacher with a megachurch.

One time, while I was stroking away at this girl like a Cambridge oarsman with Oxford half a length in front, my cox veered a little to the left and we made eye contact midorgasm. My chest tightened. I looked at her eyes and thought about how lovely they were, about how I wanted to make them light up over and over again. She was moderately funny and managed to not ask annoying questions when we watched *Akira* and *Princess Mononoke* on my laptop. As I looked at her then, something inside me shifted ever so slightly. Whatever it was, it made me cry. (Franco: "Bro, you did what?") While we were lying in her bed I told her I liked her. (Rinzlo: "Guy, what the actual fuck is wrong with you? You never tell a girl you like her after coitus. Yes—I just said coitus!") The Os would've stabbed me if I'd told them I'd actually told her I loved her. She looked sideways at me and went to the bathroom. I could hear her tinkle into the pot. She came out and asked if I wanted something to drink. I said tea. When she let me out of her apartment, I said I'd give her a call. She said "Sure" but she didn't answer when I did.

Eventually, and inevitably, if a homie can't eenie-meenie-miney-mo-catch-a-bad-bitch-by-his-strokes he's going to wind up lonely. In the great game of love, lust is last place, and the consolation prize for participation is loneliness. There's only so much disconnected sleeping around one can do before catching an umbilical or the worst of STDs: feelings.

"Love," Cicero said on his wedding day, as I adjusted his bow tie, "is the worst thing that could happen to a man's sex life." He tried to sound like he didn't want to get married, but his machismo was always weak. I'd never seen him happier than when he put his wife above the Os, a new hierarchy which took some getting used to.

What Cicero had I wanted for myself. I grew tired of scanning restaurants and clubs to see if there was any drama waiting for me. I became fatigued by having my name dragged through the streets and being shunned from the sheets. I remember telling Lindo I was tired of the lying, the acting, laying siege to women's emotions for days, and leaving Trojan horses filled with empty promises and endearing insecurities to coax them from behind their walls.

"Why, Lindo," I asked him, "why can't I just have a Vanessa Carlton kinda girl?"

"Vanessa Carlton, dude?"

"Don't even play. VC is mad pretty—the original ride-or-die-walk-a-thousand-miles bad bitch."

"Okay, bro." We were quiet for a bit and then he asked me why I just couldn't stop with the girls.

I sighed. "Because then I would have to start on myself and that is more work than I am willing to do right now," I said. I picked up my keys so I could head home to my apartment, eager to fill it with fleeting company.

GRIEF, THE FOURTH PATH

When my mother passed I gave up church but not church girls. Not that I'd been going to church anyway, but I decided pretending to be a believer was too much effort in the face of such deific duplicity. God had given Noah the peace sign and promised there'd never be another flood; instead he sent the fire to fetch my mother.

After my mother died, I wondered if I was still *her* son without her around to claim me as her own. With the cord that connected me to the mothership severed I tumbled over myself into the darkness beyond gravity's pull. Somehow my father, my brother, and I were supposed to make it through the hundred fears of solitude with just the three of us for family. When my mother was alive we talked to each other through her. She mediated peace talks. Home, to me, was wherever she was. But when she went to a place none of us could follow, we became undone like a Jenga tower with an unlucky block being pulled out.

The early days were easier, the grief glued us together. Then the grief passed but the loss remained, humming at barely audible levels. Those months were the worst, when the calendar became a *Minesweeper* game, with any day or date hiding a detonator which could be triggered by the smallest thing, even the weight of a memory, and blow up the whole week, month, or year to noxious and depressing smithereens.

Our new reality was confronted somehow, with each of us dealing with our separate loneliness in some way: my father went back to work, my brother moved back home to keep my father company, and I tried to bury it inches deep in the Third Path.

Once in the pitch black of night my brother phoned me and I sat the fuck up straight in bed (*Not this again!*), preparing for more bad news. "Which hospital?" I shouted as soon as I accepted his call. Not my father too, I thought.

"I just wanted to talk," he said.

"It's three in the morning," I said. My heart was still beating like a village war drum.

He said he knew. But it was about Mamma and he just, you know, wanted to talk for a bit. I didn't want to talk about her, about her to him, about her to him there and then. But I was learning the ways of kindness so I said yeah, we could talk.

He asked if I ever thought about her. He asked if there were times I felt like somehow I'd done something which had invited calamity upon her. He said maybe he'd aged her too much when he was younger. He could've had her summoned to school less, maybe reduced the number of detentions. Maybe that would've kept her alive longer.

"Nah, dude," I said gently, "that's not how it works."

I listened patiently as he talked about her, about her last days when she was up and about, as alive as a living person could be. She had plans for her garden, was plotting to finally finish her knitting challenges, and she would reread her favorite books. I remembered the way she vibrated when she spoke about the next day, how she angled toward it regardless of whether it was sunny or heralded a storm.

"You know you're like her," my brother said. "Both of you were always too much for this place. Maybe that's why she left." A strangled sound escaped my throat. "But Dad and I are happy we still have you."

I was glad he couldn't see me and my wet eyes. He said he needed to get to bed. I nodded because I didn't trust my voice. "Stay strong, dude," he said. "We're all waiting to read about your life and times."

I hung up, lay in bed, and cried.

They say out in space no one can hear you scream but that's not true. Space listens. It doesn't talk back, but it hears you with its multitude of silences. Somewhere in that great darkness punctuated by pinpricks of light, something must have heard me as I careened through the inky oblivion of mother's death. I recall a gradual slowing down, an end to my feet spinning over my head, and up and down becoming relative points of navigation again.

My mother's voice popped into my head: *You are not the first.*

Isn't that some shit? To remember, in the grief of your mother's passing, that you were her second but firstborn child. She only said it that one time in the kitchen when I was much younger before hastily walking out holding her stomach, but the mysterious moment imprinted itself on me for some reason.

You are not the first to carry grief with you.

I looked around for the source of the utterance but could not discern its origin. Who dared to tamper with my mother's words and with my memory?

There are others.

I stilled myself.

I wasn't the only one who had lost, the one person who was losing, or the singular soul that would lose—my fate was shared by many others, all of us connected by fine lines of suffering.

But help is always on the way.

I fell asleep afterward, dreaming of distant stars and the black spaces between them.

THE EXQUISITE AND SOLO PATH OF LONELINESS

By the time I met my girlfriend, I'd spent a while wearing so-called equanimity for cologne. I was the Black Buddha who'd successfully survived my youth, quelled my wrath, and singlehandedly—I lie, there were many, many hands involved—fucked my way through lust and almost love. I had reduced my grief to an occasional conversation seasoner, using it to deep-spice my shallow self into something tastier.

Reincarnation was calling.

The sugar weakness had been booted. I hadn't eaten fast food in two years and a bit. One time, at my place I made a butternut smoothie which nearly made the Os repent their sinful, carb-consuming ways. Ultimately nobody made the leap of faith to lower cholesterol levels and attain single-digit body fat percentages. My early-morning walks were another kind of meditation and when I told the Os they crinkled their noses. If anything, it seemed to me as though sanity was the only true possession a black person could own and even it was under attack every day from whitewashed glossy magazine covers, Denzel winning the Oscar for playing a crooked cop, and war documentaries which didn't bother to blur out the burnt black bodies.

"Trust me," I said, "black men are a dying and precious breed. I'm just trying to be on the endangered species list past the age of forty-five."

They all laughed.

But some of the laughter was brittle.

Lindo and Cicero seemed as though they wanted to know more. Lord knows the Os desperately needed to hear the message. But they were too scared to take those first tentative steps out of their shells. Masculinity is like a violent street gang—"You have to kill someone's to get in and you have to kill yours to get out," I said at a *braai* once. "The exit price is too steep for some to pay." There was a smattering of agreement.

She was at the *braai*—my future girlfriend.

By then I was one of those guys who knew how to say all the right things in the right company. I'd spent the greater part of my evening talking about "The Seven Habits of Highly Defective Niggas"—what I hoped to be part one of some extensive thesis. I regurgitated by-the-way knowledge and then segued into gender equality to distract my audience from my part in past shenanigans. I said it was time equality trickled down to women.

She asked why it had to trickle. "Why couldn't it be shared equally?"

I said, "Exactly."

Some dude said that as a father he wouldn't want his daughter to be harassed in the streets and I agreed. She asked why he had to be a father before he could be a decent human being.

Someone started a side discussion about the way the races treated each other. I said white men were the worst thing that ever happened to black people. She said I was wrong: "White men are the worst thing that can happen to black men. *Men* are the worst thing that can happen to black women. But at least with the white man you expect it—history remembers—but black men, your own people, are the worst."

She looked at me. Daring me to challenge her. I kept quiet.

When it was time to eat, everyone waited to see where she'd sit so they could choose seats as far from her as possible. I was in the bathroom at the time and when I came out, the only seat left was next to her.

I smiled as I sat down and tried to engage her in conversation. I wanted things kept in my topics of interest and consciousness, where I was comfortable and infinitely quotable. I put on my best peacock feathers, wowing, hoping to flatter, to appease. But there's this saying people from the Small Country have: *the chameleon fools everyone but the branch*.

And she snapped it underneath me.

"That's the problem with feminism, isn't it?" she said at some point. "It demands more than just treating your mother or sister or daughter with common decency."

I blew on that retreat horn hard.

She is, to date, the only woman I never tried to run my game on. She told me, simply, I had nothing to offer her. She had nothing I couldn't have anywhere else if I felt like it. She said she wouldn't be my rebirth, one of those I-once-knew-a-woman crucibles where I'd reforge myself, alloying myself with the best parts of her, leaving the residue of her sanity and soul behind, charred and useless.

That we wound up dating is one of the universe's unexplained mysteries.

Around her I didn't have to put on the mask of masculinity that gave me my superpowers. She saw me and I was seen. And because I was seen I could look at my reflection in her words, her counsel, and her disappointment. Sometimes I wonder whether I was a project, something for her rehabilitation résumé, just another horse to bring to the water. But then I remember how thirsty I was from running the macho marathon, how she and I didn't have to bruise each other's egos or psyches for chuckles. Our talk was full of vulnerabilities and wading through real shit, and somehow coming out on the other side calmer and happier. At least it was until I realized men are forever icebergs into which women are doomed to crash time and time again.

I sat with Cicero, the only one of the Os who'd had any stable relationship of any kind, who seemed happy and content in his marriage, and asked him how he knew he was ready for marriage.

"You decide," he said simply.

"Yes, but how?"

"You just do."

I changed my angle of approach. "What if it doesn't work out?"

"You decide that too, my guy."

I decided she and I were forever.

That's how I became lonely.

I remember the day I cried in my apartment when I picked up my phone. My fingers stumbled across the message thread from my mother, the one that chilled at the bottom of the screen, never deleted. I hesitated for a moment before I clicked on it and read the words she wrote to me in the week before she passed. We were talking about teaching, about how I was going to start a radical after-school writing and drama club where we read pirated manga and acted out Windhoek-adapted scenes from *Romeo and Juliet* ("*Boss, do you bite your thumb at us?*"—"*I don't bite my thumb at you, Chief, but I bite my thumb!*"). She said she was proud of me. She even managed to drop all the relevant emojis after sending all the wrong ones.

My last reply: *Wow! Mamma, you're so lame.*

I cried.

I knew then I wasn't fine. I hadn't been fine in a long time. I'd dealt with my mother's passing by doing surface shit. Sitting in silence for a few hours a day, eating all the recommended minerals and vitamins, drinking that white woman's gallon of water a day. But my mother's death was a tectonic event. The cracks went all the way to my core, turning it into a void, imperceptible to the naked eye, only glimpsed sideways through silent lulls in conversations, or painful and distancing absences in my affections and friendships.

I was alone.

When my girlfriend finally peeled back the layers, she had the grim look field medics have when they turn over a wounded soldier and look at the auxiliary ventilation holes blown clean through them. I think that day when she came home and found me sitting on the couch in the dark, eyes gummed by teary sleep, she knew I was beyond her care. Only when we talked about my mother's passing later—with my crying, swearing, and screaming at every atom in creation—did she know I was a terminal case.

But she was dating me *voetstoets*—you take a man as you find him—so she helped me fill up my crowdfund for courage to see someone about the shit. She was the only one I talked to about it. The Os could understand many things, but there are worlds so far out of our intellectual solar systems they might as well not even exist. We were iron men with iron hearts and steel sharpens steel. I told her I'd go to therapy for her. I even tried to use it as a means to score bonus points, like I was being a superspecial boyfriend. Like the time I went to yoga with her.

My girlfriend was too slick. "No. You have to do it for yourself."

BLACK BUDDHA AND THE SIXTH PATH TO REDEMPTION

When I finally walked into the therapist's office I doubted the sessions would help. Therapy was for white people. Black people know progress is the best way to get over shit. Get a promotion, make more money, buy something, take a holiday somewhere—that's how it's done. This whole therapy thing, I thought, was a scam with a good hourly rate.

I quit after a week.

My girlfriend cooed me back to the couch.

It took me a couple of sessions to open up, to talk about everything, but the breakthrough came.

I finally said it:

"My mother died on my birthday. Every single year I feel shit about getting older while she gets colder. I'm afraid my existence is the one that took her life even though I know it wasn't. Every three hundred and sixty-five days feels like a lap in the Blame Olympics."

The therapist remained quiet. She didn't write any notes.

I continued:

"More than once I've blown out the candles, with my brother and my father crying and croaking out the birthday tune she used to sing so well, and wished for the finish line once and for all, for all of it to end. But, but—"

"But what?" the therapist asked.

"But I can't just quit. I can't take a day off from being me."

"Why?"

"My family needs me."

"They can make a plan if they have to."

"My friends—"

"The Os, yeah? Sounds like they'll be just fine too. So why can't you slow down?"

"Because."

"Because what?"

"Because I'm the Sage of the Six Paths!"

"The what?"

So I explained to her about never climbing high enough for the water to stop lapping my feet; about having to be three times as good as the locals who were twice as good as the average white just to get less than half as far at the best of times; about the six paths and how they all crisscrossed; how some ended only to reappear years later but in different guises; about how some never came to an end; and how I was The One who had to make sense of it all for every black in the whole wide world even though it didn't make sense to me half the time.

"Interesting," the therapist said. "And what path do you think you're on now?"

"I don't fucking know. And it's so scary."

I thought I'd cried before, but my God.

"Okay," she said. "Let's take it one step at a time."

"Okay."

I let out that cathartic cinematic sniffle which lets the audience know every little thing's gonna be all right.

"Let's start with forgiveness."

Ah, the hard part then.

—*Forgive yourself.*

—*Forgive her.*

—*She did not leave you.*

At the therapist's urging I got my pens and notebooks out. I learned when to argue with my old man and when to let him be, which was all the time. I learned when to be kind to my brother, which was always.

I didn't see much of the Os during that time. I spent more time with my girlfriend. We had our best days together then, when I was discovering new parts of myself, adding more and more puzzle pieces to the picture that was our love.

Then, for some reason, I figured, hey, I'd gone and come far enough. Surely the rest of it was just more of the same shit, right? Cry a little, write a little, and then everything would become better after a while.

Then my foolish male logic took over.

I forgot that footsteps make the path.

I slid back into the darkness.

It was eerily comfortable, how easy it all came back, how the compass needle found Lethe without even trying, how quickly that dreaded cup filled itself.

Back in the therapist chair I asked her when the hell everything made sense, when everything was just better. She asked me if I knew how to cook a guinea fowl. She told me how. I laughed a little.

The only good thing I learned from that Second Darkness was that I had to cut my girlfriend loose to stop both of us going down with my ship—whatever lay at the bottom of the whirlpool I would have to face myself. There are caves even Yoda cannot lead you through, you just have to hope your oneness with the Force will shield you from your past. I wished there was some other way for it all to end. I hoped that we'd find each other after many years and we'd reprise the romance.

But that was foolishness.

In the real world you make choices based on available information and when faced with disappointment there're only two ways to deal: deceit or honesty. I made a break for the latter. I sat my girlfriend down and told her our love had become a neglected thing. I told her the end of the road had passed us by. I said some shit about the hero's journey and having to learn how to be alone before I could be with someone else.

She Scotty-beamed out of my life.

Man, I'd hoped we were forever as I watched her go.

But a sage negro knows forever is never as long as one thinks it is.

He also knows that a path has to lead somewhere. In my case I wanted to abandon the cyclical nature of the six paths, to drop the veneers of venerability and arrest my orbit around oblivion. I could lose anything but not myself. If my mother was right, if we lost that then we'd lost everything.

But we hadn't. We'd only lost her. And through no fault of our own.

The sixth path is this: walking out and walking away. There is courage in holding on, but there is wisdom in learning to let go. Redemption, in my case, meant realizing that people are the worst things that can happen to each other. The charging lion cannot change its teeth nor can the poisonous snake cure its bite, each is living out its nature. I wanted to happen less to people, and to stop cooking guinea fowls.

▶ǁ

A couple of nights ago, I was driving Franco home from the police station after having bailed him out for drunken driving. If I hadn't been up reading, he would've slept in jail until Monday morning.

The warrant officer was determined to keep him in lockup. "He was endangering lives," he said. "This man deserves to face justice." After I slipped him a couple of hundreds, he said a man deserves to sleep in his bed on a Friday night and called out for another officer to fetch Franco.

Franco turned to me in the passenger seat, eyes still saturated with drink, and asked why we kept doing dumb shit.

"Like driving drunk?" I asked.

"Exactly," Franco said, "like driving drunk." His blinks were so slow I wondered why he just didn't close his eyes. "Or you leaving your girlfriend."

I inhaled sharply. "What the fuck, Franco?"

"Out of all of us, I would've expected you to know a good thing when it came around but—" He yawned and kept quiet.

I cut through a red light. I needed to get him home and get to bed. We fell quiet for a while as we drove.

"When do we outgrow this shit?" Franco turned to me. He seemed alert, like the need for a sincere answer had sobered him.

"Do you know how you cook a guinea fowl?"

"What?"

"You take the guinea fowl," I said, angling the car toward his house, "and soak it in a pot of water for three days with spices and herbs— parsley, sage, rosemary, and thyme—whatever you have available, to add some depth and flavor. Then you toss in a rock and bring the pot to the boil." I parked the car outside his gate. "When the rock is soft, the guinea fowl is ready."

B-Side

Granddaughter of the Octopus

y grandmother always reminded me of Ursula, from the Disney version of *The Little Mermaid.* My sons are watching the VHS cassette—the sea witch's rumbling buttocks, purple turkey-neck arms, and enveloping bosom dance around the screen as she schemes to steal Ariel's voice. The sorceress stirs fond memories of the woman who snatched speech and ignorance from men's throats. She too wore black, sported a slash of venomous red lipstick, and kept her hair short. Her imperious size, her bloody lips, and her somber clothing intimidated people. But so long as you weren't one of the poor unfortunate souls she considered to be foolish, frivolous, or "unfuckable," she was quite lovely.

As Ariel surrenders her voice I watch Ursula cackle with victory. The sight scares my sons. I smile, looking at this illustrated woman who so reminds me of my grandmother, the woman who had eight sons from eight different men.

▶ ‖

Foolish.

Frivolous.

Unfuckable.

These are the characteristics she used to dismiss people, especially men, from her presence.

—*Look at this foolish man.*

—*A frivolous fellow—quite useless.*

—*That one is truly unfuckable—if I was her I would leave him.*

My grandmother was unashamedly indelicate. She'd long lived by herself; her personality and manners were unkempt by the propriety and modesty which defined women in the valley. She had a reputation for being a difficult woman. Years later, when I described her to my eldest son, trying to convey her character to him, he said, "Mom, she was a harridan."

I looked up the word: *a strict or belligerent old woman.*

It wasn't her. Even though we lived on a farm with an unending list of chores and duties, she was lenient when the sun was murderous and patient when the rain washed away our best-laid plans.

She had one law: *my children, my family, my house, my farm, my land, my body, my mind, my spirit, my rules.* Her fierce possession of these things, and her unyielding defense of them, was what made her seem overbearing. She'd never go out of her way to make anyone do anything so long as they didn't interfere with what was hers. Her ire only came out when she felt attacked. Her cheeks sucked in air, pumping the kind of bust an opera singer would envy, and hurled the blackest curses at any threat—man, woman, child, neighborhood dog, unscrupulous merchant, or thieving farm worker. Once she doused you with her malison you were marked with Cain-like shame. Only she had the magic words to return you to the world of the living; she was always eager to do so, bearing down on you, squeezing you into a hug, nearly suffocating you in the barely dammed contours of her breasts.

My grandmother couldn't be commanded. If you wanted to be labeled as foolish, you begged favors from her or threatened her beyond the point that she respected you.

This is what happened to the mayor of the town where I grew up.

He was a foolish man.

Three times he'd tried to get her to sell her land, an amalgamation of fields which spread across the valley, to a mining corporation. The first time he came around he'd been turned away at the gate. The second time he'd made it as far as her kitchen door before she shooed him away politely—this meant he was sworn at only once.

For his last pitch my grandmother summoned the whole clan together. All my uncles took leave from their jobs in the city to make the long drive home. Even my father, whom I hadn't seen in years, made the familial hajj. My uncles' wives were there, as were my cousins, who, like me, were all victims of varying degrees of absent husbands or fathers. I always considered this a curious fact: my grandmother knew exactly where her sons were even if their wives didn't.

That meeting commanded an attendance register even weddings and funerals couldn't. A message had gone out: *Something might be done with the land.* Everyone's inheritance was affected, everyone answered the summons.

We were in the open square in front of my grandmother's house. It had a giant tree growing in the middle of it; the gnarled trunk leaned drunkenly to one side, its boughs spread widely enough to provide a circle of dappled shade. My grandmother, my uncles, and their wives sat on wooden stools brought from the house. Everyone else sat on circular log cuttings rolled into place to create an amphitheater around the mayor, a squat man, who'd come prepared with maps of her territory. He considered the meeting portentous: the whole family must've been gathered to announce alienation of the precious land. Emboldened, he showed us the parcels ripe for prospecting and exploitation. The maps, reduced in scale, couldn't explain the size of my grandmother's farm. Even if she only sold a handful of hectares, the mining company's offer would make the youngest inheritor quite rich. My cousins gasped. The mayor smiled, glad they were impressed. When he finished his presentation, they applauded. My uncles and their wives remained silent.

We turned to my grandmother. She'd sat like a supreme and divine judge of appeal, ears turned toward the mayor, listening to his arguments and propositions, and not saying a word. Only her word mattered. She held the land in her own name and took counsel about what to do with it from no one.

—No.

My cousins were shocked.

—No?

The mayor wiped his brow. He looked at some of my uncles.

—No.

—*But they made a good offer.*

—*It is not enough.*

—*How much would be enough?*

212

—Their acknowledgment that nothing they offer would be enough.

The mayor was angry.

—The fields are not being used to capacity. Your family does not live in the valley anymore. Your sons do not even farm. Do they even know the difference between a rainy and dry season? Selling the land would bring business to the valley.

—We have business enough already: the making of our lives.

The mayor's shoulders slumped. My grandmother carried on:

—In any case, these lands are not mine to give away. They were given to me by my father, and him by his. I hold on to them for my children and their children. What would my parents think of me if I showed up in the afterlife and said I had sold their lives' works and burial grounds for money? They are in this land, which makes us a part of it too. To sell it would be to sell ourselves. And what will we have then to provide for ourselves?

A cousin, Holy Spirit–heavy and tithe-deep in evangelism, spoke up:

—Trust in the Lord, Grandmother.

She turned to him:

—Your grandfather endured worse than your Jesus for this land. When you go back to the city, please take your prayers with you.

A couple of us laughed. My grandmother's tongue-lashings were legendary.

She turned back to the mayor:

—My answer was no. My answer is no. And tomorrow my answer will still be no. I would also ask you not to speak to my sons as an attempt to get to me again. I saw you looking at them. There is no history of partitioning and there shall be none as long as I am alive. I am finished expressing myself on this matter.

Some of my uncles bowed their heads. My grandmother looked into the distance. The mayor's audience was over.

She was not a tribal queen. She was not even rural nobility. My grandmother was just a woman with eight sons from eight men who owned lands coveted by a mining corporation. But when she delivered her judgment, an edict had been handed down from the heavens. We all felt it: some power which coursed through her—from the first settlers of the valley, the tribal wars fought to protect it, and the marriages that had expanded its fertile borders—giving her the power to bind us with her declaration.

—*What do your sons say?*

An insult. My grandmother billowed into full fury.

—*What man here has a mouth that I did not give to him? If he has one let him speak!*

No one did. She turned her attention back to the mayor.

—*Foolish man. My children, my family, my house, my farm, my land, my body, my mind, my spirit, my rules!*

She got up, walked to her house, scattering the meeting in her wake.

It'd be one of the last times our whole family would be together, to hear her declare that our home would never be sold. This was before her sons' foolishness took over, when we'd lose the land from squabbles and greed, when our ancestors' power over us weakened as we strayed further from home.

▶ ‖

Frivolous.

This is how my grandmother described some of my uncles: they were frivolous when they were young and frivolous when they grew older; they were frivolous in their choice of wives and in their sowing of seeds.

"Your father," my grandmother said of her second son, "was frivolous." He'd gotten my mother pregnant while they were young, robbing her of her college education and her local honor. He'd fled the scene of their romance and the crime of my existence soon after. A young woman with child but no husband was an acute embarrassment: her own family shunned her. My grandmother took her in. She understood what it was like to carry a child no man wanted. My father had been born in a similar fashion. I always wished he'd been different somehow, that he'd been the one snake who didn't bite his own tail.

When I was born I made my father's mother a grandmother. Later, she'd joke that I'd fulfilled an old saying which followed her around the valley when she was still husbandless and carrying her third child: *she'd become a young grandmother or an old whore.*

—I was not insulted. I told everyone I would not mind being both.

Despite my status-changing birth, she accorded me a beautiful name: *she who bestows new titles and favors.*

If my mother doted on me, then her love was marginally eclipsed by my grandmother's. When my father married, bringing my half sisters and half brothers to her for naming, it was clear I was favored. They were named after clouds, the river, the soil, or the small happenings of our times. But I was she who brought new gifts; I bestowed crowns to lost kingdoms. She was a mother until I turned her into a matriarch.

Our family tree thinned down through the generations to a single point: my grandmother. She sat there like the pinch in an hourglass or the cinch in her dresses when she was younger. From beneath her skirts, and with the passage of time, our family erupted and spread out from her.

▶ ‖

Unfuckable.

This is what my grandmother thought of my first boyfriend.

—*He is short. And unfuckable.*

—*What does that have to do with anything?*

—*Short men give you short-man problems. Your grandfather was a tall man with all the gifts of such men.*

—*But he ran off.*

—*A credit to his long shinbones, which you now possess. Look at you, beautiful and tall. Do you want a man you cannot kiss on tiptoes?*

Conversations like these were common. She had a wonderful repertoire of insults she'd hurl at anything that displeased her.

—*You are as useless as a discarded foreskin.*

—*He is as short as a romp.*

—*You are slower than a man who has promised you a second round.*

If these words caused some childhood trauma, this was somewhat undone by my grandmother being the kindest and funniest woman I knew. She opened her door to any of my uncle's impregnated mistresses regardless of the truth of their paternity suits, something she disclosed to me toward the end of her life. She allowed satellite families who'd farmed the land in service to our clan to stay rent-free, even permitting them to sell a fair portion of the harvests for their own subsistence. She paid for doctors, attended weddings, and wept sincerely at funerals. Many girls in the valley bore her first name as their spiritual second.

When my mother wanted to study further my grandmother banished her from the valley until her studies were completed—she took on the duty of raising me.

Between beating dust out of bedding; cleaning floors, windows, and cupboards; fetching water; lighting fires; cooking with instinct and available necessity; and living according to the rhythm of the rains, I was without want. It was on my grandmother's farm that I learned about my family's history of fuckable and unfuckable men.

The first man: a musician, a drunken charmer. "Wayward. Handsome. Very fuckable. I never told him about being pregnant. The man could not choose between his guitars, how was he going to provide for us? No, he loved his music too much. He was not suited for the kind of life being a father entailed. But I knew I could be a mother. I wanted to be one. I let him pluck every string in my body in exchange for letting me take the parts of him I needed—a fair trade. I did not want anything else from him. My father had died and left me with this land. I had the farm to run. The musician could never fit into the life I wanted. Let me say this: you should never be secondary to a man's art. That is one way of asking to be ignored."

The second man, my grandfather: "Built like a statue, and just as cold. But a man who knew what he was mostly about. I admired that. He knew his limitations and was generous within them, beyond that he was cruel. What? I don't know where he went—I never looked for him. Yes, he knew I was pregnant. But I was not going to be treated badly. By then I was as you were, in form at least, with a woman's physique. That is not praise—any girl can have a woman's body. By your age I had a woman's mind. Do not get angry. Your breasts are persuasion. Your waist is a promise. Your buttocks are power. But the mind matters most: it controls all the others. You must know which parts of you a man likes, then you will know what he will use to replace you. If you have good breasts he will look for someone younger when they start to sag. Your grandfather liked all of my parts except my mind. It frightened him. It is why I did not chase after him. You do not want to get into the habit of chasing after men—only mindless women do that. If you quietly go about your business a man will find you soon enough, either to distract you from your labors or to help you with them. Only time will tell, and only a mind will listen. Your grandfather, for all his qualities, was a distraction. We had our time together. And that was that."

The third man: a farmer's son. "Not so tall, but tall enough to warrant interest. These were tough times to be a woman with two children and no husband. I liked handsome men but I admit I liked him because he was kind to me. It is rare to see that: kindness in a man, especially for a woman with children that are not his. Kindness— only single mothers know the meaning of that word. Him? He died. Sickness. We were supposed to marry. I could see a decent life with him. That is another thing: to see clouds in the sky is not the same as seeing crops growing from the rain. Losing that man drove me to sadness and neglect. I wanted to live long enough to give birth to your uncle and waste away so I could join his father in the afterlife. But I was not ready to meet my ancestors. I did not want to be insignificant in this world and inconsequential in the next. I was going to raise my children and make something of myself. If I died, I was going to command power in the spirit world. So, your uncle was born and I carried on living."

The fourth man: a shopkeeper. "You must know I was still grieving.

This one eyed my fields, counted my workers, and asked how much we made at market. He proposed marriage immediately. I was so desperate to be someone's wife I nearly accepted his proposal—I was already carrying his child. But I said no. He was angry and hit me. Let me tell you: any man that lets you feel the back of his hand should describe the taste of hot palm oil when you hit him with the pan. We fought. People came running up to the house fearing we were being torn apart by wild dogs. They had to pull me off him. Ha! He was too ashamed to stick around. He closed his shop and left. I will tell you another thing: people will treat you like a hero until you cost them something. Everyone would have been happy with a regular supply of soap in exchange for me being hit every night by that man. I had many enemies when the shopkeeper left. The priest said I had done the right thing. Then he sighed and said he had not had his favorite brand of tea in weeks. What nonsense is that? Foolish man. Him and his religion can go the way of all frivolous men: to Hell."

The fifth man: a teacher. "Smart, funny, highly fuckable. He taught in the village school and could charm milk from a cow. I thought I was immune to men by then. It is clever of this other god to have made women from a man's ribs. Why? Which woman would feel lonely in a garden of paradise? Anyway, I was lonely. Let me tell you this: be careful with loneliness—it is a leopard emotion hiding in the breakfast you make your sons in the morning, in the quietness of the house when they are at school, and the solitary duties you shoulder when you are a woman doing everything a woman is not allowed to do. It makes your breasts itch for a touch in bed at night. Before you know it you are being foolish and frivolous and walking down dark village paths to chase your sons' teacher. I know what I said before. I was lonely, not free of fault. When loneliness is done with you it will leave you to slink into the night, ashamed you came to its lair. No, I never told him. I had a reputation as a loose woman. He would claim it was not his. Anyway, he went off to the war. Strange, no? Teachers going to war. What can you possibly learn from dying? The real lessons are in living."

The sixth man: the soldier. "I would have gone with him willingly, but he insisted on using force. These were dark times. Most of the men had gone to the war. It was just us women left in the valley with young children. I did not have a man to miss so I took it upon myself to make sure the women did something for themselves. For once it was nice being welcomed by other women—suddenly we were all fatherless or husbandless. We milked the cows, shepherded, sowed and brought in the harvest. We did for each other what the men were not around to do for us. Why are you looking at me like that? There were no men, and women know other pleasures. You are now old enough to hear this: when you choose a man it is best to know what you are giving up. Me, I know. Some women do not. Where was I? The war. We hoped it would not make its way here but it did. The soldiers ran out of food, so they came to raid our lands. We were defenseless. They beat us. Raped us. They forgot they had come for food. No, I am not ashamed. What was done to me was not my choosing. He was unfuckable. He had to use force. Those soldiers caused a bigger war when our men returned. How could we explain all the children? Some women were driven from their houses for being taken by force instead of dying. Many came to stay on my land. Maybe you have met them. Maybe you have not. What does it matter? No, your uncle does not know. He knows his mother's love, not his father's hate. That is enough."

The seventh man: the husband. "You seem surprised. I was married once. After the war. Not all the men who came back were bad. Some were good. But even they did not know how to fit into our lives. We were used to doing everything by ourselves and they wanted us to be servants. But we also considered ourselves to be soldiers: we had survived the war. Some of our men had not. I ask you: how could we accept for things to go on as they had been when everything had changed? There were arguments in many fields between wives and husbands in those days about the right crop to plant and who dug the best furrows. My husband was one of those who came back. Well, most of him. He never raised his voice and never beat my children. He's the only one who was around for his child's birth, the only man I permitted to name his son. We were fine together. Love? I do not know if it was love. I know my husband was quiet. He left me alone when it was what I wanted. He did not care about my six boys. He said seven was a luckier number and got down to the business of making it so. Let me tell you this: my husband knew the counting end of a woman. No, I will not explain it. Him? He killed himself. Even though we had a good time together. Yes, I guess that is kind of running away. But I blame the war, that was the crime. Even now everyone mourns the dead, but no one apologizes to the survivors. When he died, I got his lands too. Big? You think my land is big? In the future everything gets smaller, the only thing that gets bigger is the past. Sometimes I think I am a foolish woman for hanging on to all of this, like I am trying to catch water in my hands. But someday all of this will be gone. Sold or lost, I do not know. Yes, I am certain you would never let this land go. But there are others before you. They have a say in this too, just like I had a say when it was my turn."

The eighth man: an engineer. "After the war came reconstruction. You know how men are: they destroy things and claim the glory of rebuilding. Listen: if one man breaks you do not let the next one fix you. He will hold it over you. This is the truth. If you are broken, mend yourself. Never let a man do it. You do not realize what a bad job they have done of it until later. This man liked restoring things. He thought he would remake the valley and me. He led a fuss of men who measured distances for roads and tested the soil for Lord knows what. There was to be a new hospital and school but there was no money for them. That is how the mining and timber companies came. They said they would create work for everyone, they would build everything everyone wanted if all they were given were the land. But the land was everything. Ha! What were they going to do with the old farmers? What would happen when our river was poisoned beyond use? I refused to sell. Do you see the clear sky? Those green fields over there? The river that looks like a green snake? That is because of me. If I sell, all of this will become nothing but dirt. I explained all of this to the eighth. He had arguments: commerce, industry, technology— things people say when their feet are separated from the cold concrete of their city homes by expensive shoes. But we who have walked this land barefoot know these things come at a price. He called my ideas nonsense, but he liked that I argued with him. His city wife never did that. O-ho. Not all men come to you in the way you wish. I did not mind. I was here. She was there. Let me tell you: there are men who can make you divide yourself in two, separate you from what you know to be true and right. He was such a man. It is embarrassing to hear your grandmother speak this way, eh? Then let me tell you, child, bestower of new gifts and titles, I must meet the eighth man in the world beyond this one, even though I am not looking forward to dying. It scares me. I do not want to work hard in this lifetime providing for my family only to die and work overtime in the spirit world too. Can you imagine dealing with the prayers for good rains and harvests or healthy pregnancies? Our ancestors work after hours and after life. It almost makes me wish for the white man's heaven. Why don't I want to go there? Child, they never mentioned whether they have fuckable men. Yes, I know. I might go to Hell. The eighth? He left when his work here was done. He worked on the big road leading out of the valley. I was not in need of rebuilding so his nature could not be satisfied with me for long. He tried to keep in touch, but I kept my distance. You need to respect another woman's territory. I had his child. If I had told him he would have left his wife. I am sure of that. But I had enough: my land, my seven healthy boys, and another child on the way. I had friends, my work, and my duty. I let him go. I was ready to grow older. Now I am old. I might not look it, but I am. I am ready for the second part of the village prophecy. I was a young grandmother long ago because of you. Now I would not mind being an old whore. Child, I said I am old, not dead. I carried eight boys who are now men from eight men who were not always men. I have no space for shame. I tell you: shame is how men will control you. And you should not be controlled. Especially by short, unfuckable men. Let me look at your boyfriend again. Ha! He looks foolish and frivolous. You must leave this one."

In this way I learned my family's history and my grandmother's part in it. She was energetic when she recited her stories, raising her voice, lowering it, mimicking pelvic thrusts, or making sensuous winds with her hips. She would even grab my waist and show me how to twist it, telling me such displays were not for men but necessary movements for me to find myself.

In her later years, when she was too old to move, she was wheeled around, directing where she wanted to go in short barks, frustrated as age slowly stole her purchase on earthly citizenship, taking away bits of her at a time: vigor, hearing, movement, sight—"And the fire in my loins. Child, you don't know the cold unless you have felt the heat, I tell you that."

She liked being left beneath the old tree. From there she could see her farmland from beneath its shady branches. Whenever I climbed the hill to visit her, her wrinkles would crinkle as she smiled, watching me walk toward her.

▶ ||

Ursula swells and attacks the prince's ship. She is impaled, killed, her body vanishes into the waves. My sons cheer, especially my eldest, who reminds me of my grandmother, especially when his will flares up against my rules. He looks at me with eyes that know more than he lets on, eyes that see me even as they hide him away. Even in this far country, far away from the valley of my home, a land he knows nothing about, I sometimes feel her in his ability to hurt with words. He is yet to come to her kindness.

My grandmother was right: everything in the future becomes smaller. Our land was sold off by my father and uncles when she died. The money didn't last as long as they thought it would.

While I was pregnant with my firstborn I felt some vestige of her power inside me, an invisible tentacle. When he was born I named him in accordance with her last admonition: not to live my life as revenge for the past.

"The past always wins," she said.

I named my son for the future, as best as I could, in the way I think she would have: he is the way, the goal, the destination on the horizon.

And I am the Granddaughter of the Octopus, the bestower of new gifts and titles.

From the Lost City of Hurtlantis to the Streets of Helldorado

(OR, FRANCO)

I know Franco is in a fucked-up place because he still refers to his ex as his girlfriend by accident when his mood is chipper. It just slips out, like a squeaky fart, and no matter how much he clenches up after that it's already too late. Things are never the same after someone hears you fart.

Sometimes, it's best when he rambles on about how she was a good one and how he should've done better. It means he is focusing on the issue. Sure, it's regret, but at least he zeroes in on the object of his pain. When he's silent I get worried. That's when a dude is liable to do something that puts him on page three of the newspaper. Some of the boys think he's doing well because he shows up to parties but I know he's in trouble. A vet knows a vet. The way he glazes over at bars midconversation means I need to get him home quick-fast. It's in the silence, when his eyes go dark, when he is slow to reply. That's when he's fighting the tiller, liable to get storm-clapped, wake up on the shores of the Lost City of Hurtlantis—demons, dementia, desperation, and all.

He is still cut up about her. It's in everything he does. The way he misses a simple pass on the court means he's thinking about Carmen being in the stands, seeing her face where it's not. When our team takes an L he sighs and trudges to the sideline, waiting to see who's got next. This is the same Franco who used to go coast-to-ghost on players, nearly untouchable when he was in the zone, snatching ankles, sliding defenders, swishing from all corners of the court. Now he's a liability. He could walk into a Cavaliers game and feel right at home.

For the first three months the whole crew was on suicide watch. Me, Lindo, Rinzlo, and Cicero—the Caretakers. We took turns going over to his house to make sure he ate and washed his ass. We phoned his workplace to make sure he checked in. On weekends we took him to the gym, the go-kart racing park when it was open, the dam for some *braais*, the lookout spots, high enough that the spread of Windhoek's city lights looked moderately impressive. We even went to the monthly salsa party on Independence Avenue. We did things we never would've done by ourselves, hoping it would lift his spirits a bit. Comfort in company, or some shit like that. Nothing seemed to work. Six months later the nigga's heart was still tottering around, punch-drunk from lost love. I almost wish Carmen had the decency to put him down for good when she finally decided to leave.

Today gave me hope though.

Franco took part in a twenty-kilometer run. When he called to tell me he was at the starting line I couldn't believe it. Carmen had been trying to couple-goals the Two Oceans Marathon in Cape Town with him for years. Franco's answer was always "What are we running away from?"

So today at half past madness in the morning I actually drove across town to see him scrape himself across the finish line. Homie was coming apart the entire time, body shining with slave moisture, chest sounding like he was inhaling a pack of razor blades. But he pushed on through. There's no fuel like high-octane heartbreak to make a nigga do the impossible. I thumped him on the back. Behind him, the marshals started taking down the route markers.

"Well done, Franco! That's my guy."

"Thanks, man."

"This shit's crazy. You didn't even train, man."

"Just felt like it." He looked at me sideways, then looked away. "Felt like something I should do, you know?"

"Nah, fam, I don't know. If I run three kilometers in any direction there'd better be a train to take me back home."

"We said we'd do one of these things together."

"Who's we?"

"Me and C—"

He needed a moment to pull himself together. We both pretended it was his body making up for the oxygen debt. I went to fetch him some water.

That afternoon, he went and got a new haircut. Nothing basic, he went and got a lineup with the premium fades on the side like only barbers from Central and West Africa can hook up, the ones in town near the Ellerines taxi rank where they blare Wizkid and Patoranking onto the sidewalk. Maybe he was on the mend. There is no finite time for recovery. Some guys take longer than others. Some never heal, some master the shit and wander through life like functioning alcoholics, heartsore, sour as fuck. But they still show up for work, they still date, they even marry, they have kids. I guess if there's a closet, a negro is always going to find room for another skeleton.

I hoped reinvention would be heavy with Franco when he got the fade. The next step in all of this would be him switching up his wardrobe, leaving his loose-fit relationship jeans for something newer and tighter. New sneakers, new clothes, new cologne, new swagger, new pussy times eight—these are the twelve steps.

How do I know this?

I'm the Sage of the Six Paths.

Lindo, Rinzlo, Cicero, Franco, and I walked the first path together. It was called foolishness. Back in high school all we did was get into fights, on the basketball court, on the soccer field, in the mall parking lot. We were boys-will-be-boys kind of boys, all from Windhoek-Worst, eager to rep our hood like we had seen the American kids do. We didn't have Twenty-First and Lewis or cool street names like that. Just streets named after scientists and dead composers. So we were trying to make a name for ourselves before we had to go home and do our chemistry homework.

When we grew older there were other paths: wrath, grief, lust, loneliness, and redemption. I walked them all.

One time, when I was stuck on the grief path, I left my girlfriend asleep in bed and snuck into the lounge to call Franco. I told him I just wanted to talk. He said, "Sure, dude. We can talk."

I talked a bit about my mother. About how when she passed on I realized God was average middle management at best and just plain cruel at worst. And how I felt like I was letting her down with small things I was doing or not doing. My voice broke and I held the phone away from my mouth so he could not hear me crying into my hand. When I put it back against my ear he said, "It's all good, man. If anyone's gonna get through this it's you."

I did. Just took some therapy and shit.

Looking at Franco with his new haircut, his effortless pretty-boy looks, the pout of his lips, and his pensive silences that made girls go mad, I thought about telling him about therapy. I decided against it. If there's another thing I know it's that guys don't deal, they deal out. Everyone has to walk his own path.

That was me then.

This is Franco now.

We clasped hands and bumped shoulders.

"Dope cut, Franco," I said. (The compliment shop had been working overtime for six months now.)

"Felt like it was time."

It was about damn time.

Then we all went to get pizza at the Debonair's, and our other boy, the moron, Lineker, the one who never knew when to shut his mouth, said the grapevine was rustling and word on the creep street was Franco's girl was dating someone new. Me and the other Caretakers winced and looked at Lineker hoping to God Belial would flame-tickle his balls for eternity. Lineker never even put in his fucking shift as a Caretaker but here he was making a homie relapse. Franco froze at the till, eyes swimming. He ducked to the bathroom quickly. I ordered a Hawaiian for him.

"Lin, you're a fucking idiot, man," Rinzlo hissed.

"What?" Lineker shrugged. "I thought that'd help the dude move on, man. You know, since she's also moved on."

"It doesn't work that way, Lin," I said. I pinched the bridge of my nose in the universal way sage negroes do—with the pinky finger out—to let other niggas know you're tired of their shit. "Just don't fucking say anything when he comes back."

"Did you guys know?"

"Of course we knew, Lin." Cicero shook his head. He was the one who'd found out about Carmen switching up. He'd dropped into the chat group and said we needed to be ready to go to Code Red. "But we didn't need to let him know. Fuck, man."

"Information is a man's worst enemy." Rinzlo casually leaned against the counter. "It's bad for morale everywhere."

When Franco came back into the atrium, homeboy's long-ass eyelashes looked like wet spider legs after rain. He managed to square his shoulders though, prop up his chest. The false steel in his voice made my airways tighten with pity, like I was watching the Iron Giant fly off to meet inevitability all over again.

"Who is it?" Franco shivered as he said it.

The other Caretakers found the devil in the menu's details.

"Yo, Franco, I don't think that'll help, man." I tried to head him off. Dudes have this obscene fascination with the truth, especially when it will harm them.

"Who is it?" He turned to Lineker.

"Bronwyn."

I made a note never to hang with Lineker ever again even though I'd been asking myself the same question.

Yeah, we all knew Carmen had a new man, but we didn't know

who it was. I'd been itching to know his name. Vultures can never resist a carcass. But, also, fuck Lineker.

"Franco, I'm sorry, man." I put an arm on his shoulder. Cicero and Lindo tried to launch a heated discussion about toppings, bacon versus ham. Franco didn't budge. He was set on performing emotional *seppuku.*

"How long?" he asked.

"Maybe three weeks," Lineker said, ignoring the death stares we were all giving him. He shrugged. "Maybe longer. I don't know. Just heard today."

Franco's face became a satellite image of Africa at night. The lights were few and far between the spaces of his being. The rest was filled with darkness.

The homie was back in the void.

The other Caretakers and Lineker hoovered their pizza and tagged themselves out of the ring, paying their bills, vanishing like genies after a third wish.

I was left with my guy Franco.

At his place he was ethereally calm. I regretted not heartbreak-proofing his house. Realistically, I thought, how much damage could a spatula do? Could he choke himself by swallowing a whole eraser?

He went to the kitchen and got himself a beer. I boiled water for tea. I made it black, no sugar, no milk—a new path for me. He sipped his beer slowly. I blew on my tea and tried to keep the conversation light by talking about how crazy the recession was, how people were being retrenched all over the place. I told him how Angie was pushing promo codes for high-waisted jeans on Instagram for extra cash, how Lindo was thinking of part-timing as a physical trainer. I told him about Rinzlo's shady investment scheme that was strangely shaped like a pyramid. Everyone was trying third, fourth, and fifth side hustles just to survive. I said I might have to sling crack to my students' parents because, Lord, I didn't know how they dealt with their own spawn. I realized Franco hadn't said anything the whole time. His brow was furrowed.

"Bronwyn? Really?"

That is men for you. They see a cliff and they hunger to break their fall with the jagged rocks below.

"Yeah, I'm pretty surprised too."

I was and I wasn't.

Bronwyn is a dude we kind of totally absolutely play ball with on some Sundays when the NBA highlights get our blood racing. He's always on the fringe, the last-round pick. Even now when I conjure up an image of Bronwyn's best plays I can't see him making a successful dribble or a fadeaway jumper. Even under the hoop with no one bearing down on him the nigga could fumble a layup. I looked across at Franco. I could tell all he was doing was picturing Bronwyn with Carmen.

Peaking in the Top One of Things a Nigga Would Not Like to Think About is his girl with someone else. It's never the sexual thoughts that send him into the Bermuda Triangle of heartbreak. It's the million and one little things they used to do together or the things he never did with her that come to mind immediately. Like the time the flu had her leaking fluids and all she wanted was some food brought over but a homie lied and said work was dragging on so he couldn't? Some other guy is going to nurse her real good. That time her dumb friend needed help moving house but you were too busy watching *John Wick* for the eighteenth time? Yeah, somebody is going to triple-jump their way into that opportunity.

When my girlfriend left, all I thought of was another squeeze curling into bed with her, holding her hand under the sheets like I used to. She called me Teaspoon. I told her it was a dumbass name. And when she left, I wanted the word obliterated from the dictionary. There could only be one Teaspoon and I was he.

"Man, I'm sorry, Franco."

"It ain't your fault, man."

"Yeah, but it still sucks, bro."

I am right, and so is he.

It sucks. It is not my fault, but it's definitely Franco's.

Carmen caught Franco cheating with her cousin, and even though I haven't managed to coax the full story out of him, I'm certain there were other girls. But, damn, her cousin. That's the kind of cold shit that makes Windhoek women sour for years. And guys from Helldorado are trash. That's where Franco lives now. Women would be better off finding boyfriends from stable, institutional beige neighborhoods like Avis or Klein Windhoek or Eros. But the sticky, humid fuckboy tropics where it rains tears and insecurity like clockwork? They need to leave them the fuck alone.

Franco, my number one hombre, got caught. He lied about it. Then Carmen called her cousin in from the next room and he had to slam on the apology brakes real quick.

Skrrr! Skrrr!

She left him. It was the right thing to do.

But, Lord, I've never seen anyone apologize like Franco. He went to her place, chest ripped open, offering her whatever she could get her hands on. He went to her work and embarrassed her, crying like a motherfucker. He went to her church. He sang louder than the most stalwart choir auntie, off-tune. But he *sang*. He even showed up at her mother's house, trying to apologize, but the *zali* was not having it. She told Franco it was between him and her daughter. Then she proceeded to do some gangster shit: she broke the Seven Seals of Motherhood and summoned her daughter onto the *stoep* and told them they needed to talk it out like grown-ups and not to come back into the house unless they had sorted out their mess.

Carmen had called me to come and get Franco before she heard her mother putting a double-step, chicken-and-gecko-blood, three-incantation binding spell on her ass.

"Hold on," she said all of a sudden. "I'll call you back quickly."

She did not. I was worried.

I drove out to get my homie.

But when I got there the war was already over. There they were on the *stoep* holding hands like they weren't the anthem for doomed youth.

Franco never told me what he said to her but it must have been the very Words of Creation because Carmen forgave him.

That's the one thing the missionaries got right when they landed. They managed to stamp automatic forgiveness into every black man's soul. Forgive and forget. That was the game plan. First give them Jesus and the Sacred Power of Forgiveness and put the Fear of Eternal Damnation in them. Then take the land. And make sure the forgiveness gene is passed down from poor father to pauper son, dispossessed mother to despondent daughter, so in three hundred years' time their children can't come back to claim their shit.

Forgiveness runs deep with girls from south of the Tropic of Capricorn. They don't have options in their dusty-ass desert towns. The petrol station serves as a mall, date-night restaurant, and community hall all rolled into one. Not far away is a church where they preach about turning the other cheek. Toss boredom, brain-scrambling heat, seeing her mother ladle generous portions of pardon from the failed marriage *potjie* pot, and the Big Ol' J. C. together and a girl's going to grow up ready to excuse any transgression against her.

Carmen came from one of those towns of latitude unknown where rape was recreational and addiction was a vocation, one of those places with names ending in *-fontein* or *-kraal* or *-dorp*. She knew the many names of sheep. She could open a beer bottle just by looking at it. Homegal was always going to grant a pretty city boy like Franco that Desmond Tutu amnesty.

She didn't even make him go through the kind of public purgatory white girls make guys go through, letting him know he fucked up, inviting him to dinner with her whole family, who also let him know they know he fucked up. There is a way of passing the peas that lets you know your girlfriend's grandmother despises your guts. That's how you know white girls are serious about dating a black guy, they take him back. When a white girl gives up you know she was just going through a phase because dating us is a lifestyle.

Not even a week after Carmen saved him from the Lake of Sulfur and the eternal pecking of livers Franco was back in her guts, and then, because this is Franco we're talking about, her cousin's.

Negroes, man. Negroes.

The second time around, Carmen wasn't having it. That's why he's been sad for so long. That shit was supposed to be automatic. That is how the Lord's Prayer goes: *As we forgive those who trespass against us!*

By his estimation, Franco had at least ten more forgiveness tokens remaining. But Carmen left for good.

She chose her mental health. And, apparently, she chose Bronwyn.

Yeah, she went for a dude in his social circle, but that is just part of the game in the Oh-Six-One. You will break up with a girl and then your cousin will bring her to a wedding. Guys will change barbers and have the common decency to find someone new on the other side of town, but if they break up with a girl they will start hollering at her best friend the next day.

Karma being what it is, Franco should have known better.

We did our part to help him recover. We through-passed some company to him who could nurse him back to health. Cicero introduced him to a colleague who said she wasn't looking for anything serious. Lindo had a shy friend who'd always had a crush on Franco. I called up that one woman who had a thing for me but things never added up for us. On our one-sided date Rinzlo showed up with Franco and I slyly handed her off for him to run to the end zone.

I told them not to catch feelings. I told them Franco was going through a breakup. No matter what the arrangement, no matter the extensiveness of the contractual clauses, no matter how broken a black man is, women from Windhoek will get out their porcelain glue and jeweler's glasses and try to put him back together. All the king's horses and all the king's men have nothing on women from Nam'.

It's actually foolish the way women think dating a man fresh out of a relationship can end well. Maybe they think it's like lying in someone else's warm spot in a frigid bed—half the work is already done. That's what Angie says: "At least you know he has feelings."

Recently broken-up men should be treated like Chernobyl. After forever has expired, it will be fine to settle there again. But, no, Franco was howling at the full moon with that directionless sorrow and women found it cute.

At the very least Franco should've let some of the women scoop his bits into a dustpan, make sure the hurt was contained. But, no, he wasn't interested. He just wanted to lie in bed with the curtains drawn, letting his beard that didn't connect become more raggedy each day while I dealt with all the angry women who blamed me for their hurt.

I did my part for Franco. I counseled, I encouraged, I soothed, I even tried to pass the blame biscuit to his ex.

Damn right it wasn't my fault.

But it was definitely Franco's.

"Do you think she's serious about Bronwyn?"

"I don't know, Franco. Can't tell, man."

Bronwyn wasn't a bad guy, really. Sucked at ball, couldn't for the life of him say something funny on or off the court, but he was chilled. I never heard him say a bad word to anyone or about anyone. I never heard his name in the streets. He was not a starter, but maybe that's what Carmen needed. After all, if you want to date an All-Star you need to deal with All-Star Weekend.

Franco slouched on the couch. I sat on an ottoman and shuffled through the day's newspapers on his coffee table.

"Was I that bad?"

At times like these a sage has to be a lantern-bearer for those lost in their own treacherous dark.

"Franco," I said, "you're my guy, man." He relaxed. "But you were the fucking worst."

"Fuck you!"

239

I kept cool. "Your anger's compass has the wrong north," I told him.

"Fuck you and your sage shit. Nobody needs your palavering."

"You need it more than most, Franco. But, listen, I ain't Morpheus and you aren't The One. I can't code a matrix around you forever. You need to fix or fold, my G, and I can only help with one of those."

He sighed.

"You made it through," he said after a while.

"What?"

"Your breakup."

"Did I?"

We looked at each other for a long while.

"You know what?"

"What, Franco?"

"Deep down I think she still likes me."

I stared the shit out of the sports page.

"You don't think so?" He was looking at me.

"I don't know, Franco. I—I think you should just focus on yourself for a while, you know? She's with Bronwyn now. That's a sign of something. I don't know what exactly, but it's a sign."

"Yeah, but that'll pass."

Franco leaned forward, elbows on his knees, chin resting on his balled fists.

"She'll come back."

Then Franco started crying.

Oh, Franco.

B-Side

NINE MONTHS SINCE FOREVER
(CICERO'S INTERLUDE)

The one thing marriage gives you is someone to blame. James was always late for work, but a week after his nuptials, he blamed his tardiness on his wife. *The wife took extra-long getting ready this morning. You know how that goes. Women, right?* And I knew Des always wanted a way out of our social circle, so when she married Dean she blamed her slow distancing from us on him. *I'm sorry I can't meet up this weekend, Dean and I have a function with the in-laws.* I've been telling the homies marriage takes a lot of my time whenever they say they haven't seen me in a while. When they head off to a Sunday pickup game, I tell them Nicole and I have to do the week's grocery shopping. *Gotta do our meal prep, gents.* When they meet up in the week to sweat at the gym from sundown to late evening, I tell them Nicole and I are spending time together after long days at work. *We're shattered, guys, just going to take it easy tonight.* At every given opportunity, I tell them Nicole and I need to grow together. *We need to figure each other out,*

241

you know, and we need to find our stride. Once, to avoid meeting them for Rinzlo's birthday, I said Nicole and I were going through a rough patch and we needed to work things out.

Rinzlo wrote in the group chat: *It's only been nine months since you said forever. How can things be going wrong already?*

They weren't. Things were just fine. More than fine. And based on his multiple Instagram stories, Rinzlo had a decent birthday: *Chilling with my Day Ones! Real Gs pull through (and don't pull out)! Four Os Forever!*

When the guys invite me over to watch Champions League soccer I say, "Nah, not tonight. I have to put in quality time with the wife."

I've never liked soccer. I don't even particularly like playing basketball, but the homies and I have been jamming since high school so I stuck it out for the sake of the crew. Marriage, though, is the fire escape I never knew about.

I blame my wife for my absences, but, really, she's a better friend to me than my friends. I prefer her company. I can't tell them that, though. They wouldn't take it well. Rambo, my other friend, tried to leave the crew in high school. Not leave, per se. He was weary of fighting, tough-talking, and being a ride-or-die member of our cowboy posse. There's only so much rolling into town you can do before you start wanting a welcome. Those hastily closed shutters can do a real number on any reasonable person and Rambo was more reasonable than most. Lindo and I would've defected with him but Franco and Rinzlo—our alphas—iced him hard, made him persona non grata, and threatened to do the same to us. We were too dumb to do the math and realize we were the majority. I guess cool has more voting rights. Franco and Rinzlo cut Rambo out of everything. They wouldn't even talk to him in class or basketball practice. I didn't have the balls to ride solo, without the crew for shelter, so I did my part in enforcing his banishment.

Eventually we made up. We needed each other to get through high school and university. We were alloyed together by a good sense of humor, proximity, poverty, and not wanting to be singled out by the privileged gaze. Together we were something, a crew of funny, self-deprecating guys; apart we were just another group of broke black boys. Now I understand what Rambo meant when he rode into the sunset back when we were younger: "You guys need to find yourselves, and then see if you still find each other." I found myself with Nicole, and now I'm not so sure if the squad and I are still down for life. I mean, I've already promised this life and the next to my wife.

I blame Nicole for the part-time vegetarian diet that exorcised the guys from my house even though I'm certain it saved me from a cholesterol-related heart attack in my soon-to-be thirties. I blame her for switching out the club nights for date nights, which saved me money and rescued me from the shame of being the only dude who couldn't pull ass at the end of a night. I blame my wife for giving my old comic books to the secondhand store in town even though I've been longing to do that for years. I kept them because the crew used to steal them from shops when we were younger and they reminded us of our young warthog days. She gave them away and I fumed to the guys: *She's just changing shit all over the place! Like, WTF?*

I huffed and I puffed about all the modifications Nicole made to my life when we got married—the morning meditation routine (relaxing), the lunchtime meetings at our favorite café (so necessary), the evenings spent watching *Grand Designs* (dopest show ever)—but when the homies were out of sight, I breathed easy, found a telephone booth, and exited it looking forward to going home and putting vases on our now comic book–free floating shelves.

The other guys at work ask me if I want to go for drinks, and I tell them my wife is at home waiting for me. She isn't. She's either at pottery classes or yoga with her friends. Nicole keeps her own timetable. I could chill with my colleagues any day of the week if I wanted, but even her absence from home shoulders the blame for my inability to do the most basic of dude things.

"Ah," Tapiwa says—he's still reeling from his divorce—"the old ball and chain." He chuckles a little. "I'm glad to be free of that." (He isn't. I see the reluctant crow's-feet crinkle around his eyes when he forces a laugh or a smile.)

"Yeah, you know how it is," I say.

In the car, I'm glad when the engine coughs and slowly carries me to the solitude of my house. I shoot some things on my PlayStation for a while and then cook, waiting for Nicole to come home so we can resume our life together. She finds me rapping along to Naughty By Nature's "Hip Hop Hooray" halfway through the risotto and effortlessly slides into the second verse like we're a world-class wrecking crew.

It wasn't easy being with Nicole at first. I was scared of how unorthodoxly beautiful she was. Tall, thin, almost no breasts to her, and just enough ass to harass with my eyes. I kept her a secret for a while. When the guys eventually met her, Franco said she was funny. Lindo said she was smart. Rinzlo, whose opinion I least looked forward to, said the kindest words to ever come out of his mouth: "Well, she looks human." Rambo, the only one who could think beyond his tip, said he'd always been waiting for me to stop chasing the thirst traps

244

I pursued for rep and be with someone who made me happy. I asked him why he didn't tell me this sooner, and he said, "Cicero, a man has to find his own path. I'm just glad you found yours."

That's Rambo. Sage negro numero uno.

Nicole says Rambo isn't okay. She says he's a nice guy, no lies, but he's really hurting. I tell her he misses his mom. "She died on his birthday," I tell her. We're playing Boggle after supper, and she's kicking my ass. "Even I'd be messed up if that happened to me."

Nicole says it's something else. "It's a hollowness inside him." I snort and say that's abstract women talk. She rolls her eyes. "You should pay more attention to your friends. Especially him. He isn't all the way here. Not all the time."

I don't know what she's talking about. Rambo's the toughest guy I know. I don't think I'd survive half the shit he's been through. That dude is a born soldier. I don't know what they feed guys from Central and East Africa but they're made of something else. Harder than a coffin nail and more resilient than a plague. First time I met Rambo was at the school athletics meeting. That's the day I found out why track-and-field commentators always talk about any man who breaks the sprint record as the fastest *recorded* man. They're making provision for some barefooted Flash from Rambo's region who's never heard of lactic acid or sweat. Rambo jogged his way to the finish line while we pushed our calcium-deficient legs to pump harder and faster. When we finished, we were all awed by him, asking him where he was from and if there were others like him. He said he was the slowest at his school in the green tropics of Africa. Since then, Rambo's always been a step or life lap ahead of us, experiencing things before us, plowing through the hardships of his life, and always willing to help us through our own shit. Despite his disappointments and setbacks, Rambo keeps showing up to serve in the trenches of our lives, throwing himself on grenades and carrying the wounded across mine-ridden marshes with bullets zipping past him. He's a cold and cool dude. Once, I asked him what he thought about Nicole, and he said it didn't matter. All that mattered was what she made me feel, the man I was around her, and how loved I felt. He used the word *love*. That's why we call Rambo the Sage, he's the only one brave enough to use cataclysmic words like *love*.

"My man," he said. "All that matters is that you're seen." He dead-ass looked me in the face, like with eye contact and shit. "I see you, Cic, and now you're seen. I'm really happy for you."

I had to look away.

When I married Nicole, Rambo was my best man. I had to include the other guys to keep the peace.

I was so happy to become Nicole's husband. I always felt like I was the sidekick in the crew, just some dude who was there for the lead character's development. Nicole made me a headliner, a marquee player around whom she would build her whole franchise and future. Rinzlo, at the wedding, after grabbing the mic from Rambo at the end of his speech, said even I managed to get a ring. "There's really no excuse for Carmelo Anthony."

I remember how Rambo was that day, how silent he'd become when there was no one around him. I asked him how he was doing during a lull on the dance floor, and he said he was cool, fine, okay, and a'ight. When I told Nicole about it later, just after we'd tasted the first delights of our marriage (we'd been chaste the whole time we were dating—something only Rambo knew about), reviewing the wedding ceremony and the reception, she said he was lying. I was new to marriage. I hadn't yet realized I'd acquired more than a wife, an equal partner, a crutch upon which to lean whenever I needed an excuse. I hadn't yet become acquainted with the unnerving quality wives have of sussing out poisonous weaknesses in their husbands' friends.

Nicole has this weird ability to know what I'm thinking even before I tell her. Franco said it's wife-vision: "They can see straight through you, fam. They can see the boy you were, and the man you could be. They can see everything. That's why I ain't getting hitched. There're certain truths I don't need in my life." I don't know how Franco is able to say that around his girlfriend, but he does.

Lindo says it isn't that hard to see through guys, all you have to do is look. Lindo, I think, is the closest to Rambo in terms of temperament. With Franco and Rinzlo on one end, Rambo and Lindo on the other, sometimes I feel like I'm the middle child who doesn't have enough of either parent to proudly claim him. Which, I guess, is why I gravitate even more strongly toward Nicole.

Rinzlo doesn't get along with Nicole because she's the only person who doesn't entertain his bullshit. She puts the lid on his gutter mouth even before he opens it. That's why he can't stand her. I like having Nicole around when Rinzlo's in the area. I feel exposed around him when she isn't. The other day he said I was pussy-whipped. He said the wife had me on a leash like a broken slave. I think it's the way he referred to her as *the wife*—in lowercase, like Nicole didn't command the respect of the Caps Lock button, even in speech. He made her sound like a routine duty. I told him wife was a privilege she bestowed upon me by being married to me, for as long as she deemed me worthy. "Wife isn't her job description. Same goes for me—hubby isn't my name. It's Cicero."

"I didn't say *hubby*, bra," Rinzlo replied. "I said guppy."

Rambo, Franco, and Lindo had to pull us apart.

When Rambo drove me home, he asked me what had set me off. He'd never seen me like that, not in all of our years surviving this place that corroded our childhood and forced us to calcify armor around our soft characters. I'd never thrown down with Rinzlo before, the scrappiest of our crew. Rambo asked me why the heck I was prepared to be sent home bruised or broken.

I thought about how fed up I was with the guys, how duplicitous we were around each other. I was going to tell him I was tired of juggling my consciousness around the homies, my work personality around the guys, and the husband I was when I was with Nicole. I wanted to tell him that I was, for the first time, being me and being appreciated for it. I wanted to tell Rambo that even though he was the coolest guy I knew he had nothing on Nicole and the truth of her. I would have told him there and then that I was bowing out of the sad, cyclical story. I wanted to tell him we were like the third season of a Netflix show—thin on substance, a tad heavy on hard humor, with characters who lost their shine a long time ago. We were still in the same place. None of us had moved away. We were probably never going to. I wanted to tell him that I really, really wanted to go and find myself, and then see if we found each other.

Instead, I looked at him sideways and blamed Nicole. "I couldn't let him say that shit about my wife, man."

Rambo looked at me long and hard and then said, "Okay."

HOPE IS FOR THE UNPREPARED
(OR, ME)

"Love has no exit interviews," I say. "Closure is the poor man's time traveling."

My voice is cold over the phone. I tell myself the situation calls for it; I'm speaking to my ex-girlfriend, after all.

She's not any ex-girlfriend. She lingers on my skin like an old tattoo, still visible on my persona. I explain her to everyone I meet because she's the first person they see on me despite my best efforts to keep her up my sleeve. Even now, about a year later, I'm in danger of being pulled back to the promises of our better days and the betrayals of the worst. Her voice has the familiar curiosity that pokes and pries beneath the flaps of my being, trying to lift them and see what lies beneath.

I was certain she'd never call again. But she did.

▶ ‖

Before this call was the text message from an unknown number I nearly blocked, before she clarified it was her. The shock put me on the flats of my feet. I should've known better; around the year mark is when sentimentality hits the hardest: the anniversary of all the could-haves, would-haves, and should-haves. I played for time, my fingers made small talk about smaller things: *Teaching is going okay. Yeah, I'm writing a bit at the moment; can't say what though. My dad is fine and my brother remains the best of us.*

—*He always was.*

—*Ouch!*

—*Don't act like you didn't know it.*

I deflected her questions this way and that. Serena, yo-yoing Shara-pova at an Open, would've been proud of me.

She asked if she could call.

—*Unless you don't want to talk.*

I wondered if this was a sneaky Kasparov maneuver: move a phone call to G7 to checkmate my emotional stability. This was my signa-ture move back in the day: Spirit Bomb–calling on all the misplaced heartbreaks to Kamehameha some poor girl into taking me back. But I realized it wasn't me I was talking to. It was her.

That, I guess, is why we dated, why we worked (until, of course, we didn't). I figured if she'd wanted to gut-punch me, she'd have done it earlier, when I was reeling from the strangeness of being alone.

—*Sure, no problem. You can call.*

I let the phone vibrate in my hands for a while.

Brrr! Brrrrrrr! Brrr! Brrrrrrr! Brrr! Brrrrrrr!

So this is what power felt like.

"Hallo," she said.

"That's my line."

"Not anymore."

I flinched, glad she wasn't around to see me. We talked about inconsequential things: the heat and the mosquitoes thugging at ten o'clock in the morning ("Crazy!"), her work ("Cool!"), how her sister's abstract expressionist painting was going ("Uh-huh, mmm, of course . . ."), the endless drought and the deepening recession ("Damn!"), and her recent trips to Thailand and Costa Rica.

"How'd you know about those?" she asked.

"The Gram."

"You still follow me?"

"Standard breakup procedure: stay tuned in to the ex's social media feeds to see if they lost the breakup."

"How do you know if you're winning?"

"The ex usually gets a dumb tattoo." She laughed a little. I could still make her laugh. "But the giveaway is when they start quoting Rupi Kaur." An intake of breath on her end. I could still make her cry too. I asked about her travels again.

The beaches and the sundowners, the food and the ruins harboring history and memories, the people, the miles, the takeoffs and landings, and too many parties. "Just what I needed at the time," she said. After a pause: "The distance."

"I'm glad you went. And now you're back."

"I'm back."

I asked the obvious question: "Why'd you call?"

"To talk."

"Talk about what?"

"Us."

251

"There is no us." (A fact, true, but I don't know why I said this.)

"There was."

"Was." Another unscripted response rubbed against the moment's grain. I looked for shelter in the unknown but secretly felt. "Seriously, why're you calling?"

A camel caravan of silence ambled by, heading toward some secret desert oasis.

"Clarity," she said.

"Ah." I went to the kitchen and sat on a barstool, tenting my elbows on the counter. "The closure talk."

"If you don't want to talk, just say so."

"After all this time, how'd anything I have to say help you?"

"I don't know. I'm hoping it will."

I told her what was in my diary, what the homies called "the coldest shit ever written": love has no exit interviews; closure is the poor man's time traveling.

►ΙΙ

She's quiet.

I'm no Spandau Ballet, but I know this much is true: a woman should never phone her black exes. Former high school crushes are cool—they're harmless (the validation of the call will make their week, possibly their year). Even the ex-fiancé is worth a ring or two. But black exes are a hard no: they're an unending cycle of underpaid optimism and predators of patience. Any woman calling up such exes should know the facts as Charles Darwin found them on the Galápagos Islands: after a breakup, instead of going on a journey to the center

252

of their hurt, they'll go around the world in eighty baes, avenging themselves upon everyone like they're the wounded counts of Monte Cristo. They're a losing stock not worth betting on—sell them cheap, sell them fast. The market will always recover. But any sane woman should know she might not.

The hush from her end makes my eardrums pulse. I press the phone harder against my ear. For some reason, I stupidly hope she can feel it.

When she talks, her voice is strong. She says she's sorry she phoned.

I'm about to say something to keep her on the line. I stop. I've been here before, with her emotions in front of me like a Normandy beach, my Allied and Lying Forces prepared to storm it, dreaming of all the womanly gifts lying behind enemy lines willing to give it up for a bar of chocolate, some cigarettes, and that most precious and poisonous thing: hope.

I keep quiet.

She says, "I liked you a lot."

"I liked you too." My throat tightens. "But that was a long time ago."

"It's been less than a year."

"Exactly."

I sense it on the other end of the line, the reaching, like God's finger stretching out to Adam on that faded picture at the taxi rank, a few inches between them, contact capable of creating life. The static pulses of a new relationship vibrate between us, calling for a return to innocence. They are low but strong.

I cough and tell her we've been down this road before. There's a muffled sound from her end. I think she's stifling a cry. When she speaks up again, she says she understands. She asks if I have something special planned for my birthday. I'm going to be thirty soon.

Maybe that's why she phoned. Perhaps she hoped I'd be a little wiser, a smidge kinder. That I'd managed to carve myself out of my character clichés and learned to keep the darkness of my grief and depression at bay. I often wonder if I have. And I worry far more often that I haven't. I fear I'm still as predictable as the dawn, weaker than a newborn fawn. Perhaps there's no cure for the negro junkie chasing the rush of his own folly.

I don't have any birthday plans. "Just dinner with my father and brother."

"Send them my regards."

"I won't. We aren't those people for each other anymore. My father will ask too many questions. My brother will be too happy, too hopeful. I would've appreciated it back when we were still together"—my throat catches—"back when it was love."

She asks if it really was.

Was it?

How we met. How we wound up dating. How we walked unshod of deception around each other. How I was the one who brought doubt to our paradise.

I admit it now, the gall rising in my throat, the reels of romance rewinding and reminding me how things could have ended in another place, another time: maybe marriage, maybe family; maybe foundations, burrowing to new depths to withstand the winds of a fleeting world; or pinions and new altitudes for life on the wing.

Another Place—I wonder where it is and how to get there.

Another Time—I yearn for its clock and the hours that could be ours.

"Melanie, sweet Melamine," I say, using her royal title, the one I bestowed upon her back when she called me Teaspoon, the only man who could stir her the right way. "We could've ruled this universe together."

She cries and hangs up.

I start typing her number. I still remember it. There's a stash of memories connected to her that I can't delete despite changing grocery stores, my gym, and frequenting the other bookshop in town even though it's not as good. What was the purpose of the distance, the time, and the silence if I could still dance a decent jig when habit pulled a phantom string?

Is this a sign? Do I want it to be?

I stop myself before pressing the call button.

I breathe in deeply. Exhale. Breathe in again. I go to the bathroom and wash my face, pat it dry, and look in the mirror. My skin scratches against me, like some scaly thing that doesn't quite fit anymore. I pull a piece off my cheek and look at the man beneath: soft, vulnerable. I move to put back the missing chink in the armor but stop.

I lied and I'm sorry: I know how to get to Another Place. I've felt the seconds and minutes of Another Time.

My mother told me how.

▶ ‖

She told me about my name's secret meaning.

I cringed. "Hope? Hope is for the unprepared."

I couldn't understand how much that flippant comment hurt her. The way it burrowed deep into her, touching every well of resolve she'd kept deep within herself as our family changed houses, trying to scrape enough money together to stay in one place longer than a couple of months. Walls with photographs or tables with vases—these were luxuries we couldn't afford. We moved too much to pamper ourselves with the trappings of a permanent life. Once, in his kindergarten class, my younger brother said his family lived in a house made of boxes. Our parents had to explain to the concerned teacher he didn't mean it literally. But it was common to have brown moving boxes in every room. I took special pride in being the chief biter of Sellotape when it was time to change houses. My mother cloaked herself in high spirits then, saying we were descended from a nomadic and hopeful people.

"But where are you going if you don't have hope?" My mother appeared untouched by my retort. Only now, years later, do I sense the hurt she concealed in her question, scared her parenting had been found wanting, or that our migration was, in some way, her fault. After all, if hope was for the makers of bad plans, then my parents must have been the only dreamers or fools who couldn't read the signs of trouble back in the Small Country.

We were in my mother's herb garden at the new house, the final one. A fresh salvo of rain had barraged the city, and glass beads of moisture clung to the basil, chives, and parsley—ambitious plants considering the New Country, shouldered between two ancient deserts, wasn't conducive to growing anything at all. It was dry, brown, perennially hard, perpetually tough to survive in. My mother plowed, fertilized, and watered as best as she could. Then she hoped her hard work would be repaid.

"How," my mother queried, reaching down to inspect a leaf, "will you know your way?" She poked her finger in the soil, pinched a clod of dirt, and rubbed her hand on her stained overalls. She smiled at me. "You can prepare as much as you want, as best as you can, and things will still go wrong. Your father and I had big dreams, grand plans—in another place, another time—we prepared as much as we could. Things still went wrong."

I crossed my elbows, defiantly warding off her wisdom. "I know, that's why we're here."

"We are not where we are because we didn't have plans, but because we pushed on when they failed. Even when things were hard, we worked and hoped things would change for us. Things are not the way we thought they would be. They are different. Sometimes different is all you have."

I said the New Country was more than different. It was difficult too.

"So was home. You only yearn for the best bits we told you about. The bad parts we kept for ourselves." She looked around her green and tenacious garden, with my teenage beanpole standing in its middle, defiant and eager to tell her about the workings of the world. "And if you really think about it, this is where you brought us." She looked at me slyly.

"How?"

"This is Another Place, Another Time. We could not have reached it without hope. Without you."

My mother laughed as I walked away, angry that she'd managed to pivot and flank my indignation.

▶ⅠⅠ

I look in the mirror.

Sometimes different is all you have.

I tear off a little more of the old hide and feel the brush of possibility against my skin.

Hope takes you to other places.

I start pulling it off in chunks, exposing my neck and my arms to the harsh world. When I reach my chest, I hesitate. I feel the lure of the coward's path, the hamster wheel I'm trying to escape.

Hope takes you to other times.

I tear off the rest of the old me. I have the power to restart the world.

I go back to the kitchen and reach for my phone.

ONLY STARS KNOW
THE MEANING OF SPACE
(LOVE'S INTERLUDE)

He is a boy, a man, and a poet. I'm forced to take turns being with each one.

I don't tolerate the boy.

I endure the man.

But I love the poet.

He's the one who tells me the arms of the Milky Way spiral outward from us. "Baby," he says, holding my face in his hands, "the planets tilt their axes toward us." He kisses me, a meeting of lips, a communion of souls. When he comes home to me, to our corner of the galaxy, he says time slows down when he's with me. "Like when you read a good book, and the weather outside your window changes without you even realizing it."

The poet says when we're apart he struggles to find his feet:

Lost—

(Like the empty space between line breaks in a poem)
—Eager to continue the sentence that is us.

He writes things like that to me. It's common to find an envelope stuffed with his compositions on my pillow when I go to bed, hidden among my shoes in the early morning before I go to work, or folded into my handbag when I'm shopping. I unfold them and read the neat handwriting, squeeze myself between the stanzas, and revel in my role as muse and girlfriend.

I've been loved by men before. None of them have been artists. To be loved by someone who creates, who does, who tries to communicate his innermost being for a living is akin to being present during the First Seven Days. Can you imagine bearing witness to the awesome powers and the creation of life? It's intoxicating. When the poet writes to me I see his past, his present, and his hopeful future come to a point on his pen.

The poet says: "Baby, you're my true North."

He is South.

Our love spreads out from the furthest East to the westernmost side of West. He says our children will be named after the compass directions of our future travels. "Pick a place," he says, "and we'll go there."

I say I want to go to Ghana and the poet says Ghana is mere geography. "We are gods. Accra-cadabra! We shall see Ghana." His self-assuredness books the flights. His words check in the baggage of our dreams: Thailand (because it's affordable), Colombia (for his beloved Gabo and whatever he believes is awaiting him in Barranquilla), Senegal ("To track down the last of the griots," he says), New Orleans (for the Cajun cuisine and the Creole cool), Montego Bay ("So you can flaunt that *island gyal* body, baby!"—his Jamaican accent isn't on point, but I appreciate the sentiment). "All the lines of longitude and latitude shall know of our love," he says. "Because the world's flat until we go around it."

I mean, come on.

(I asked him, once, why the Small Country in Africa—that's what he calls it—he's from wasn't on the list. He hasn't been back since he left it as a child. He said, quietly and resolutely, that trauma made for a poor visa application. "It's what sent my family traveling. There's no point in going back when forward is all you've ever known." I never asked about his home again. I was too happy and too busy planning a new one for us in what he called the "New Country.")

When we lie in our bed his breath becomes my air, my heartbeat pulses through his veins. He traces his fingers on my navel and swirls the supernovas his touch ignites. He says we're stars, burning far, far away. The poet says we're from the future—"From tomorrow!" Apparently, that's why everything lags behind us, struggling for speed. When he's the poet, I can scarcely keep pace with the worlds he creates. He flits from one vision of the present to a distant sighting of the future. In everything, he says, there is us.

When he says what he says, his brow certain, his voice commanding and coordinating cosmic energies, it's hard not to be in love with him, not to believe like he believes—only a fool would doubt him and I'm no fool.

I'm true North. He's solid and smooth South.

History follows in our wake.

▶II

The man is something else.

He can't escape the physics of his life. The gravity of his failed dreams sucks him down, down, down. He is fearful. He panics when roads branch into the undergrowth. He can't take the lead in such moments and rushes, headless, toward me, his shelter. The man calls me that.

Shelter.

I'm a cave in the woods. A hut on a hill. A cottage by the sea. A house on a street. Just a home. I'm his lodgings. If all I was going to be was an inn for a man tired from his road in life, I'd have had more relationships prior to this one. But I didn't. I saved all my best parts for the poet. Men have come, and men have gone. They've brought me all their inadequate offerings and selves, dented by disappointment and scarred by love. I've turned all of them away.

I'm mad when the man comes home. He says he's happy to see me. He asks about my day, listens with one ear and less than half of his soul. Then, because I'm his shelter, he unzips the costume of his being and reveals himself to be what he is: just a man.

The poet, though, is a lion, astral, not completely of this world.

I wish he could be more poet than man.

But man he mostly is.

▶ ‖

He says: "Look at this."

We're in a mall.

I hate malls. I despise the consumerism cult and the tithe-payers who've come to pray to their capitalist god: shopping. But even poets and their muses are forced to make their heathen pilgrimages to buy food. So we don our clothes, leave our bed where we consume each other endlessly in a sensual ouroboros, and go to stock up on supplies.

"I think we can get this," the man says, holding a pineapple. He looks at the price to make sure it's within our means. I tell him, sure, if he wants it. He hesitates. Then he asks if I want it. I sigh and tell him I do. He drops it in our shopping basket. We move on to complete our shopping and flee this place that invites stares and poorly disguised disapproval. Our union is largely frowned upon even now—especially now. The hopeful promises of color and creed sold by the New Country weren't communicated to those who had to deliver on them. Still, I stand straight. I shoulder the stares. I hold the man's hand defiantly.

He might be a man, but he's my man.

The man doesn't notice anything untoward. He's too lost in his inner cavernous and winding being.

Later, when we're at home, the poet cuts the pineapple into thin slices and puts each one on my tongue with great reverence. He licks a stray strand of juice on my chin like it's ambrosial. He uses his words to undress me, sending flocks of shivers careening down my back. He uses his words to pin me down and prize me open.

—"Mmm . . . like this, baby?"

—"Yeah, just like that."

When he's inside me he says he can see the whole universe, like his telescope can pierce the nebulousness of my soul and see my essence— my God particle. The poet whispers to me with each oar stroke of his body, pulling our boat toward mutual pleasure.

Melamine—push.

Melanie—pull.

Mel—push.

The drumbeat of desire beats a steady tattoo.

He pulls my hair. He grips my thighs and thoughts. He puts me on and off, and when I climb on top and soar to my climax I look down at my territory, taking unbridled pleasure in his submission. When I peak he pulls me to him, to himself.

O, Melamine!

When we descend back to this life and time, I alight on this mortal plane as a goddess only to find him quiet, near tears.

He's a man now.

I lie next to him and wait for him to speak.

I wait and I wait.

The man doesn't use words like the poet. He remains taciturn, sucking in joy from our company, regurgitating space and distance between us.

The poet is loud and brash, uncontainable, lustfully loquacious.

But the man is silent.

So I wait.

▶Ⅱ

I find him standing in our lounge watching the day seep into the evening from the bay window. With the dusk behind him, silhouetting his pondering shape, I can't tell whether he's the poet or the man. Their shapes are the same in the dark. I wait and see which one turns to meet me. He says, when he sees me, "Baby, only stars know the meaning of space."

Ah. The poet.

I ask him what he means by that. He says nothing else in existence shines so as not to be alone. "Can you imagine the distance between you and something else being so vast it's measured in the time it takes for its light to reach you?"

When he's like this it's impossible to know what he's thinking or how he's thinking it. The best thing to do is to wait him out, like the man. The difference, though, is that the poet eventually reveals himself to me, ethereal as he might be; the man echoes silence from his shell.

Then, just as quickly, the stargazing poet becomes the man again.

"What if the light arrives too late? What," the man asks—maybe me, maybe the world—"if the light never arrives at all?"

Sound leaves the room.

I prepare to wait out his loud nothingness. I sustain myself with memories of the poet from a better time, like a desert traveler with a gourd of water ruing the forgotten rain. I try to love the stillness of the man.

I tell myself there's beauty in its bleakness.

And I wait.

▶ ‖

The man is annoying.

He stacks green peppers on the side of his plate and leaves them uneaten. He rubs the bridge of his nose when he's bored—or when I talk to him. He refolds the clothes I've already folded. He moves the picture frames around. He kisses my cheek absentmindedly in the morning when we part for work like my lips weren't on offer. He's the man around his father and brother—callous, calamitous, jonesing for a fight, any quarrel that will show he's the man.

The man is a lesser man around his friends. Even as a man he's a better version of himself when he's with me. There are few things as painful as seeing him drawing margin lines around himself, boxing his star fire so he doesn't burn cockroaches. I tell him this and he looks at me like a man would, accusingly, wounded and ready to hurt. "They're my friends," he says. "I had them before I had you."

The poet would follow that up with, "But now you're my after, and you're all that matters."

Instead, the man says, "You wouldn't understand. We've been through things together. They know me in ways you can never know."

I'm always aware of where I stand with the poet—at the top, front, and center. But with the man, I don't know where I rank. I could be in second place, lapped by any number of anxieties. I could be a last-minute consideration. I could be nothing.

I look at the man and realize I despise him. He's not what I was promised. He's not what the poet promised me when he started the count of our time together.

▶︎‖

I tell the man I want the poet.

Where's my Grecian hero, trained in sword- and wordplay? It's been a while since I've had both. I refuse to let the man make love to me. I refuse to reward his defeat with my desire. It might be easy for him to morph between poet and man and experience the same hungers, but my elemental fires and floods can't be started by the earthborn.

I ask him where the scientist who told me I was the prism through which life is refracted went. I harangue him for an answer. I virago myself to the point where even I ask myself when I became *this* person.

But I persist. I want answers.

"Where," I ask, "is the sage who told me I'm the Final and Hidden Path?"

I'm met, as usual, with reticence.

▶❚❚

The boy wastes my time.

He reminds me of me before I realized I was more, multitudes upon multitudes—more man than man, more woman than both.

I was once a girl.

But girls from my neighborhood have to grow up quickly before they're lied to and made someone's plaything. I became a woman before my time. I wasn't going to blunder from crush to crushed sheets with my whole future hanging in the balance. The stakes were too high. Like Artemis, I fed men who dared to look upon me to their own hounds, and that kept many others at bay for a long while. I decided, long ago, only gods would be given the privilege of my time. Only a titan would touch me.

When I met him he was a boy, forgettable, the kind of boy other people consider amusing company—*just one of the boys*. A boy without a purpose, a boy who thought I was a girl. He quickly found out I wasn't his second childhood. The boy scaled up. The man ascended to my heights. He became the poet, what he should've been all along. What he really was.

267

But the poet can't hold back the darkness of the man. His light fades, and he lapses back into disappointing mortality. He becomes the boy. And I hate the boy. The boy is unsure; he gives up too easily. The boy is full of tantrums, a product of misplaced rage.

The boy misses his mother and somehow blames himself for her loss. The man and the poet do too, but the man, at least, has a miserable dignity about him even I can respect. The man grieves through soft reminiscence, trying so desperately to plug the gaps in his being he didn't have time to fix with his mother's presence. The poet mourns through creation. Even as the void snatches for his strings he weaves new dances for himself—he tinkers with the geometry of grief and creates new shapes and ways of being around himself. The poet is his own flag, and it's amazing to see how he rallies to himself.

The boy simply abandons everything, all hope.

►ΙΙ

"I'd rather have the man," I tell him when we argue about our changing seasons. "But I prefer the poet."

He tells me he is as I find him.

I tell him I'm not willing to settle. It's all or nothing. I tell him he must decide.

I watch the boy listen to me. The poor child says he understands even though I can tell he doesn't. He shape-shifts into the man—his shoulders stiffen, his spine straightens, his raking silence spreads out— and then he says: "If that's what you want, then I'm fine with it."

The man is a coward. He even deflects decisions that would free him from the burden of confronting me.

I prepare my mind and my heart for what needs to be done.

I am my own true North. He is someone's South. He must make his own way.

I leave him and love behind.

▶ ||

At first, we had good times. Then, like everyone else, we had bad times. Then we had more good times than bad, and then we just had a lot of the bad. We thought we were in a better place than most. For a while, even I convinced myself we were balancing things out, doing the best we could with what we had. Then I thought back to what the poet had said: what we had was *us*. We were supposed to be infinite. Only then did I realize I wasn't the man's all-powerful deity. I was merely a temple, a shelter, a haven for the ritual of romance.

I couldn't accept that. I had to leave.

But if you'd met the poet you'd understand why I kept going back.

You see, it was *the man* who broke up with me. I was certain *the poet* had a different answer.

▶ ||

Once, with the poet, I said I wanted to change my job. He told me to change it. "Everything around you will expand and stretch to accommodate it." The poet saw the possibility in all things.

Another time I said we were a good thing and he said: "Baby, we're that good-good that's so bad." He had this way of making me feel like we were the best thing that happened to each other. No matter who you are—girl, woman, other—you can't help but be validated by words and action like that.

I said we needed to think about the future—our life together, apart from everyone else—and the man scrambled for safety in praxis. The boy spurted childish fears of the risk—the size of the loss if we put our luck and love on the wrong number.

"On the wrong color?" I mocked him. "On the wrong day? I thought you said fortune was our domain." I was angry. I shouted for the poet. Maybe I shouldn't have.

But he became the man. The man became the boy. The boy ran away.

▶ ❚❚

The poet and I orbit each other for some time as we try to detach. We manage it for a while but we're eventually drawn to each other's gravity by desperation and desire.

"Maybe our destiny," I say in the fleeting aftermath of my latest attempt to resurrect the poet within the man. I tell him about us being stars. "Raw beauty, pure light from another place, another time."

All he says is "Hmm."

Maybe the poet was right. Perhaps our light is so distant it's already gone.

Maybe we're already in another place, another time.

I leave.

▶ ❚❚

We collide, many times, in a spray of sheets and sighs and sorries.

We separate with swear words, tears, and more silence.

I leave again.

Our paths peel themselves apart. I fly toward the compass directions the poet said we'd explore together.

The man goes toward himself. I hope.

▶II

I see Ghana. I see the slave castles, hollow with memory. I walk down to the coast, where my toes are caressed by the seductive kiss of the Atlantic Ocean. I pull back.

This ocean knows the taste of black bodies! the poet would have said.

That night, a boy at the beach club ventures up to me. I let him kiss me but go no further because of the shame of it all. *I'm letting boys kiss me.* I'm so far outside myself anyone thinks they can get in. When I go to sleep I think of the poet and the distance between us, about us shining but not shining together.

Only stars know the meaning of space.

I cry in my bed.

▶II

I visit Kenya and Tanzania, where I'm pursued by boys and men. I'm big game. But their walls are too small for me to hang my pride so they can mount me as their prize.

▶II

I see Mozambique, a country of land, sea, and air. In Maputo, at a party I'm invited to, I make out with a man and let him feel parts of me no one has felt in a long time. He calls me his *carinho* and begs to be with me. Only boys beg. I would've been willing to give myself over to a man.

"*Tudo bem, foda-se. Não é como se você fosse tão bonita assim!*" he shouts at me when I leave him to go back to the hotel.

▶ ‖

I book a getaway to Thailand with a girlfriend.

I kiss a stranger at a bar. He's no poet, just a man who's happy to be a man. We don't have sex bordering on suicide, just the surgical doling out of pleasure. He asks me how he did when he's done.

"You did well, baby," I say. Men like to hear that.

The poet never asked me such trivialities. He knew my rhythms. He conjured up my waves and rode them like an ocean master.

However fiercely they rage,
However long they blow,
I was built for your storms.

The poet, again. I'm thinking about how well he knew my body, and how I knew his. Even his shadow could scorch.

I'm in Asia, thinking of poetry from a supposed-to-be-forgotten poet.

A deep want vibrates within me as I lie beside the other man, sated and soon to be asleep. I arouse him with my body and take him again and again, trying to fill the gnawing need inside me with him, but he isn't enough. I tire him and leave his place in the early morning, with him still stumbling through slumber.

272

I wonder if the poet has found someone else. Whether he has settled on a way of being.

Is he a man?

Or a boy?

Is he someone else's world?

▶ ‖

Another girlfriend offers me a couch in Costa Rica.

We visit the beaches and the bars. We take pictures at the La Paz Waterfall Gardens and the Ruinas de la Parroquia, and post thoughtful captions about them on our Instagram profiles. A Latin jazz orchestra performs at the Teatro Nacional—a sound that tempts my body to move. In the evenings we go dancing and manhunting.

Even on the other side of the world, I think about the poet. I think about him when I'm under the man who moans in Spanish when he expends himself. I think about the poet when I'm with the man who uses his tongue so roughly I have to shiver myself into a lie to make him stop. I push him off when our rhythms don't match and put on my clothes as he apologizes and asks, "*¿Qué pasa, hice algo mal?*" I leave his place, slightly embarrassed.

Even when I'm with my friend, who's gentle with me, letting me explore her form and mine, I think of the poet. When we lie next to each other, with her arm across my breasts, she looks at me and says: "He must've been something." She'd asked me about him.

I tell her the poet was everything. He was, like everyone else, fighting this losing battle against life, but he did it with such verve. He swaggered away from defeats without suffering loss. He was generous with his victories. He loved me with passion, he loved me with constancy, he loved me because I loved him. "I was more," I say, "and together we were the most."

The rest of the trip is awkward since the poet's absence is always between us. I can never completely shut him out, even when my friend makes me feel things only she can. I find that love molds you to your person and makes it impossible for anyone else to fit inside you. They either spill over or do not fill you up at all.

At the airport, I kiss my friend goodbye and she says: "Good luck harnessing the wind and capturing the sun." I ask her what she means and all she says is I know what I have to do. She says I should either give up the poet completely or reclaim him and be done with it. I fly back home with the truth nibbling at my ears.

However fiercely they rage,
However long they blow . . .

▶ ||

I ring a familiar number.

The man picks up the phone.

I ask how he is and I receive bland answers in return. We synchronize our speech. We bruise each other with the familiarity of our flagrant youth. We talk and then stutter into silence. I try to draw the poet but feel the man's new walls. Wherever the poet is, he's beyond my reach.

The man is careless with his words. He hurts me with what he thinks is kindness. He says closure is a fool's hope.

I'm a fool now.

I cry and hang up.

▶II

Silence.

▶II

Space.

▶II

Stars.

▶II

My phone rings.

He says he's coming over.

He shows up at my place. I heat up, ready to throw myself in his flames.

I ask him where he is in life because one thing I have learned about men is they're either coming from or going to someone else and my peace has always depended on knowing which is which. I tell him I'm no middle ground. I'm not a haven for heartbreak. I'm not a transit lounge for a man waiting for a plan. I'm not some port for pause, for pleasure and plunder.

He says he's come to wrangle comets with his bare hands.

I ask him why.

Why me?

Why now?

"Because, baby, only stars know the meaning of space," he says, his voice firm, reaching out to me without a single trace of the man or boy lurking behind his eyes. "And space is boring."

I look at him.

Not boy. Not man. Not poet.

Just him.

I see him for the first time.

And I love him.

SOFA, SO GOOD, SORT OF
(OR, JOHN MUAFANGEJO)

THE OTTOMAN AND HIS LIEUTENANT

The ottoman in our lounge marked us as a family on the rise. We were the family who could afford a piece of furniture which served no particular purpose. Everyone else had rickety wooden stools which rocked under their weight, sun-beaten plastic garden chairs with scratches, and ugly sectional leather pieces they bought on lay-by at extortionate interest rates which took months—sometimes years—to pay off from Ellerines, Beares, Lewis, and that one uncle in the furniture business.

But we had a lovely ottoman my father paid for in cash, a low, gray, almost-chair, not-quite-table thing. It didn't match any of the other pieces in the lounge but I think that was the point. Our family had reached that sought-for stage of life where nothing had to match. We were, finally, a family with options. We were not constricted by our choices. We lived with them like equal neighbors, not in fear of them.

My father could walk into a shop and ask about a lovely sky-blue two-seater my mother liked or a coffee-brown wingback armchair he fancied, and when the price was given to him he didn't flinch or ask when the shop closed, lying that he'd come back later with money. He was the kind of man for whom stores would open a bit longer even if all he was doing was browsing. The gray flecks in his hair made the salespeople take him seriously—black men with just a bit of white in or on them are quite commanding. To polish off his imperious demeanor he had a broad-shouldered walk with a measured pace. When he walked it looked like time itself yielded the right of way to him. My mother said it was one of the things which drew her to him. "He walks like his destination rushes to meet him," she said.

When I went with him to the furniture store—this big, wide warehouse—the aisles seemed to part for him, bringing us to the lounge furniture section manned by a man named Darrell. He greeted my father politely. My father greeted him as well and swept past him toward the suites and sets.

My father's soft and severely formal English spoke of a strict upbringing in the equatorial tropics, up where the *sapeurs* flooded the dirty, trash-strewn streets with their riotous and outrageous costumes, strutting down smelly alleys to crowded markets and bars, clad in the most ostentatious jackets, trousers, ties, and socks. Coupled with his deep voice and the francophone lilt that would be the legacy of Leopold's ghost, my father's English made cashiers and tellers stand up straight when he asked them a question. It made floor managers in department stores skittish, unsure of his station in life in relation to theirs. Was he a Big Man? Could he somehow change the trajectory of their lives for the worst if they displeased him? Was he able to

278

have someone fired if they didn't know whether a particular trouser size was available or when the avocados would be in stock again? My father's voice was the waiter's bane. They could never tell whether he was asking a question or compelling them to do something. It was the "no" he added to the ends of questions. It seemed to suggest the possibility of a contrary opinion while simultaneously ruling out such a notion. Even I could never tell if he was vexed by something I did. For example, I'm not sure whether he was displeased by my choice to quit soccer and swat tennis balls in the middle of high school. "This is the sport you have chosen, no?" he said. I hesitantly said yes. He took me to choose my rackets the next day. To this day I'm not sure he approves of what I studied at university.

—"Literature? You are sure it is what you want, no?"

—"Err, yes?" *No. Wait, what?*

My father had that effect on people. The only one who ever seemed to know what he was saying was my mother.

Darrell, the salesperson in the furniture section, seemed to know how to handle clients like my father. He hung back, kept quiet, let him sit down on the sofas, watched him stretch his legs and lean back. My father moved from set to set, never saying anything. I shadowed him, following this man full of choices and decisions and tastes I couldn't fathom. At the last lounge set my father spied the ottoman.

He looked at it curiously and then he sat on it. His back was straight as a mast and his hands were on the knees of his dark blue trousers. He sat like that for a minute or so in silence. Darrell stood nearby. I kept sentinel watch over the scene. My father hated interruptions when he was deep in thought, like when he was reading his newspapers or his French classics in his study or listening to Chopin.

He once said silence was golden but every other precious metal or gemstone screamed and that's what made them cheap. Gold, he said, never had to explain what it was because everyone knew its essence, its longevity, and its power.

I was determined to be a golden child. I watched my father sit on his gray throne surrounded by his auric silence. Then he made a deep sound in his chest, like a purr, which meant he approved. Later, I'd hear that sound whenever he scanned my flawless report card, or whenever I climbed into the car with a trophy or a medal or a certificate. He'd make the same sound at my graduation many years later.

My father asked Darrell for the ottoman's price. Darrell said it was not an individual piece, it was part of the lounge set.

"No, I only want this one," my father said.

"Sir?"

"I only want this one, no? How much will it be, Mr. Darrell?"

Darrell did the right thing and excused himself to fetch the manager. My father continued sitting on the ottoman. He beckoned me to sit in the gray two-seater across from him. When the manager arrived, he was friendly and smooth. He tried to butter up my father but barely made it past the crust of his inquiries.

"The price of the other items in the set can be calculated, no? Then I would like to know the price of this one. It is the one I want. You can add a markup for the inconvenience," my father said. He remained seated, hands on his knees, with the manager standing in front of him and Darrell just off to the side. The manager looked at the ottoman for a bit and then he quoted a price, tentatively, looking at my father to see if he was near or far from the money. My father looked at him impassively and said he would pay the price plus fifty percent for the trouble. The manager was silent for a while. Darrell coughed.

"Are you sure you don't want something else for that amount of money, sir?" the manager asked. "Something more, err, substantial?"

"This is what I want, no?"

The manager looked to Darrell and then to me but I couldn't offer any help. I was doing my best to keep earning those seen-but-not-heard points.

"Yes. Of course, sir," the manager said.

"Splendid," my father said. He stood up and from the manager's expression I could tell he was surprised by the sudden height of the man, how he went from sitting to standing tall in one blink-and-miss-it movement. My father extended his hand, and the manager shook it with what must have been a hastily spoon-beaten mix of respect and fear. "And you will make sure Mr. Darrell will get the commission, no?" My father held on to the manager's hand as he shook it slowly.

"Yes, of course," the manager replied.

"Thank you, sir," my father said. He released the manager.

At the payment counter my father inquired about the precise time of delivery, a time many people wouldn't be given. Most people would be told "sometime today or maybe tomorrow." But the manager, who insisted on ringing up the purchase himself, said, "We'll be at the house at two o'clock this afternoon, sir." It was a Saturday. The shop would've been closed for an hour by then.

The first time Aunt Margaret, my mother's sister, saw the ottoman, she asked what it was. "Is it for putting your feet up?"

"No," my mother replied. "He would be angry if you did that."

"Is it a table of some sort?" My mother said it was an ottoman. "A what?"

"It's for sitting on," I piped up. "Daddy got it."

Aunt Margaret looked at the ottoman dubiously. Wider and longer than a coffee table but not long enough to lie on; lower than a stool but not as comfortable, no backing for support, and the upholstery material looked quite expensive. She shrugged in the way she did when she came to our house and encountered some new trapping of modernity she couldn't fathom. "Rich-people things," she said.

She said the same thing about the two forks and two knives thing, which was confusing even for me—"Rich-people things!"—and the pictures on the walls which were not of distant and close relatives celebrating weddings, christenings, and graduations. There were some paint splatters in black frames, some photographs of a bleak, desert landscape, and some rare woodcut prints. "So this is what they call art," she said when my mother gave her a tour of our new house, "rich-people things."

Looking at the ottoman, Aunt Margaret did what people without money do when they encounter something outside of their financial comprehension. She steered well clear of it like it was a dangerous animal crouching in the lounge, liable to spring up and savage her.

The ottoman sat like a jewel in our living room empire of custom-made or eccentrically chosen furniture, like a marquee conquest of some sort. Of all the furnishings in the room, I think my father liked it best, even more than his armchair, which throned him like a sinister science fiction villain.

Maybe he liked the ottoman's color or its shape. I could never tell. But he loved to sit on it, with his back straighter than straight and his hands on his knees. One day I asked him why he liked it so much and he gave me the same look he gave me when my mathematics average fell into the shameful percentages, the one he called *la parfum de la moyenne*. He said, "You would not understand. You have never been home."

I said, "But, Daddy, this is home."

And he said, simply, dismissing me, "That is why you would not understand."

DADDY'S ARMCHAIR

In my house, when I was growing up, you could sit anywhere except Daddy's armchair. You could park your butt in the five-seater or the other armchairs. You could even sit on the coffee table if you wanted to, but my mother would give you a stern look that would make you move your bottom off the square of sturdy oak and welded metal. You could sit at the dining room table when you were busy with homework, but when it was time to eat you had to remove your books so the surface could be decorated with Malagasy print mats and plates without chips or cracks and cutlery that reflected the light. If you really, really, really wanted you could even sit on the floor, but you had to do it when my mother was not around—if she saw you, she gave you an even sterner look because you'd be shaming their struggles and diligent provision of their children's needs.

You couldn't sit in Daddy's armchair. Not when he was around, because that was just plain disrespectful, and not even when he was away, because that'd be akin to pronouncing yourself heir to some supposedly vacant throne. I did it once when I was little, and my mother bustled into the lounge and shooed me out of it. "Your father isn't dead," she said by way of explanation.

Even when he was away my father's aura hovered around the house, ensuring rooms remained neat and arranged and his study stayed locked and private. You could feel his presence in the house when he was on the other side of the world, in New York, in Rio de Janeiro, in Sydney, or in Manila conducting his pharmaceutical procurement lectures. The smell of him lingered in the house. I am certain my mother sprayed some of his cologne in the house's rooms whenever he was away, like it was a holy fragrance that would ward off evil and keep the forces of distance and separation at bay until he returned to us and to her. I teased my mother about that when I was much older, when I could finally say something smart about the world. I said, once, when I walked into the house—my father was away in one of those -tan countries in Asia on some conference—that she had a hard time "decolonizing her mind." She laughed and said, "You idiot. What do you know of such things?"

If my father was away and guests came to visit us, my mother graciously welcomed them with hugs, double-cheek kisses, and trays of juice and snacks. She ushered them into the living room, where they'd take their seats. All of them avoided sitting in Daddy's armchair. Even if seating was running low, no one would sit in it. I remember thinking that the armchair was endowed with mystic powers only my father could harness. Maybe the seat permitted him to look far into the future; perhaps it was a conduit for some hidden power only he could harness. I imagined there would come a day when my father would relinquish the seat to me like Jean-Luc Picard while he went away to dispense wisdom about ethical and sustainable medicinal purchasing processes. For a while, I'd be in charge of steering our family to frontier worlds far beyond this one.

Nobody sat in Daddy's armchair except Trevor.

We were supposed to work on a science project, building a scale model of the planets. Before we could vanish to the privacy of my room, my mother insisted, as she always did when any of us brought our friends over, on detaining us in the lounge for a prying conversation. I had, for my part, done my best to explain his backstory to her so the questioning wouldn't have to be longer than necessary.

"He's at my school. His father is a businessman—no, I don't know what kind of business—and his mother is a lawyer. Trevor's a cool guy. He's white," I said by way of summary.

I hoped that would satisfy her before Trevor arrived, but I really couldn't be sure. The scope, depth, or duration of the maternal inquisitions was known only to one person: my mother. Once, Franco, one of my friends, answered questions about his parents' occupations, where his grandparents came from, what his older sisters were studying at university—"Medical microbiology? That sounds interesting. Tell me, do they find it challenging to be in such a male-dominated field? Oh, you haven't asked them. Well, that is a pity, isn't it?"—and what he wanted to study after high school for an hour. After those sixty minutes of excruciating inquiry Franco kept his visits to my house to the barest minimum.

Trevor had heard of my mother's interrogation sessions and, to be honest, he wasn't really keen to come over, but his parents were going through a divorce and his house was a war zone with either parent using anything within sight as ammunition against the other:

---

the family's flagging finances; Trevor's younger sister and her bipolar disorder; Trevor's poor report; the school trips that were canceled because either parent refused to pay for them, stating it was the other's responsibility, and then using Trevor's subsequent disappointment at not being included in trips as evidence of the other parent's disregard for his happiness. Even Trevor's friends who looked like they were the offspring of a happy and ongoing marriage were hors d'oeuvres for drama. I went over to his place once and his mother asked me how long my parents had been together, and I, not knowing the lay of the land—this was in the early days, when the news of the divorce hadn't yet done the rounds—said they'd been together since before I was born. Their marriage was a couple of years older than the republic of our relocation. Thinking I was being asked to provide testimony of my parents' love for each other, I said, "They've been through every thin and now they're getting fat together in the thick of things."

What did Trevor's mom say?

"That's very sweet, dear. Your father stayed true even where others wavered. There's a joke for you. Trevor's father and I are going to fizzle out without so much as a struggle. That's got to be some kind of irony, right? You understand what I mean, right?"

We decided my house was a better place to finish our project after that.

As soon as we entered my house my mother swooped down on Trevor and pulled him into one of her bosom-mashing hugs. She walked him to the lounge and told him to take a seat. She'd be back with some drinks. She shouted to my father in his study that I had a guest. My mother called me into the kitchen and asked what Trevor wanted to drink and I said juice and when I came back into the lounge

I was carrying a tray with some orange juice and a glass for him. My father was coming out of the study at the same time and my mother was behind me.

Trevor was sitting in my father's chair.

In Daddy's armchair!

My mother exclaimed sharply and I could feel my father focus his terrible attention on Trevor. My father crossed the lounge quickly. Trevor stood up to shake hands with him.

"You are Trevor, no?"

"Yes, sir."

The two of them unclasped hands. My father ushered him into a seat but Trevor missed the cue and sat back down in my father's chair.

("Again?" Franco was shocked. "Yo, that white dude was tripping, man.")

My mother breathed so loudly I was scared her adenoids would have to be checked out. I made Morse-code eyes at Trevor—*Get! Out! Of! The! Seat!*—but he didn't seem to understand my meaning. My father remained standing and looked down at Trevor.

"You are in my seat," he said curtly.

There was no "no" at the end.

Trevor looked at the seat, then at the three of us standing, me still with the tray, eyes pleading, and did some mathemagic. He shot right out of Daddy's armchair. My father sat down. I put the tray on the coffee table. My mother sat in the other armchair next to my father's. I gestured to Trevor to sit with me on the five-seater.

Perhaps because of the impropriety my mother didn't ask Trevor the usual game show questions which tested his general knowledge and, therefore, determined his place in my parents' intellectual solar system. As far as they were concerned, he was way out of their radiant benevolence, further than Charon, a rock of such insignificance to them they felt no need to lavish their curiosity upon him. "Well, we should let you get on with your project, no?" my father commanded.

"Yes, sir."

When I closed the door to my bedroom I breathed out deeply. Later, at supper, I would have to answer questions. There'd be a long talk about white people and how they invaded spaces.

"Dude," Trevor said, "was it just me or was it hella weird down there?" He threw his backpack on my bed and followed it.

"Both."

"But why?" he asked.

"My father's not dead, Trev. If you sit in his chair, you kill him." I opened my science file and turned to the worksheet with the sizes of the planets and the compositions of their atmospheres.

"Wait, I don't get it," Trevor said, "didn't your parents study in Europe and stuff?"

"Paris."

"And they, like, travel and stuff. I mean, your dad gets a new passport every month."

"So?"

"So how can they still believe things like that?"

"It's hard to explain," I said. "It's just who they are." He didn't seem satisfied with the answer. "Look, Trev, you can be old-school and new-school at the same time. It doesn't hurt me so I just let them have their strange ways."

"Yeah, I get that. Even my parents slip into the *plaas taal* every once in a while when they're stressed out. But mine don't hang on to all that stuff."

"Talk shit, Trev. Twenty bucks says your mother freaked the fuck out when Lezaan came over for supper. No way the idea of *kroeshare* in her gene pool sat well with her."

"Okay, she did a little. But then she got over it."

"So she said." I fetched the box of models from the cupboard. I handed him Mars. I'd work on Neptune.

"They don't actually believe your dad's going to die because I sat in the chair, right?" I kept quiet. "Do they?"

"You know," I replied, "I actually don't know."

"But why?" he asked. "Why would they choose to believe that?"

"Because it probably reminds them of home."

"Isn't this your home, bro?"

"That's tricky to answer, Trev."

THE LOVE SEAT

The theater lights have just been turned off when my girlfriend and I walk in. We're just in time. The trailers are about to start. *I hate missing the trailers.* My girlfriend knows how much I hate that so she fretted the whole time when we stood in the popcorn queue waiting to be served. If we missed the trailers or, worse, missed the start of the film, it would be her fault. I didn't reply to her when she sent me the text message saying she had to drop her mother off at the shops twenty minutes before the film started. When she rushed up the stairs to the cinema floor, apologizing for arriving late, she tried to hug and kiss me but I turned away and said, "Let's just get the popcorn."

We look for our seats.

J . . . I . . . H . . .

"G—this is us," I whisper.

1 . . . 2 . . . 3 . . . 4 . . . 5 . . . 6 . . .

"We're seven."

Our seat is taken. A small child in the row behind us whispers to his mother that he can't see the screen.

"You're in our seat," I say.

"Oh, yeah?"

"Yes, you are. This is G seven."

"Are you sure?"

I take out my phone and turn on the flashlight. I show them the tickets. The man turns to his partner and then back to me. "Do you mind if we sit here?" he asks. "You can have the seats next to us."

The first trailer is playing: a period drama—the kind of thing my girlfriend used to like before she met me.

"It's okay," my girlfriend says. She puts a hand on my shoulder. The pressure asks if it is okay to move on. The pressure *hopes* we'll move on. I shrug off her hand.

"You're in *our* seat," I say.

"Come on, man, there're so many empty seats in the cinema—"

"Mommy, I can't see!"

"Sorry to disturb, but the film's going to start soon and if you don't mind—"

"—then you can take any of the empty seats," I say. "Or you can take the seats you paid for. But you can't have our seat."

The next trailer: a nameless animation with a forgettable plot-line. Disney is trying to cash in on everyone's desire for the good old days.

"Come on, our drinks are already out."

"Mommy!"

"Excuse me, could you just—"

"Then take your drinks and your popcorn and move on to the next seat," I say. "I really don't mind sitting next to you. I just don't want to sit on top of you."

"Mommy, can you tell them to—"

"Really now, my son can't—"

"Jeez, buddy, it's just a seat. We're all watching the same film."

"Listen, ma'am, your son will see the screen as soon as I'm seated, thank you." I look at the couple in our seats pointedly.

The last trailer is playing: a spy thriller I've already seen thanks to high-definition leaks and fast bandwidth.

"Let's just sit somewhere else," my girlfriend says.

"No," I say. "I want *our* seat."

The cinema screen is dark. The aisle lights are dimmed. A familiar drumming and trumpeting heralds the start of the film.

"Let's just move," the man's partner says. "I don't understand why these people—"

"Which people?"

"Just drop it," my girlfriend pleads.

"No, I want to know which people she's referring to."

The man and his partner take their drinks and their popcorn and shuffle down the aisle to a safe distance.

"Thank you," I say. The man answers with a familiar swear word. "You too, buddy!"

The film's title floats onto the screen and then fades into the darkness. My girlfriend and I sit down and place our drinks in the cup holders.

"Was that really necessary?" she asks.

I turn in my seat. "Ma'am, tell your child not to kick my seat. Thank you." I turn back to my girlfriend. "Of course it was worth it. This is the only love seat in the whole cinema."

The film starts playing.

I reach for her hand and hold it. It is limp. After a couple of seconds, she returns the pressure, slightly.

THE STROKE THAT BROKE THE CAMELBACK

Her hands grip the backing, her knees are spread apart on the cushions, and her back is bent like a flexicurve. The black vines of ink snake from the inside of her left hip and around to the middle of her lower back in intricate swirls and whorls of tribe unknown. I used to tease her about them in our early exchanges. I might've used the word *cliché* to describe them more than once. Now, in this position, they ripple, fold, and mesmerize like tiger stripes passing through the undergrowth. Earlier, when she sat on my lap, my hands caressed the puckered skin left by the needlework under her dress. I called them sexy as she breathed into my mouth and pulled on my lower lip. My fingers felt the edges of her panties' elastic, gently, inquiring about whether they were ready to come off.

I hold the back of her neck with my left hand and use my right to keep her waist in position. She has new ink on her neck, a quote from Camus. Dead center between her shoulder blades is the tattoo I hate the most, the one I called the fault in her stars when we first met: a stylized scorpion in a smooth black ring which holds her worldview in its pincers.

Scorpios are resourceful. True. "Who goes to the movies without a big handbag?" she asked. "How do you sneak your own food in?"

Scorpios are sensual. So, so true. "We have to try this new massage oil. It's got a herb oil that's an aphrodisiac." (Like I ever needed help to get going when she was around.)

Scorpios are stubborn. Only facts here. "Just say you were wrong, and I was right," she said after an argument that flamed and smoldered for days.

Scorpios are not compatible with Geminis. Hmm. Perhaps.

But here she is.

Again.

When her neck becomes too sweaty I place both hands on her waist for better purchase, gripping until I feel the pelvic bones. I plant my feet, lean back, and thrust harder. I chance a look down at the perfect collision of our movements. I can feel the pinch of pleasure at my tip, running away from me and into her. It's just a few inches out of reach. I strain to touch it, feeling for it further and deeper within her. The chair rocks on its back legs. My search for the elusive sensation flushes out its quarry. She shivers uncontrollably and lets out a wail that's both lewd and forlorn. I rush to join her and hurl myself over the finish line. The camelback tips over and deposits us on the floor. I manage to angle myself to the side so my full weight does not collapse on her. She swears. Then she laughs, deep, throaty. I laugh too.

Slowly, we untangle ourselves from each other, taking deep breaths, our chests going up and down like bellows. She stands up first. I follow. We look at each other naked, from the toes all the way up. We don't make eye contact. I right the sofa in one easy movement. It's cheap, poorly constructed, prone to fall over when too much weight is placed on the backing. She reaches beneath the couch for her panties. Her shape as she bends one leg to put on her underwear, with her vertebrae poking through her smooth, shining skin, stirs deep memories of watching her as she dressed for work, with me still lying in the covers, reluctant to face the day. I once told her the sight of a woman dressing is more erotic than a woman undressing. The way everything is covered up, all the inches of skin vanishing behind their armor. It's like watching a sunset slowly yield its empire to the territories of night, the last few slivers of sunlight are the saddest and the most hopeful. Perhaps tomorrow it will shine again.

As I squeeze into my jeans, adjusting my boxer shorts, she pulls down her halter-neck summer dress, the final curtain fall. She squeezes her bra into her handbag and adjusts the dress over her breasts. The movement beneath the fabric, the curvature I know that lies beneath, makes me look away. She has another tattoo underneath her left breast, on her ribs: the Death of Rats. It was another jealousy trigger for me because its location made me think of a stranger being that close to her, touching her, putting his mark on her forever.

I put on my T-shirt and stretch. She sits back down on the couch. I join her.

We look at each other and laugh again. When we stop she rubs her face like she is performing *tayammum*, cleansing herself of the last hour of wistful recollection which led to the lusty resurrection of regret. She looks like she's wiping the last two days of calls and carefully negotiated forgiveness from her mind, like she's determined to erase her breach of the unilateral request for silence from the record of time. I try to smile kindly at her, hoping it doesn't come across as smug.

She reaches into her bag and pulls out some hair ties. Her hair is whisked into a topknot. Then she fishes in her bag for her lip gloss and applies a light sheen. She takes a deep breath and says, "Well."

She stands up. I stand up too. She makes her way to the door. I follow her, barefoot, the cold tiles beneath echo the mood change in my flat. When I open the door for her she says, "Don't call me again."

I look at her, at the hoop in her tragus she talked about getting for months, the Thailand-bronzed skin on her slender neck, and her fiery brown eyes alight with a fire.

"I'm not the one who called," I say.

She walks out and stands in the hallway, searching for her car keys in her bag. She finds them somewhere near the bottom. "Next time don't answer," she says.

I sigh and say I won't.

"Please," she says, "don't."

CHESTERFIELD SLEEP

My friend and his wife let me crash on their couch while I looked for a new place. I let my girlfriend keep the old place. She was losing a lot in losing me. It would've been too cruel to evict her too. My friend and his wife didn't pry with their questions. They didn't ask me what the plan was. They didn't insist on action. Instead they opened their bijou apartment—which also housed their fledgling marriage—to me. The Chesterfield their parents gave them wasn't the most comfortable of beds but it certainly was the most expensive I'd ever slept on. My friend said he was always around if I wanted to talk but I think he was secretly pleased I didn't.

On some days I lay on the Chesterfield in silence with my arm covering my face, and when they found me like that, they tiptoed past me, trying to stir their tea or coffee without hitting the sides of their mugs. Sometimes, I cloaked myself in melancholy just to see what new ways they'd come up with to play the good and understanding hosts.

My friend's wife was phenomenal in the kitchen. She cooked without carbs and liked the same shows I did. When we sat down for supper my friend was always a step or two behind in the pop-culture ping-pong. He used to do the washing-up before I moved in; I displaced him from his duty. While I ran some hot water into the kitchen sink and got started on the plates, he watched news on the television. His wife joined him on the couch, where they talked about the goings-on of their days in quiet voices. I tried my best not to intrude at such times. When I was done washing up, I walked out onto the balcony to give them their space.

I offered to chip in with the rent, but they waved my money away. "It's no good to us," my friend said. "Anyway, we're the ones who should be paying for your presence. Remember us when you're famous."

I bought them expensive groceries, the organic stuff. One night, at supper, while eating giant turkey drumsticks with a spinach, spring onion, carrot, and red pepper stir-fry I'd made, my friend's wife said I'd always been good at choosing birds. I flinched and she said sorry. I said it was okay even though it wasn't.

I was actually a little thankful for her remark. It showed me it was time to leave. Proximity breeds callousness and my prolonged duration had upset their routines. I hadn't been staying with them for long but the strain I placed upon their marriage was palpable. My presence cut short their marital gossip time, when couples should be together talking about everyone else, finding assurance in lying that they're not like other couples. They muffled and subdued their lovemaking out of respect for me lying loveless on their couch. I saw how they debated which film to watch, carefully choosing short ones so they could let me sleep. They included me in their plans. Shopping trips, long walks, their Pilates classes, and going to see their respective in-laws. I tagged along sometimes. Other times I told them to go on without me. I used the time alone to look for a new place. When they returned home, I told them about my progress or failure and they said there was no rush for me to move out.

When I found my place, I took them out for supper at a nice restaurant, the kind that came with a waiting list stretching back to the day I was born, even though it had only been around for a couple of months. When the waiter came with the bill my friend tried to pay. I told him no. "Your money's no good to me, man," I said.

When we arrived back at their place, we toasted my last night on their couch. He said, once more, that I really didn't have to rush moving. They loved having me around. Plus, who'd keep the apartment clean now that I'd be leaving?

I told them it was time I moved out. I needed my own space. I needed to get back to my things hiding in storage. They offered to help me move and I told them I'd let them know if I need help.

The next morning, I asked another friend for his *bakkie* and made the move by myself.

My new place was worth less than I was paying for it. There were no distinct borders between the lounge and the bedroom. The agent said the apartment was "dynamic," which, apparently, was what all the young people were looking for these days. "Flexible spaces for flexible lifestyles," she said. (But anchored in rigid rental contracts: first of each month first thing and a deposit as large as a dowry.) The bathroom and the kitchen had their own individualized spaces and the balcony didn't face the right direction to see the sunsets. I signed the lease papers anyway because I needed a start. It wasn't a grand start, but it was something.

Moving into my apartment wasn't hard since I didn't have much to move. I'd like to say I was a minimalist, but minimalism meant being rich enough to go without. I simply went without. I carried my single bed and my writing desk up in the elevator on separate trips. When I carried my bookshelf through the corridor, I met a Cameroonian who insisted on helping me.

"My brother," he said, "you're strong, but two together are stronger." Before he left, he said if I needed help of any kind I should just knock on his door.

I unpacked my books, my board games, my wide-screen monitor, my console with its controllers and games, slowly, trying to find the best place for everything. I reverently put my mother's guinea fowl painting on the shelf above my books. In time I'd buy a coffee table and another bookshelf.

My friend and his wife asked for a picture of my place. They said a friend of theirs was selling a camelback that'd look good in the lounge. Maybe, my friend said, when the place was fully furnished, I could have a housewarming party. I said I'd think about it even though I hate having people over. There would be no housewarming party.

While I was busy rearranging my books on the shelves my father called me to ask how the move was going. I told him my place suited my needs, that the lounge needed a decent couch. He said he wanted to get rid of the five-seater at home. I could have it. I asked him why. He said he wanted to move things around like the vases and get some new pieces for the walls.

"There are not that many people living in the house anymore," he added matter-of-factly.

My throat tightened and then I relaxed. The unspoken loss passed. I was learning.

We were all learning. Even he was. He was adjusting to the changes, willing to move with time instead of fighting it. I told him I'd take the five-seater.

I asked how he was doing.

He said, "Sofa, so good. Sort of."

A joke my mother made when we first moved to the new house in the new neighborhood, when she realized permanency was going to be part of our lives. No more flight, no more fleeing—a new home, a new hope.

She insisted on getting new furniture. They could afford it. My parents had looked at each other. *They could afford new furniture.* A shiny fridge with a water and ice dispenser, a slick gas stove, kitchenware in all colors of the rainbow. They could even afford private-school fees.

When the five-seater was delivered she lay on it. My father asked her how they were doing and with a smile she looked up at him said, "Sofa, so good." Then she laughed and said, "Sort of."

Hearing him echo her made me laugh-cry. I told him, gently, that I needed to finish making my place habitable. He said he'd call later. Before he hung up, he said, "You also want the ottoman, no?" I nearly dropped the phone. "Your mother hated it. I'm getting rid of it. It's yours if you want it. Let me know when you want to come and get it."

JOHN MUAFANGEJO

It's a few minutes to midnight. I'm sitting at my writing desk, flicking through my diary, looking for a particular page. I find it. The words are written in big, black block letters. I put a thick border around them and then I go over the letters again, making them bolder and blacker, the texture of the page changing as my pen adds new layers of ink.

I look at the desideratum of the present, of the past, of the future. The words from the linocut print I keep on my phone: *Hope and optimism in spite of present difficulties.*

I say it once—the hope.

I sent the words to my girlfriend earlier when she asked if we could work again. I decided we would.

I say it twice—as a prayer.

John Muafangejo's words for the New Country. My mother's favorite words from her favorite linocut print. She said maybe that is why we moved all the way here, just to find these words.

Then I say it a third time, loudly—the anthem.

The spell is cast.

It is midnight.

My phone buzzes with messages from Lindo, Rinzlo, and Cicero.

—*My guy! Happy birthday!*

—*Thirty? Jesus, you're fucking old.*

—*Happy birthday, man. Here's to many more!*

And her:

—*Happy birthday, boy. See you tomorrow. L*** you.*

Franco calls me. "Happy birthday, bro," he says. "Everything you gain now, you gain yourself. And everything you lose, you lose by yourself too."

"That's some sage shit, Franco."

He laughs. "So how do you feel, old man?"

"So far, so good."

Sort of.

END CREDITS

Before the day ends, before the night comes,
Before I forget what should not be forgotten,
Before this wonderful adventure concludes,
I would like to thank the following people:

My wife—   • Cara Mia Dunaiski
for being the hope,
the prayer, and the
anthem:

My mother—   • Gemma Akayezu
we're still here;   (17 June 1954–
so far, so good: 05 November 2016)

My family—   • Gilbert Habimana
for their hope and   • Clement and Elizabeth Dunaiski
optimism in spite of   • Amélie Dukunde
present difficulties;   • Ange Mucyo
we might be unprepared,   • Querida, Alexandra,
but we'll always   and Hannah Dunaiski
have each other:

My agent—   • Cecile Barendsma
for her trust;
Semper Fidelis:

The sages—
for bestowing new
gifts and titles:

- Michael Kelleher
- Peter Orner
- Naughty by Nature

The Scout Press team,
who were patient with
me when I needed it
most, and who did things
for me that I could not
do for myself:

- Alison Callahan
- Taylor Rondestvedt
- Jessica Roth
- Sophie Normil
- Hope Herr-Cardillo

My first readers—
for showing me
only stars know the
meaning of space:

- Tshuka Luvindao
- Mathabatha Sexwale
- Marielle Montenegro

My muses and amusers—
for showing me the
way, the goal, and
the destination; for
being the supporters of
things, for their humor
and kindness; for their
innumerable kindnesses;
for the laughs; for
showing the yoof dem
that help is (and will
always be) on the way:

- Leye Adenle
- Mekondjo Angula
- Jakob De Klerk
- Bonita De Silva
- Chiké Frankie Edozien
- Kalaf Epalanga
- Zerene Haddad
- Abubakar Adam Ibrahim
- Mubanga Kalimamukwento
- Louis Kato Kiggundu
- Bongani Kona
- Joonas Leskëla
- Mohale Mashigo
- Maaza Mengiste
- Reuben Mkandawire
- Shalom Ndiku
- Zanta Nkumane
- Natasha Omokhodion-Banda
- Ondjaki
- Troy Onyango
- Oatile Phakathi
- Heike Scholtz
- David Smuts
- Mukoma Wa Ngugi
- Zukiswa Wanner
- Roland Watson-Grant

And you, dear reader—
both met and unmet:

Now that we have come this far,
where to from here?

RECOGNITIONS AND AWARDS

"Granddaughter of the Octopus" won the Africa Regional Prize of the Commonwealth Short Story Prize in 2021 (United Kingdom) • "The Giver of Nicknames" was shortlisted for the AKO Caine Prize for African Writing (United Kingdom) in May 2021 • "The Hope, The Prayer, And The Anthem (or, The Fall So Far)" was shortlisted for the Afritondo Short Story Prize in 2021 (United Kingdom) • "The Neighbourhood Watch" was shortlisted for the AKO Caine Prize for African Writing in 2020 (United Kingdom) • "Only Stars Know the Meaning of Space" was longlisted for the Afritondo Short Story Prize in 2020 (United Kingdom) • "From the Lost City of Hurtlantis to the Streets of Helldorado (or, Franco)" was shortlisted for Best Original Fiction 2019 by Stack Magazines (United States).

ABOUT THE AUTHOR

RÉMY NGAMIJE is a Rwandan-born Namibian writer and photographer. He is the cofounder and editor in chief of *Doek!*, Namibia's first literary magazine. He was shortlisted for the AKO Caine Prize for African Writing in 2020. He was also longlisted for the 2020 Afritondo Short Story Prize. In 2019, he was shortlisted for Best Original Fiction by *Stack*. More of his writing can be read on his website RemytheQuill.com.

Previously published short stories: "The Seven Silences of the Heart" in *One Story* (United States), November 2021 • "The Hope, The Prayer, And The Anthem (or, The Fall So Far)" in *The Hope, The Prayer, The Anthem: The 2021 Afritondo Short Story Prize Anthology* (United Kingdom), August 2021 • "Granddaughter of the Octopus" in *Granta* (United Kingdom), May 2021 • "Hope Is For The Unprepared (Or Me)" in *The Selkie* (Ireland), December 2020 • "Only Stars Know the Meaning of Space" in *Yellow Means Stay: An Anthology of Love Stories from Africa* (United Kingdom), September 2020 • "Annus Horribilis" in *The Forge Literary Magazine* (United States), September 2020 • "Wicked" in *Barzakh* (United States), July 2020 • "Tornado (or, The Only Poem You Ever Wrote)" in *My Heart in Your Hands: Poems from Namibia* (Namibia), June 2020 • "The Giver of Nicknames" in *Lolwe* (Kenya), May 2020 • "Love Is a Neglected Thing (or, Corinthians)" in *Silver Pinion* (United Kingdom), May 2020 • "Nine Months Since Forever" in *Necessary Fiction* (United States), April 2020 • "Black, Coloured, And Blue (or, The Gangster's Girlfriend)" in *New Contrast* (South Africa), March 2020 • "Important Terminology For Military Age Males" in *Columbia Journal* (United States), March 2020 • "The Sage of the Six Paths (or, The Life and Times of the Five Os)" in *Sultan's Seal* (Egypt), January 2020 • "Little Brother (or, Three in the Morning)" in *Sultan's Seal* (Egypt), December 2019 • "Sofa, So Good, Sort Of (or, John Muafangejo)" in *Azure* (United States), September 2019 • "From the Lost City of Hurtlantis to the Streets of Helldorado (or, Franco)" in *American Chordata* (United States), July 2019; republished in English and translated into French, Portuguese, and Spanish in *Periferias* (Brazil), August 2020 • "Crunchy Green Apples (or, Omo)" in *The Amistad* (United States), May 2019 • "The Neighbourhood Watch" in *The Johannesburg Review of Books* (South Africa), February 2019 • "Yog'hurt (or, Just Breathe)" in *Litro Magazine* (United Kingdom), December 2018